MADE FOR YOU

Vivienne

I did the last thing I ever expected to do.
I bought a boat.
A beautiful boat that was all mine to spend the summer on.
Only thing I was looking forward to was the calm being on the water brought me.
A place where I wasn't a hockey dynasty princess or the only single girl of the family.
What I wasn't looking forward to was the broody man in the boat next to me.

Xavier
I was at the top of my game two years ago.
Then it all came crashing down.
I hung up my skates and vowed to never play again.
I was good at hockey, but hockey was bad for me.
I planned to spend my life on my boat with my dog.
Alone. Happily alone.
Until she came along.

BOOKS BY NATASHA MADISON

Made For Series
Made For Me
Made For You
Made For Us
Made For Romeo

Southern Wedding Series
Mine To Kiss
Mine To Have
Mine To Cherish
Mine to Love

The Only One Series
Only One Kiss
Only One Chance
Only One Night
Only One Touch
Only One Regret
Only One Mistake
Only One Love
Only One Forever

Southern Series
Southern Chance
Southern Comfort
Southern Storm
Southern Sunrise
Southern Heart
Southern Heat
Southern Secrets
Southern Sunshine

This Is
This is Crazy
This Is Wild
This Is Love
This Is Forever

Hollywood Royalty
Hollywood Playboy
Hollywood Princess
Hollywood Prince

Something So Series
Something Series
Something So Right
Something So Perfect
Something So Irresistible
Something So Unscripted
Something So BOX SET

Tempt Series
Tempt The Boss
Tempt The Playboy
Tempt The Ex
Tempt The Hookup

Heaven & Hell Series
Hell And Back
Pieces Of Heaven

Love Series
Perfect Love Story
Unexpected Love Story
Broken Love Story

Standalones
Faux Pas
Mixed Up Love
Until Brandon

SOMETHING SO, THIS IS ONLY ONE & MADE FOR FAMILY TREE!

Zoe Stone & Viktor Petrov
Matthew Petrov
Zara Petrov
This Is Love
Vivienne Paradis & Mark Dimitris
Karrie Dimitris
Stefano Dimitris
Angelica Dimitris
This Is Forever
Caroline Woods & Justin Stone
Dylan Stone (Formally Woods)
Christopher Stone
Gabriella Stone
Abigail Stone
ONLY ONE SERIES
Only One Kiss
Candace Richards & Ralph Weber
Ariella Weber
Brookes Weber
Only One Chance
Layla Paterson & Miller Adams
Clarke Adams
Only One Night
Evelyn & Manning Stevenson
Jaxon Stevenson
Victoria Stevenson
Only One Touch
Becca & Nico Harrison
Phoenix Harrison
Dallas Harrison
Only One Regret
Erika & Cooper Grant
Emma Grant
Mia Grant

Parker Grant

Matthew Grant

Only One Mistake

Jillian & Michael Horton

Jamieson Horton

Only One Love

Frances Grant & Brad Wilson

Stella Wilson

Only One Forever

Dylan Stone & Alex Horton

Maddox Stone

Maya Stone

Maverick Stone

Made For Me

Julia & Chase Grant

Made For You

Vivienne Grant & Xavier Montgomery

Made For Us

Arabella Stone & Tristan Weise

Penelope

Payton

Made For Romeo

Romeo Beckett & Gabriella Stone

Mine to Take

Matthew Petrov & Sofia Barnes

Mine To Promise

Stefano Markos & Sadie

Cover Design: Jay Aheer

Editing done by Jenny Sims Editing4Indies

Editing done by Karen Hrdicka Barren Acres Editing

Proofing Julie Deaton by Deaton Author Services

Proofing by Judy's proofreading*

Formatting by Christina Parker Smith

MADE FOR YOU

NATASHA
MADISON

ONE

VIVIENNE

I HEAR THE front door open and slam closed, I hear footsteps, and then I smile. "In five," I say to myself, holding up five fingers. "Four." I close down one finger. "Three, two, one." I point at the bedroom door as it swings open.

"What is taking you so freaking long?" my sister, Franny, huffs, coming into the room. "We said five minutes." She stands there in blue jeans, ripped at the knee, and a white cotton T-shirt tucked into the front. Her blond hair is braided at the side, and her blue eyes are staring at me. We are opposites in every single way. Where she has blond hair, I have auburn hair, just like our grandmother. Where she has blue eyes, I have green eyes, they change with how I feel, and our height is the only thing we have in common. She also has bigger boobs than I do, but that is what the miracle bra is made for.

"How was I supposed to know you really meant it this time?" I ask her as I zip closed my luggage. "How many times did you say five minutes, and then I'm sitting in the car waiting for you guys to be done?" I close my hand in a fist and smack it with my other hand to mimic sex. I walk over to the side table to grab my laptop, putting it in my Louis Vuitton big bag.

"Valid point"—she laughs—"but we are in the car, and Dad already called twice. We are officially late."

I shake my head, walking around the guest room, making sure I didn't forget anything. "Why is he like this?" I ask, grabbing my luggage and Louis. "It's not like there aren't people at the house already. It's Sunday." Sunday lunch is notorious in our family. It started once and just kept going. It's a day when we all gather at someone's house and eat ridiculous amounts of food. "I bet you, right now, at least forty people are in his house, and he's still pacing around like no one is there."

We walk down the stairs toward the front door. "You know, unless the four of us are there, he feels like he's missing a piece of himself." She mimics the words he says all the time. I can't help but chuckle at the irony of it. He's big bad Matthew Grant, but his life is all about his family.

The hatch of the Range Rover swings open, and Wilson, Franny's husband, gets out of the SUV. He's wearing shorts and a T-shirt with a baseball cap backward. "What took you so long?" he asks, reaching for the bag in my hand.

"I thought you guys were banging," I answer him honestly, and he laughs. "You know, since you don't have the baby, you got to get a couple of rounds in before she comes back and cockblocks you."

"As if my daughter would cockblock me," he jokes as he puts my luggage in the back and presses the button for the hatch to close.

"It's all fun and games until you walk in on your parents grinding uglies." I close my eyes when I think back to walking in on my parents not so long ago. "I swear I'm suffering from PTSD." I walk over to the back door of the SUV and open it, getting in.

The drive takes us less than three minutes, and I see the street lined with cars. "Why was he calling when he has a household full of people?" Wilson mumbles as he gets out of the car.

I laugh, getting out and walking up the driveway to the front door. My parents split their time between New York, where my father was the GM for the New York Stingers but is now the team owner, and Dallas, where my brother, Cooper, plays on the team. My other brother, Chase, is their team doctor.

The minute I open the door, I can hear the chaos from the kitchen spreading out into the foyer. The number of baby bags at the door is on another level. "There is your mom," I hear my mother say as she walks into the room holding Stella, Franny's one-year-old daughter.

"Hi, baby girl," Franny coos, holding out her hands for her daughter, who just stares at her like she did her wrong.

I roll my lips. "Someone is holding a grudge," I state, walking over to my mother and kissing her cheek. "Did your mom desert you, Stella Bella?" I ask her, and she just looks at me. "Trust me, this is so much better than walking in on her trying to ride your father."

"Would you stop that?" my mother shrieks. "We were dressed."

"Not even close." I shake my head. "Not one stitch of clothing was around either of you."

"Look at my princess." Wilson smiles at Stella, and she side-eyes him, too.

"Tough crowd. I would ask you to come to me, Stella, but let's be honest," I tell my niece. "You don't really want me either." I lean in to kiss her cheek, and she whines and tries to push me away. "I'm going to go see my other favorite niece."

"Don't threaten her like that," Franny scolds, pushing me away. "Come and see Mommy." She holds her hands out.

"Ask her to wash her hands first," I throw over my shoulder. "Chances are she had your dad's pickle in her hand."

"There you are," my father says, coming out of the kitchen. "I've been waiting for you." I just laugh at him.

"Dad, there are about a hundred people here." I look around, seeing kids running everywhere.

"Yes, but I missed my baby." He grabs me and brings me in for a hug. "It pains me that you don't use your bedroom here."

"It pained me to see you naked," I counter back, and he laughs.

"Are we still leaving after dinner?" I ask, and he nods his head.

"Plane leaves at seven," he says. "Should get in about eleven local time."

"Sounds good. I have something to do tomorrow," I tell him and walk away before he asks me what. I step into the kitchen, stopping to kiss a couple of the kids and say hello to my sister-in-law, Erika. "Where is my favorite niece?" I look around. "Who just turned four."

"Good save." She laughs. "She was in the backyard discussing why we should get a dog with your brother."

"Aw," I say, putting my hand to my chest. "You're getting a dog?"

"Immediately, no." She shakes her head. "I said they were discussing it."

"You know he'll just say yes." I laugh, grabbing a plate and walking over to get some food.

"He says yes, and I'm leaving him," she huffs. "We already have a million kids. I don't have time for a dog."

"You think he's going to allow you to leave him?" I throw my head back and laugh. "How far do you think you'll get before he drags you back?"

"What are you two talking about?" my brother, Cooper, asks, coming beside Erika and pulling her to him. The two of them were best friends who then fell for each other when he got divorced.

"She said she's leaving you if you tell Felicia that you can get a dog," I fill him in, and he laughs.

"Never." He shakes his head. "It's not that bad. I asked Dylan."

"Cooper Grant," Erika warns. "I'm not kidding with this one."

"I know," he says. "I sent her to ask my dad." We both gasp. "Let him say no to her."

"That's low, even for you," I say, turning and walking outside, where round tables are set up everywhere. Most of them are filled with people eating, and I spot an empty place at my brother Chase's table. "Hello, lovebirds." I sit down and look over at my brother and his new fiancée, Julia.

"I didn't think I'd see you today." Julia smiles. "You hit the wine really hard last night."

I laugh. "Just following your lead."

"Next thing you know, you'll be in love," Julia teases, and I glare at her.

"Bite your tongue," I retort, eating my food. Now, it's not to say that I don't want to be in love. I know that love exists because it's all around me, all the time. I look at Chase putting his arm around Julia and kissing her lips. Cooper comes over and sits next to me, followed by Erika, who he pulls onto his lap. Michael, my other cousin, is the next to join us with his wife and Julia's twin, Jillian. Franny, Wilson, Dylan, and Alex are the last ones to crowd the table.

"When are you coming back?" Jillian asks me, and I shrug.

"I'm not sure," I say, taking a bottle of water on the table and opening it. "I sort of am making plans for the summer right now."

"Really?" Franny says. "Like what?"

"Um." I look around to make sure my father won't hear this. "You can't tell Dad yet," I inform her.

Cooper already shakes his head while Chase looks up at the sky and mumbles, "Dear God."

"I like where this is going already," Alex says before she shouts out, "Oh my God, are you going to spend the summer in Europe?" She puts her hands together. "That was my dream."

"What the hell are you talking about?" Dylan says from beside her. "We did that 'summer in Europe' shit. You don't remember all the fucking Instagram pictures we had to take. You only booked hotels you found on Instagram. A whole month of switching hotels because the other one had better views. Do you know how many freaking steps we went up in Italy?"

"You're welcome." Alex glares at him. "Besides, who invited you on that trip?" She rolls her eyes at him, and he leans in and kisses her. "Yeah, whatever, I can hate you and kiss you all at the same time."

"Oh, trust me," he huffs. "I know."

"This is what happens when you marry your cousin," I joke with them, and everyone laughs. They really aren't cousins in that way. My uncle Justin adopted Dylan, who then became best friends with Alex. Only a couple of years ago, they finally declared what everyone already knew; they loved each other.

"Can we get back to what we aren't supposed to tell Dad?" Cooper asks, and then my father pops up behind him with my uncle Max.

"Yes, please, let's keep secrets from your father," Max says, chuckling at him.

"Just like a Band-Aid." Franny leans over, and I take a deep breath.

"Well"—I clear my throat—"I was thinking about what to do this summer." I tap the table with my finger. "And I bought a boat." I look around the table, seeing everyone just looking at me.

"What do you mean you bought a boat?" my father says, glaring at me.

"I mean that I bought a three-bedroom, two-bathroom floating cottage." I take a drink of water.

"Hold on a second," Cooper says, putting up his hand. "What do you mean a boat?"

"I have pictures," I reply, grabbing my phone out of my pocket and opening it to the photo gallery. Handing it to him, I can't help the smile that fills my face and the calmness that comes over me.

"This is a yacht!" Erika blurts out. "This is not a boat."

"Where are you parking this?" Michael asks as he grabs the phone from Cooper.

"It's going to be parked at the marina," I inform them.

"You can barely drive a car," Franny joins in. "You live in New York."

"I can so drive a car," I reply through clenched teeth, "and I got my boat license."

"So you can drive the boat?" my uncle Max asks me, shaking his head.

"Eventually," I answer honestly.

"How the hell did you get a license?" Michael asks me, leaning back in his chair.

"Online," I tell him, and Franny just gasps. "I did it in one day."

"That can't be right," Wilson says, looking at me and then my father. "Or safe. Right?"

"Who the hell would get a license online to drive a boat?" Alex asks me. "Like, that is bigger than a van we had in Hawaii, and you ran over a flower bed."

"You will not be driving this boat anywhere," my father orders. "What the hell are you going to do?"

"I plan to spend the summer on it," I tell him what I was going to tell him at a later date, but now the secret is out. "So there you go."

"Absolutely not," my father says, shaking his head vigorously. "That is not going to happen."

"Dad," Franny says, laughing, "she bought the boat. I think it's pretty much happening."

"What if there are pirates?" Uncle Max now chimes in, and the whole table laughs.

"It's New York. I don't think there are any pirates," I reassure him, shaking my head.

"I am putting my foot down," my father insists, and I just look at him.

"Fine," I reply, getting up. "See you in October!"

Two

Xavier

MY EYES FLICKER open slowly as the sound of the soft bells fills the room. I blink a couple more times before I roll over the king-size bed, reaching out to stop the ringing. Lying in the middle of the bed with my hand on my chest, I hear the clicking of nails on the floor before I feel her jump up on the bed. "Good morning, Beatrice," I greet her when I hear her sniffing as she walks toward me. "Did I wake you?" She lies down beside me, putting her head on my chest. I stroke her head. "How did you sleep?" I look down and all she does is blink her eyes for a second before closing her eyes. The room is still pitch black. "Are we not getting up this morning?" I ask her, and I can hear the thumping of her tail on the bed. I toss off the covers, getting up and walking to the bathroom. "You get five more minutes," I tell her as she lifts her head to look at me before putting her head back down and closing her eyes. I shake my head, walking into the bathroom and turning on the dim lights.

I wash my face and slip on a pair of basketball shorts before turning and walking out of the bathroom. The bed is now empty as I walk out of the room, walking up the five stairs to the galley. The soft lights from under the cabinets fill the almost dark room as I open the shades and start my coffee. I walk to the back with the sliding door and push the curtains open. "I think it's going to be a nice day," I state when Beatrice comes beside my leg. "They said it was going to rain, but I don't know about that." I turn and walk back down to my bedroom to grab a sweater and the baseball hat I always wear. Slipping on the black sweater, I push my hair back, then put the cap on backward.

Clapping my hands together, I turn back to the galley as the smell of coffee fills the air. I open the drawer and take out my big white coffee mug, filling it with coffee. "You ready?" I look over at Beatrice, who is sitting at the door. I grab the leash from the couch by the door before unlocking it and sliding it open. The cool air hits me right away. "Oh, it's chilly this morning," I observe, walking out and sliding on my boat shoes. The sound of the water hitting the boat is almost peaceful. Birds chirping can be heard. "Let's go," I say, walking to the side and stepping off the boat to the dock.

I wait for Beatrice, who jumps off the boat like it's no big deal. The sun is slowly starting to peek out of the sky. "Another day." I take a sip of my coffee. "Another dollar." We walk down the dock to the end of our row, turning to the left and strolling to the metal walkway that leads up to the street.

I press the button to open the security gate to the outside parking lot. The door opens, and we slowly take our morning walk. I look down at all the boats, all the slots now filled up. When I came in from the Gulf Coast three weeks ago, four or five boats were docked. But as the weather started getting nicer and nicer, more and more boats started coming into port.

I walk down the sidewalk, seeing the water calm as I drink my coffee. "What do you think, Beatrice?" I look over at the dog, who ambles next to me. "Is this year going to be as good as last year?" She looks down as she walks over to the corner and stops to pee. "I think so also."

I laugh at my own joke as we walk quietly down the pier. How different the past two years have been for me. I shake my head and take a sip of the coffee. My heart speeds up a touch when I start to think about how different my life is. Two years ago, I was at the lowest point in my life. I was playing in the NHL, living the dream of so many people, yet inside every single day I was dying. My headspace was an absolute nightmare. I was in a downward spiral, and if I hadn't gotten help, I would have been six feet under right now.

So what did I do? I hung up my skates and walked away from the game that brought me so much joy, but also kicked me all the way down into the black abysses. It was a vicious cycle, one that is not really talked about.

It's pushed under the rug, as they say, everyone knows what is going on, but no one has the balls to stand and say it. So I took myself out of the running. I shocked a lot of people when I walked away. My agent was the only one who knew the truth about why I was walking away from it.

Everything else was speculation, and even though I didn't want to know, I heard through the grapevine and from eavesdropping on some conversations that the press spun it a totally different way. I also knew that there was nothing I could say to make anyone change their opinion of me. I learned that the hard way. There is nothing quite like waking up after a hockey game and seeing your name plastered on the front cover of the sports section because you sucked so bad. Not even my father knew what to say, not that I shared much with him. We had our ritual Sunday calls, which lasted a good four minutes, depending on the news that day, and that was it. I did my duty as a son to reach out to him, because I knew it was what my mom would have wanted.

Every single day I went through the motions of what it was to live. But what I really needed was someplace to go where I would be able to get out of my head and unplug. The ocean was that place. I had no idea, and when my therapist suggested renting a boat and going out onto the water, I did it solely to tell her I did it. But the minute we got out in the middle of the ocean, it just grounded me. I couldn't explain it, but I knew I needed to get my own boat.

For the last two years, I've been living on my boat.

Was it a spontaneous purchase? Yes. Did I regret it? Not even for one freaking second. Let's be honest, I'm not living on some rinky-dink boat. This one is a four-bedroom, three-bathroom, sixty-five-foot yacht. I laugh, shaking my head as I think about how I felt when I visited it. I knew the minute I stepped onto the boat I loved it. As I looked around, I tried to make excuses that this was too much boat for me. I was one person, after all. Why did I need four bedrooms? It's not like I had any family who would come on board. But as I walked around the boat, it just felt like home. Which sounded silly at the time. Fuck, it sounds silly now. I left the boat and then went on a long walk. A walk where I tried to make a pros and cons list about having a boat. The only thing on the pro side was peace. Which I guess was enough for me because I got on the phone and made an offer. I then turned around and sold my house on Long Island. Sold the house as is, with everything in it, and bought a boat. I decided to focus on me, for the first time in a long time. I didn't want the house or the memories it had anymore. I closed the on that part of my life, and I was okay about it.

Once I bought the boat, I knew I needed someone to come with me. I got a captain to come on board. Every single day, he came on the boat and we went through everything. The training went on for four months. Four months of ten-hour days, we would take the boat out, and he would show me different things. I loved every fucking second of it. When summer turned into fall, he introduced me to Steven, who came with me as I took the boat from New York to Miami. It took us way longer than it should, but I knew the boat inside and out by the time we got there. When it was time to return to New York, he flew out and made the trip with me. It took us half the time. The only reason I loved coming back to New York was it somehow felt like coming home. Even though I went through the worst times of my life, it still somewhat felt like home.

"What do you have planned for the day?" I ask Beatrice as we walk down the path we take every single day and night. The sun is slowly starting to peek out. "I think it's going to be a hot day." I take another sip of my coffee as Beatrice turns around the bend. After the boat, the best thing I got was Beatrice. I was in Miami one day when I went for a run in the morning. Stopping for a second, I looked over at the window, and there she was, sitting in a pet shop just looking at me.

I walked in, and an hour later, I was leaving with a puppy and more shit than I knew what to do with. Because of my travel schedule, I never had a pet. I was never home long enough to want a pet, but now the time was my leisure. I laugh when I think back to the training stages. She really fucking hated those pee pads. She would pee right next to it while looking me in the eye. Just to tell me she was the boss, and even though I denied it, she was. She was the only woman in my life, and I was more than happy about that fact.

"I think we should take the boat out today," I say once we get back to the dock. The sun is now up in the sky. There is more action on the dock as I scan my key card, and the door opens. "Yeah, the water seems calm. What do you think?" I ask as we walk down the dock, nodding at a couple of people out on their boats.

We walk down our dock row, and I see movement on the boat next to mine. "Morning," Samuel, the manager of the marina, says to me when he sees me walking by.

"Morning," I reply, looking at him as he takes down the for-sale sign on the boat.

"Looks like you're getting a new neighbor," he tells me, stepping off the boat and onto the dock. "I think they are going to come on today."

"Sounds good," I say, looking back at the boat that just went up on the market the week before. Beatrice doesn't wait for me before she jumps onto the boat. "Have a nice day."

I walk around, stepping on the boat and taking off my shoes right away. "Looks like we are getting new neighbors," I inform Beatrice as I open the sliding door and walk in with her. "Who knows, they might have a friend for you to play with." She sits beside her food bowl. "Yeah, yeah, I'm coming." I grab the silver bowl and fill it with her food. I stand in the middle of the galley, looking out the big side window at the boat beside me, not knowing it will be another big thing in my life.

THREE

VIVIENNE

MY PHONE RINGS from somewhere under the mess on my bed. "Shit," I mumble, trying to find the phone. I move around some clothes and find it at the bottom of the pile right next to my laptop. "Hello?"

"Ms. Grant," I hear the man say. "It's Samuel from the yacht club."

"Hi," I reply, sitting on the bed. "How are you?"

"Just fine, thank you. I was calling to let you know that I have your boat keys on my desk."

The smile fills my face right away, and if I wasn't dead tired, I would jump up with glee. "That's great. Can I swing by and get them today?"

"You sure can." He chuckles.

"Would I be able to stay on the boat tonight?" I ask with nerves, making my leg shake.

"The boat is yours, Ms. Grant. You can stay on it when you want," he says, and I fist-pump the sky.

"Thank you so much." I look around the room. "I can come by"—I look at my watch and see it's ten o'clock—"this afternoon around three."

"That sounds great. If I'm not at the desk, I'll leave them in an envelope."

"Thank you so, so much," I say and hang up the phone. "It's happening," I announce out loud. "It's finally happening." I look around the bedroom at the suitcase I started packing this morning. I knew there was a chance I would be getting the keys today or tomorrow, so I was going to prepare everything.

I get up now, and my stomach starts getting little butterflies with anticipation. I literally just toss shit into the luggage. At this point, I have no idea what I'm taking and what I'm not. I just want to get to the boat.

I bring down four pieces of luggage to the front door, and then walk to the kitchen, where I take out my cooler bag. I pack the milk and eggs I bought for the boat, along with the coffee and, of course, the wine. I put the cooler bag at the front door before running upstairs to change out of my pjs. Slipping on a pair of jeans and a loose white camisole, I grab a gray knitted sweater and rush back downstairs to the front door. I put on my Nikes before grabbing my SUV keys. I make five trips to the car by the time everything is loaded. I almost forgot about the five bags of decorations my aunt Zoe had sent over for me.

I get into the car and head over to the marina. The

whole time, I'm so happy I feel like singing with glee. I take out the parking pass I was given from the last owners and scan the machine as the gate opens. I park my SUV next to the front, getting out and walking over to the office building.

There are five red tables with umbrellas set up right in front of a barbecue grill on the side, and when I pull open the door, the cool air hits me. I step inside, seeing a woman behind the desk. "Hi, is Samuel here?" I ask her. "I'm here to pick up the keys to my boat. My name is Vivienne." I smile.

"Yes." She grabs the white envelope from the stack of papers beside her. "This is your key."

My hand reaches, taking the white envelope in my hand. "Thank you. Are there any loading bins?" I ask, and she gets up.

"Yes," she says, "I can show you." She moves around the counter before walking to the door. I follow her as she walks around the corner of the building where five gray carts are. "Would you need assistance to unload anything?"

"No"—I shake my head—"I'll be fine."

"Just bring it back when you're done."

"I will," I assure her, walking over and grabbing one. It looks like a wheelbarrow. I bring it to the back of my SUV, opening it, and starting to pile things in. I don't take into account all the shit I've put in there has made it heavy to push. I grab the handles and then push it toward the gated door. Seeing that I have to go all the way around to the other side, and by the time I get there, I have to take off my sweater because I'm a sweaty mess. I get to the gate and see that it's locked. I look around, trying not to seem like I'm breaking into the place. People are all over the dock talking to each other and people on their boat cleaning. "Don't be suspicious," I mumble to myself as I try to see if there is a button or anything. I grab the envelope that I stuck in my back pocket and open it. Two sets of keys come out and a white credit card key thing. "Please work," I murmur. Taking the card, I scan it against the door and hear the click of the lock. I throw my hands in the air like I just scored a freaking overtime goal during the Stanley Cup playoffs. I pull open the door and keep it open with my hip, bringing the cart in with me. I try not to huff and puff as I go down the ramp with a too heavy cart. "Maybe next time," I tell myself as I try not to fly down the ramp. I smile at a couple of people as I walk past them.

I get giddier by the second as I get closer to my boat. Stopping right behind it, I take a second to take it in again. All mine. I leave the cart on the pier before I step aboard my boat. Mine. I giggle again as I walk up to the small door on the side, opening it and stepping into the sitting area in the back. A long bench on the right side faces the two big sliding doors. A small wooden table on the side has two chairs; that table was one of the reasons I bought this boat. I literally pictured myself sitting on one of the chairs. The stairs on the left side go up to where you drive the boat. I walk to the sliding door and stick the key in the lock and turn it. "Welcome home," I say to myself with a smile so big on my face, my cheeks hurt. I slide open the door, and the cold air hits me right away as I step inside and down the two steps to the cherrywood floors I fell in love with.

"Oh my God." I put my hands to my mouth and bend over, filled with excitement. It's everything I remembered and more. I take two steps down to the galley. The door to the first bedroom on the right is open. I take the two steps down into the cabin and sit on the twin bed. "Bedroom one," I say before walking back up the steps to the galley. The big-screen TV is on the wall right in front of the door. The long beige counter fills the whole right side, two stools tucked under the low part of the counter is where I can picture the kids having a snack. The massive U-shaped leather eating area is right in front of the galley. A silver bucket in the middle with a bottle of champagne sticking out greets me. I step up the two steps to the table and take the card out.

"Ahoy, matey." I laugh. "Don't let the pirates get you. I don't know what will happen to Dad. Can't wait to see you drive this thing. Love Chase and Cooper, and your cheap-ass sister who didn't Venmo us." I throw my head back and laugh, putting the card on the counter before walking down the steps and continuing to the two steps that go lower again. The second bedroom door is open, and it's just like it was when I visited. The blue and brown covers with the pillows. Right next to the small bathroom that I peek into before walking into the master stateroom.

"This is all mine." I open my arms and turn in a circle. The queen-size bed is in the middle of the room. With two mirrored closets on each side, I step to the right side, crawling onto the bed and lying down like a starfish. The hatch window on top of my bed lets me see the sky. "It's going to be so pretty when the stars are out." I sit up for a second, right before getting off the bed. "First thing we have to do is change this bedding," I tell myself. Even though it's a beautiful silver and black cover, I want something more me.

I quickly strip the bed, which takes me a lot longer than I thought it would since I have to get onto the bed to grab the back of the cover, and then I don't realize that my knees are stopping me from actually making progress. By the time it's done, I need a bottle of water.

I walk up the two steps to the galley and open the cabinet where the fridge is, finding it stocked with ten bottles of water. I open the bottle and drink half of it before walking back outside. I quickly tie up my hair in a bun that falls sideways as I step off and grab two bags. "Don't fucking face-plant." I can hear my brother Cooper's voice like he is right here. I put the bags on the long bench before walking over and unloading the rest. I'm super proud of myself when I start unloading the cart the second time. I finish unloading the SUV, turning back to make the last trip to the boat. At this point, I think I'm a fucking pro. I also have a feeling of déjà vu, like I've done this before. Or at least what I'm supposed to be doing now.

I stop again by the side of the boat, and this time, I open the sliding door to bring my suitcases inside. I place them all lined up in the galley before walking out to grab the other bags. On my last freaking step off to return the cart is when I become so sure of myself that I stumble just a bit. My hands come out to stop myself from falling on my face, trying to balance myself on my feet. "Shit," I say just before I hear a bark right to the side. I turn my head at the same time there is the sound of sniffing right next to me. I look over and see the cutest dog I've ever seen in my whole life. I squat down, putting my hand out so the dog can smell me. "Well, hello, you," I say as I rub the dog's neck, the tail moving side to side excitedly. "Aren't you the cutest little thing." I use my baby voice, and she starts to lick my face as I slip back onto my ass. I can't help the laugh that escapes me. The dog never stops licking my face as I try to dodge the kisses. I can't stop from rubbing the dog's neck as she excitedly licks me, the laughing making the dog even more excited.

"Beatrice," I hear a male voice call, and she stops. She looks over at the boat next to me, where a man stands on the back of the boat. "Come here," he says and motions with his head. She takes one more look at me as I look at her with a we-got-caught look, my eyes going big and my lips in an O shape. She takes a split second to lick me one more time before she walks over to her owner, jumping back on her boat and sitting next to him.

"Sorry about that," I say, getting up and dusting off my hands. "It's my fault. She wanted to smell me."

"Well, she doesn't like when you talk gibberish to her," he says, and I tilt my head to the side and pause a second to take him in. He's wearing shorts and a sweater. He looks to be about six feet tall, maybe a touch taller.

The baseball cap on his head doesn't let me see what color his eyes are, but I do see he has scruff on his face. If someone had asked me if he was hot, I would say no, just because—well, for one—he didn't even walk over and ask me if I was okay. I was on the floor. What if I hurt myself? Okay, fine, it would annoy me more if he thought I was a damsel in distress, but still, he could have offered. Bottom line, he's hot in an "I don't want to think about it" kind of way.

"I'm Vivienne," I introduce myself, and he just nods. "I'm your neighbor."

"Good to know," he replies, putting his hands on his hips.

"Are you docked here all summer long?" I ask him, trying to break the ice. I mean, everyone always likes me. I'm charming and personable. What is there not to like about me? I can tell you—nothing.

"We are," he says, and I just chuckle, nodding my head.

Well, good talk," I say to him. He just nods and walks away from me, going inside. "I like your dog better than I like you," I declare to his retreating back, not letting his grouchy mood ruin my day.

Four

Xavier

"ARE YOU DOCKED here all summer long?" she asks, trying to make small talk. Little does she know, I don't do small talk. I mean, I'm polite, but that is where it ends. Yes, no, maybe, the end, that is the extent of all conversation I have with about everyone.

"We are." That's the only thing I say as Beatrice jumps back on the boat and walks toward me slowly. I can tell from the way she is walking that she is doing this under protest and not because I called her over. She stops beside me, turning and looking over at the woman who is my new neighbor.

"Well, good talk," she says, and all I can do is turn away from the auburn-haired beauty who has rattled me. Walking over to the sliding doors, I open them and step into the cool air.

I close the door behind me before I look over at Beatrice. "What did we say about making friends and talking to strangers?" I ask her as she walks over to her dog bed in the corner and gets on it. "Yeah, that's what I thought." I shake my head and walk over to the fridge, making the stupid mistake of looking out my side windows, which give me a view of the back of her boat. She looks around, smiling as she grabs her suitcase and disappears inside. "Seriously, Beatrice." I put one hand on my hip. "The last time you tried to make friends, what happened?" I ask her as I open my Gatorade bottle. "Let me remind you of the little girl you thought would share her cookie with you. She put gum all in your hair." Beatrice just looks up at me. "And it took a week to get it out. I had to cut the hair, and you had patches all over you. That wasn't a pretty look."

I walk over and sit on the couch, trying to ignore the need to look out the window by turning on the television. I was upstairs on the top deck, sitting down, enjoying the warm air while I reread one of my favorite books when I heard Beatrice bark. She really isn't a big barker, even when you walk past the boat, unless you come too close, then she lets me know. I looked up right in time to see her walking over to my new neighbor. I sat up, not sure what was going to happen, and then all I could see was Beatrice getting excited when the stranger fell back as she tried to lick her face. I heard her talk to her in gibberish, and I got up. I put my iPad down, not sure how it was going to go. As I made my way down the steps, all I could hear was her trying to talk gibberish, which annoyed me. Maybe I was more annoyed that I stared at her for a second longer than I should. Maybe I was annoyed because I literally checked her out as she was getting up from the ground. Maybe I was more annoyed because she was fucking good looking and that annoyed me, too.

Beatrice comes over and gets on the couch beside me. She turns in a circle before falling down and putting her head on my lap. "We don't like when people talk gibberish to us. Remember, that's rule number one." I pet her head, and she takes a deep huff. "So we are going to mind our business with the girl next door and not provoke her. Do you hear me?" I look down at Beatrice, who now perks up when she sees something. I make the mistake of looking out the window and I can see her auburn hair blowing in the wind. She stands on the dock with her phone in her hand as she holds it up, showing the boat. "Where is her husband?" I ask Beatrice, who tilts her head to the side as she looks outside, her tail hitting the couch. I watch my neighbor as she laughs, shaking my head. *She's getting too close to the edge*, I think in my head, and it annoys me even more that I give a shit. "Like, who lets their woman bring all that shit onto the boat by herself?" I look down at Beatrice, who I swear gives me a smirk. "I wasn't watching her, okay? She was making noise, and all I did was look over the bench, and I saw her, okay?" She gives me a *sure* look before she puts her head back down on my lap.

I turn my head to face the television, switching the channels, until I settle down on a golf game. "Tiger

Woods, I think he's going to make a comeback," I state, slouching sideways. It takes me maybe ten minutes before I close my eyes and drift off to sleep, only waking when Beatrice jumps off the couch and walks over to the door and scratches the glass. I open my eyes, stretching. "What time is it?" I grab my phone and press the button on the side and it shows me it's almost six o'clock. "Damn," I curse, getting up. "Why did you let me sleep so long?" I ask Beatrice, who waits by the door. "Let me go to the bathroom and then we'll leave," I tell her, jogging down the steps going to the bathroom and then rushing back. "I even washed my hands," I joke with her, grabbing the leash. "Now remember what I said." I look down at her as I grab the handle of the door. "We don't like new people." I pull it open. "We don't need friends." I step out and slide my shoes on. "Smile and wave," I mumble to her as I step off the boat with her following me. I force myself not to look onto her boat, even though my curiosity is killing me. I walk down the dock, my stomach grumbles when the smell of a barbecue grill fills the air. I take a second to look up and see that most of the people on the boats are starting to sit down and have dinner. I walk up the ramp and press the button. "Beatrice," I call her name. "Leash," I say, tying her up on her leash. In the morning, when it's dead, I don't bother, but at night, more people are out, and just in case another dog gets loose, I can protect her.

We do our routine walk around the park, and when we get back, she's panting for water. I step onto the boat, opening the back door, and she goes straight to her bowl.

"Thirsty?" I ask her as I walk over to the fridge, grabbing my own bottle of water. I lean back on the counter and see the lights in the boat next door are on. "Guess they are staying on the boat tonight." I look over at Beatrice, who walks over to her bed and lies down. "What do you want to eat for dinner?" I ask her, opening the fridge and grabbing stuff to make a salad, placing it on the counter before going back to the fridge. "Chicken or beef?" I ask her while I open the fridge, taking out the beef. "Beef it is."

I turn on the television while I prep my salad. I put the lettuce, tomatoes, and cucumbers in a bowl on the counter, grabbing the steak and walking out to slap it on the grill. I open the door, take a step out, and stop in my tracks, with one hand on the door and the other holding the plate. She sits at the small table outside her door, which is right next to my grill. A glass of white wine is in the middle of the table, her feet on the chair next to her, as she looks down at the book in her hand. I'm about to take a step back when Beatrice barks and her head comes up. *I'm going to kill her*, I think to myself when she walks over to the side of the boat, trying to smell her from our side. "Hi there." She smiles at Beatrice and then looks over at me. "Nice night, isn't it?" she says, sitting up and all I can do is nod at her.

I move to the grill with the food, opening the top and starting it. I think about aborting this whole mission to eat my steak on the grill and just pan-frying it at this point. Her eyes are on me, and when I look up, she smirks. "What's with the smirk?" I ask her without wanting to.

"Just trying to figure out if it's me you don't like or small talk." She picks up her glass of wine and brings it to her lips. Her hair is tied on the top of her head in some sort of bun.

"I don't even know you," I tell her, cleaning the grill off. "So I can't not like you."

"So it's the small talk you don't like?" She puts her glass down on the table and I want to tell her that I don't want to do any sort of talking, small or big. All I want to do is cook my steak, go inside, and then not talk to her for the rest of the night. I want to wallow in my own misery.

"Small talk is fine," I grumble out, trying not to be the biggest asshole in the world, but hoping she catches the tune.

"You have a nice boat," she compliments and all I do is nod at her. "I like the front part."

"Thanks," I respond, as I look over and see that Beatrice has her two front paws on the side of the boat and she's almost leaning over to her boat. "What did I say?" I mumble quietly to Beatrice, who just looks at me and blatantly ignores me.

"Oh, I got you something," she says, jumping up out of her seat, making Beatrice bark again because now she's excited because the woman is clapping her hands together. Beatrice jumps off the side of the boat and turns in a circle around me. "Let me get it." She turns around and I make the mistake of watching her walk away and she's wearing yoga pants. The type that molds onto your body and you see everything, they should be illegal.

Who designed these pants?

"You are in so much trouble," I hiss at Beatrice. "What did we talk about before?" She looks at me and steps back and then looks over to the boat where Vivienne now steps back out.

She has two white boxes in her hand. "I got you this," she says, walking over to the side of the boat. Beatrice beats me to the side and pushes her snout out to smell what Vivienne has in her hand. "Don't you worry, pretty girl," she assures Beatrice, with a smile on her face so big that her eyes get a touch lighter, "I got you something, too, because I like you the most." She looks at Beatrice and then at me. I can't even stop my feet from moving toward her. I walk over to the side of the boat as she holds out the big white box. My hands move to take the box from her. "It's dessert. Sort of a 'hi, neighbor' kind of thing," she tells me and I just stare at her and then the box.

"Isn't it the other way around?" I ask her. "Wasn't I supposed to get you a 'welcome to the neighborhood' thing?"

"Well, I wasn't holding my breath." She smiles at me and I can tell it's the fakest smile I've ever seen. It's more of a fuck-off smile than anything else, definitely much different than the look she is giving Beatrice. "Can I give her a c-o-o-k-i-e?" She spells out the word, looking at Beatrice.

Beatrice barks at her to answer her question. "She knows how to spell," I tell her, holding the white box in my hand.

"I take it that is a yes?" she asks me, and I notice how green her eyes are. I nod at her and she ignores me and looks back at Beatrice. "Does the prettiest girl in the whole world want a treat?" she asks her, sitting on the side of the boat and I'm tempted to tell her she could fall in, but not my monkey, not my circus, I remind myself.

"I'm going to put this inside," I inform her and look at Beatrice. "You can go and see her but you come right back," I tell her and Beatrice looks at me. "Go," I say with my head and she walks over and jumps onto the dock.

In a matter of seconds, she's on the other boat. "I got you something special," is the last thing I hear from her before I open the door and walk into the galley.

Walking over to the counter, I put the white box on the counter. "Why the fuck would she get me anything? I'm not going to eat this," I state, more annoyed than anything. One, she called me on being an asshole, and two, she still got me something. I open the box and see she got me my fucking favorite, apple fucking pie with crumbles. "Motherfucker," I grit between clenched teeth.

FIVE

VIVIENNE

"YOU ARE SO lucky that you are a cute little girl." I pet Beatrice while I give her one of the dog cookies I ordered from the same place my aunt Zara used to order from for her pups. "I got you more, but I'm only going to give you one. We mustn't upset the master," I tell her, laughing. "Can you imagine how much crabbier he can be if he's upset?" I shake my head. "I don't envy you." I kiss the top of her nose as I hear the slider next door open and the grumpy man comes out.

"You bought me apple pie," he huffs, coming back over to the side of the boat. When I came out here to have a glass of wine, I never thought I would see Mr. Grumpy again, but then he came out and I heard the bark.

"I did," I confirm, trying not to let his mood get to me. Kill them with kindness is what I always learned growing up, and if that doesn't happen, kick them in the balls. "Figured it was the safest choice." He puts his hands on his hips and I ignore the way his shirt pulls across his chest. "If it insults you, I'm more than happy to take it back."

He doesn't say anything to me, instead he looks over at Beatrice, who has just finished her cookie and is now standing beside me as she smells my hand, licking it. "How many cookies did you give her?"

I smile at him, the big smile that shows him his mood does nothing for me. "I gave her one," I tell him, walking over to the box on the table beside my wine. "There are five more in here." I hand him the box. "You can give them to her when you please."

His hand comes out to grab the box. "Thanks," he mumbles.

I squat down and look at Beatrice. "Well, it's the best I'm going to get." I rub her neck. "Thank you for coming to visit me, Beatrice."

I get up and grab my glass of wine. "Have a great night, Beatrice's dad." I tilt my head to the side. "Enjoy your pie."

I turn around and walk away, not giving him a chance to ruin the night. I step into the cabin going down the two steps. My phone is ringing from the top of the table, so I step up the two steps, sit on the couch, and see it's Franny calling, FaceTiming me. I smile big, pressing connect. The little circle goes around and around as it connects us. "Well, well, well," Franny says, putting her face to the phone. "There she is, Captain."

I laugh at her, getting up and walking over to the counter to grab the bottle of white wine I opened when I sat down to eat my dinner of apple pie. "I'm not a captain yet," I remind her, replenishing my glass. "I think I need something like ten years' experience or something like that."

"Show me the boat," Franny urges, clapping her hands. "Let me see everything."

"With pleasure," I reply, grabbing the phone in one hand and my wine in the other. "So this"—I turn it around and walk back to the door—"is bedroom number one." I open the door and step down. "I just redid the bed." I tell her of the new cover and throw pillows I bought. I show her the whole boat and then finally sit in the middle of my bed. "And look at this." I lie down on the bed and show her the window that I can see the stars out of. "Isn't it pretty?"

"Wilson." I hear her whisper-shout and he comes into the room. "Can we buy a boat?"

"Oh, here we go," he says, coming to look in the phone. "How are you doing? Are you seasick yet?"

"Not even a bit. You need to buy a boat," I state to him. "And kick the guy next to me out. He's such a grumpy little shit." I look at them and Franny's eyes go big as she listens to me bitch about the guy next to me. "The only good thing about him is…"

"Is his dick?" Franny fills in for me and Wilson just gives her a side look. "What? I don't know if she picked him up and made him happy. Who knows, she might turn that frown upside down?" She laughs. "Look at how I turned you. You barely smiled before and now you beam with sunshine." She shrugs. "You're welcome." She turns to look back at me. "Please continue."

"It is not his dick," I inform both of them. "He has the sweetest dog." I put my hand on my chest. "I don't even know his fucking name," I tell her, taking another drink of wine and neither of them interrupt me. "I introduced myself and what did he say?" I ask them and they both look at me. "He nodded!" I say, frustrated. "Who doesn't give the other person a name?"

"Maybe he's wanted by the mob," Wilson suggests and Franny just looks over at him.

"You need to stop hanging around with the men in my family," she huffs.

"Maybe he's on the run because he killed his family and drove across country with his wife's head on top of his—" He opens his mouth and she puts her hand over it.

"What the hell is wrong with you?" Franny asks. "You really need to lay off those crime podcasts."

"You are both literally insane," I inform them. "He doesn't look like a killer. Nor does he look like he's running away from the mob."

"How the hell would you know?" they both say at the same time.

"I don't know, but I'm assuming if he is one of those things, would he be on a boat?" I look from Franny to Wilson.

"Of course he would," Wilson snaps out as he slaps the table. "No one is going to find you." He smirks at me. "Have you told your father yet?"

"No," I retort, "there is no need to tell him anything." I point my finger to the screen. "I swear to God, if either of you tell him even one word." I glare. "I will cut you."

"And you wonder why he's not talking to you." Franny laughs. "Seriously though, Vi, are you really staying on that boat?"

"Yes," I tell them both. "Why wouldn't I stay on my boat?"

"Well, for one, you have a serial killer who is wanted by the mob living next to you," Wilson says. "And—and"—his voice starts to rise a bit—"if your father finds that out…poof." He puts his hands to his head and pretends his head explodes.

"My father is not going to find out anything," I assure him. "Because, well, one, he's not a serial killer but maybe he's wanted by the mob." I put my hand on my lips. "Or maybe Snow White has lost one of her men and he lives next door to me." I look at Franny, who tries to roll her lips to stop from laughing. "Did I tell you he got pissed off that I bought him an apple pie?" Franny gasps. "I know!" I shriek. "Who doesn't love apple pie?"

"I'm more of a blueberry kind of guy myself," Wilson says.

I glare at him. "No one asked you," I hiss between clenched teeth. "Now I'm going to take a nice hot shower and then…"

"You are going to lock the doors, and do you have a stick?" Wilson asks me and I just look at him, confused. "You put it behind the bottom of the sliding door. It makes it impossible to slide open." He folds his arms over his chest as if he just told me the biggest secret. "What?" he asks me, and Franny laughs. "You know that trick."

"We learned that when we were five." I hold up my hand. "It was part of the summer fun program we took about being safe." Wilson laughs now. "Anyway, I'll be fine."

"Do you even have an alarm?" Franny asks me and I shake my head.

"No, but you can't get in here unless you have a key for the gate," I reassure her, "so it's safe."

"Yeah, and no one can climb a gate," Wilson says, rolling his eyes.

"Goodbye." I press the red button and disconnect them. I get up off the bed and walk toward the sliding door. I make sure to lock it, looking outside one more time, the smile still stuck on my face.

I avoid looking at the boat next to me. Instead, I check and make sure the door is closed before bringing the shades together. I walk to my bedroom, starting the shower before undressing. Once I finish the shower, I slip on blue-and-white pj bottoms with the matching long-sleeved shirt. I make my way back to the kitchen where I eat apple pie straight from the box. I grab a bottle of water, walking back to my bedroom and slipping into bed. I check my phone and see that sunrise is at five ten. I set my alarm for four forty-five. Putting the phone under the pillow beside me, I grab the remote and turn on the little TV that is on the right side of the bed.

I don't even know what I put on, all I do is put my head

down, and in a matter of minutes I'm asleep. I sleep like a baby, only waking when the soft alarm fills the room. With my eyes still closed, I reach under the pillow where I know the phone is. I take it out and shut off the alarm, turning onto my back. The television is still playing when I open my eyes. I look out the window, seeing it's still dark outside. I flip the covers off me, walking to the kitchen to start my coffee before going back to my room and the bathroom. "I'm definitely going to have to nap today," I mumble to myself as I grab my phone.

I add some milk to the cup of coffee before walking to the door and opening the shades then sliding the door open. I step outside at the same time as Mr. Grumpy next door. I raise my head and our eyes meet. He is wearing joggers with a sweater, the baseball cap on his head again. "Morning," I mumble and want to kick myself for even acknowledging him. I don't wait for him to answer me before walking up the steps to the upper deck. I unzip the door and step in, grabbing the throw blanket I bought for up here. I walk over to the little door in the middle of the wall and open it, walking down the four steps, leading me to the two sun pads on each side of the window that is in my bedroom. I sit down in the middle of one of the sun pads and cross my legs. The breeze on the water makes it cooler than it is. Putting my coffee and my phone down in front of me, I wrap the blanket around my shoulders. I get up and put up the sun pad so I can sit with my back on it. When I finally have everything done, I sit down, grabbing my coffee and taking a sip. "Magical," I say as I hear the water hitting the boats. I look at the bridge in the distance. The dock is so quiet at this time of the morning, and when I look over to the right side, I notice a clock tower. "That is so pretty." I take my phone and snap a picture.

I sit here enjoying my coffee as the sky goes from a black to a blue/orange tint. The reflection on the water is even prettier than I imagined it. I snap another picture of it as I watch it then turn the sky almost a pink as the sun starts to lift higher into the sky. Finally turning the sky a gorgeous blue. "Sunrise number one complete," I murmur to myself as I pull up the text thread that the girls and I use. It's called *Fam Jam Girls*. The guys got so jealous of our chat that we had to make one with the guys, but it's called *Fam Jam with Dicks*.

I put the picture in the text with the message.

Me: Good morning from the boat.

I smile and start to get up, taking one more look at the sky before turning around. I take a step to the middle walkway and notice the front of my boat is really close to Mr. Grumpy's. I look back to the other side and see I have moved way over. I walk over to the side and look down at the dock and see the line in the front is off and so is the middle one. "Oh my God," I say, as I reach for the line and pull it up, the line coming out of the water. I wait to have it in my hand before I throw it on the dock. It lands there with a thud and then slowly, like a snail, falls back into the water. "What the fuck?" I say, looking over my shoulder and seeing that any second, I'm going to be kissing his boat and then it'll be even worse.

I scramble to get the rope up again, and this time, I

turn it into a circle like when you see cowboys herding their cattle. I toss it on the dock and it lands. I hold my breath to see if it's going to slip again. I wait a whole two seconds, maybe even less, before I run up the stairs and then down the stairs, jumping off the boat and onto the dock. I run down the side of the dock, grabbing the wet rope and pulling the boat back to its side. I'm huffing out at this point, and my shirt and pants are wet from the rope. I look down at the silver T thing as I start to wrap the rope around it, and then try to knot it together. I stand, looking down at the rope and see it becomes untied again. "Motherfucker," I swear to myself as I grab my phone. "YouTube is going to have the answer," I say as I pull out the phone and open Safari. I'm about to type in *how to secure a boat* when I hear him from the side.

I inwardly cringe when he asks me, "What the hell are you doing?"

Six

Xavier

I OPEN THE gate and wait for Beatrice to walk in ahead of me. "Don't forget what I said," I remind her as we walk down the ramp. "Rule number two, don't go to the neighbor." She looks up at me. "It's the same as rule number one, don't talk to strangers." We walk down the dock. Empty cup of coffee in my hand, the pit of my stomach is now starting to burn again as I get closer to my boat.

This morning, when I walked out on my deck, the last thing I expected was to see her walking out also. I inwardly cringed and then looked at Beatrice. "Don't even think about it," I mumbled to her while I watched Vivienne walk up her steps. "What the hell is she doing up so early?" I asked myself while I walked off my boat. My eyes were going to the sliding back door, waiting for her significant other to come out. There wasn't even a light on in the boat. It was pitch black. I shook my head and walked away thinking, *who would let their person be outside in the dark, alone?* I tried not to think of it the whole time during the walk and I only brought it up once to Beatrice.

I even tried and forget the way I resisted the apple pie. Until I just said fuck it and cut a piece of it. I was already committed to hating it, just because. But the minute I put a piece in my mouth, I moaned out loud. It was so fucking good I ended up eating three pieces, which then made me even more pissed at myself for liking it. It made me pissy the whole night, and then when I woke up and went to make coffee, I literally had a piece of pie in the kitchen in my boxers. I figured if I finished the whole thing, I could get it out of the galley and be done with it.

I'm getting closer to her boat and I am about to walk past it when I see her on the side of the dock. Her phone is in her hand as she starts to type something. "What the hell are you doing?" comes out even before I can tell myself to mind my own business.

She looks over at me and I can tell from the look in her eye that something is wrong. "I don't know what happened, but it got untied," she states absentmindedly as she looks down at her phone.

"So, then, tie it," I say to her and she looks over at me. I always heard the saying if looks could kill, and I'm sure I've even been on the receiving end of them, but never has it been clearer than right here, right now.

"What the hell do you think I'm trying to do?" She

glares at me.

"I have no idea what you are trying to do." I put my hands on my hips, looking at her and then back to the boat that starts to sway closer to mine.

"This." She points down to the rope at her feet. "Got loose," she says and even I can tell by her tone that she's nervous. I walk closer to her, seeing she literally just wrapped the line around the silver cleat. "It was like almost kissing your boat." She looks over to me, like a deer caught in headlights. "It didn't touch your boat, I caught it in time, but now I have to make sure it stays secure."

"What do you mean, it untied itself?" I ask her and maybe that shouldn't have been what I asked her.

"Would you get off my dick for a second and let me handle this," she huffs, looking back down at her phone, "I'm going to just YouTube how to tie a boat together and it'll be fine." Her hands shake as she starts to listen to the video.

Oh. My. God. "Are you saying that you don't know how to tie up your boat?" I ask her, not sure I actually heard the words coming out of her mouth. I am too stunned by a couple of things. One, her beside her boat, two, her telling me to get off her dick, and three, her saying her boat almost touched mine.

"What I'm saying is if you give me a second"—she holds up her hand—"I will fix this."

"So you know how to tie your boat?" I question her, folding my arms in front of me.

"No," she answers, "but again, in a minute I will."

I open my mouth to say something but instead I look at her. "Move," I urge her as I step beside her and she actually moves over. "Come here, and I'll teach you." She squats down next to me. "So this is your cleat," I inform her of the silver T.

"Is that its official name?" she asks me with a serious tone.

"It's called a cleat." I nod at her. "The first thing you have to do," I instruct, unlooping the rope from the cleat, "is have your rope at an angle to the cleat." I show her. "Passing it under the far side of the cleat, and then wrapping it around your hand to do a circle." I show her the loop I just made. "Tying it to the other side of the cleat." I put the loop around the cleat and pull it closed. "And then repeat it on the back side." I do another loop and then tie it to the other side. "And that's it," I say to her and she looks at me.

"But is it sturdy enough?" she asks me and I nod at her.

"If it makes you feel better, you can do as many loops as you want," I tell her, undoing the loops now and letting the rope loose.

"What are you doing?" she asks me, shocked as she sees her boat untied again.

"I was showing you how to do it. Now it's your turn." I hand her the rope and she just looks at me. "I'm right here if you fuck up."

"Well, that's very encouraging," she mumbles, and it makes me want to laugh out loud but instead I just watch her hands. "Pull," she talks to herself. "Angle."

She repeats what I did. "Loop de loop." She makes up her own words. "And stick it in the hole," she says as she puts the loop around the cleat, "and repeat." She then looks at me. "I'm going to do three for good measure," she tells me and does another loop. "And boom." She does the "throw down the mic" action.

"What boat did you have before this?" I ask her as I rise up. She stands up beside me, looking down at her handiwork.

"Um," she says, "this is boat number one." She holds up one finger.

"You didn't have a boat before this?" My eyebrows pinch together.

"That would be correct." She takes a deep breath. "I don't think these ropes are going to move." She ignores the shock that is all over my face and walks past me to the middle cleat. "I'm going to tie this one."

"You don't need to," I inform her, but of course she ignores me and does what she wants to do. "But of course, do what you want," I mumble.

"Thanks, Mr. G," she says to me and I just stare at her.

"Mr. G?" I ask, tilting my head to the side.

"I call you Mr. Grumpy," she admits to me without an ounce of embarrassment. "But I figured it was rude, so I shortened it."

"Good call." I shake my head, walking past her toward the back of her boat. I look over and see Beatrice lying on the back of my boat. "You bought this boat?" I stop and look over at her.

"That I did." She smiles as she walks over to me. I see

48

that her toenails are painted a bright red.

"Do you know how to drive it?" I ask her, even though it's none of my business.

"I have a license." She cocks her head and glares at me. I just raise my eyebrows. "I have a captain coming to show me the ins and outs of the boat," she informs me, "so eventually I'll know how to drive it." She walks past me and gets on her boat. "The boat seems more secure," she says to me. "Now I have to go have a piece of pie." She smiles at me.

She walks to the sliding door and opens it, and before she steps into it, I speak up. "Xavier," I say, walking over to my boat with her looking at me, "instead of Mr. Grumpy." I get on my boat and Beatrice comes off the bench. I look over at her. "Or Mr. G." I walk over to the door, opening it, and stepping in, leaving her just staring at me.

I step into the cabin and look at Beatrice. "Now what did I do wrong?" I ask her as I walk over to her bowl picking it up. "I can tell you. I did rule number one and rule number two completely wrong, and I even messed up rule number three." I put food in the bowl and then place it in front of her. "It wasn't my problem and I didn't have to fix it." I stand. "But in my defense, I did it more for me than her." Beatrice ignores me and my struggles. "She could have hit my boat," I huff to her, walking over to the fridge. "You think she's alone on that boat?" I look out the window at her boat and the shades are closed, so I can't see anything. "Jesus, I'm a Peeping fucking Tom." I shake my head.

Beatrice looks up once she finishes eating. "You want a cookie?" I ask her and she wags her tail. "This is from the lady next door." I open the drawer and take a cookie out, holding it to her. "Sit," I instruct her and she sits, but her tail still wags and makes knocking noises. "We don't like her," I remind her. "Right?" I ask her and she just gently takes the cookie from my hand. "She called *me* grumpy?" I put my hands on my hips. "Me, grumpy," I huff, looking at Beatrice.

I can't even put into words how I feel right now. I'm like a full-blown ball of emotions. I'm angry but then irritated and that is making me angry. I think about the words my therapist said: talk it out, put pros and cons to everything. "Could I have been nicer to her?" I say, walking back and taking another bite of the pie. "Sure, I guess."

Beatrice sighs at me and walks over to her bed and lies down with a snort. "Could I have offered her advice?" I look up. "Probably." I sigh. "Did I judge her for buying a boat without knowing how to drive it? Yes. Did I do the same thing? Again, yes."

I take my fork and take another piece of the pie. "Will I try to be nicer to her? No," I admit. "Will I be cordial? Fine." I look at Beatrice. "Only because she likes you." I chew the bite of pie. "Will I let her get to me?" I look out the window toward her boat. "Absolutely not," I vow. Beatrice sticks her head up now and barks at me, probably calling me on my bullshit. "Oh, please, whose side are you on?"

SEVEN

VIVIENNE

I WALK INTO the boat before he says another word. "Xavier," I mumble his name, putting my phone on the counter. "Definitely not a name I would give him," I say, walking to the back of my room and stripping off the wet clothes and putting them in the sink. I turn on the shower. "Xavier," I repeat his name again, touching the water to make sure it's hot enough before I step inside.

Closing my eyes as I let the hot water rush over me, I still hear his voice. "What the fuck?" I swear. At that moment, I wish it was anyone else but him. I would have even gone with the asshole I last dated, who decided we were going to have an open relationship and never told me until I caught him with his dick in a blonde's mouth. At that point, I would have gone with every single ex I'd ever had instead of him.

I step out of the shower, grabbing the towel I hung up the night before and wrapping it around myself. Walking out to start another cup of coffee, I press the button, moving over to the fridge and grabbing the pie. I'm slicing a piece of pie when my phone rings. Leaning over to grab it, I turn it over and see that it's Lisa. "Hello," I greet, smiling.

"Vivienne," she says my name, and I look over and see that it's just a bit past eight o'clock.

"Uh-oh," I reply, grabbing the pie and a fork before walking over to the dining area. I walk up the two steps and sit down. "It's not even nine." She laughs. "Is this a good or bad phone call?" The nerves in my stomach start, my leg moving up and down as I wait for her to answer. I put the fork down beside the pie, holding my breath.

"I stayed up all night reading," she gushes. "Even though I know better than to pull all-nighters I just couldn't stop reading." The smile fills my face now. "It was so good, Vivienne. I can't wait for more."

I put my head back and sigh loudly in relief, picking up the fork and stabbing a piece of pie. "I wasn't sure, it's a bit different from the rest."

"It's so refreshing. This has to be the best book to date."

"Out of the forty books I've written, this one is the best?" I ask her as I chew a bite of pie.

"Yes," she confirms. She's been my editor since book five when I was signed with the publishing house. "Now the question is, when are you going to be done?"

"In about a month," I tell her.

"Ugh, fine," she huffs. "I can't wait to see where this is going to go."

"You and me both," I admit to her and she laughs. "But I promise, as soon as it's done, I will send it over."

"Fair enough. I have to get going. I'll be dragging my ass the whole day." She chuckles. "But it was worth it."

"Thanks for calling, I'm always nervous when you start fresh." I hang up and walk over to grab my coffee, going back to eat more pie.

I never thought I would end up becoming an author. I mean, I didn't even like writing in high school, but that all changed when I started college. I wasn't even sure what I wanted to do with my life, so I just took the basic college classes.

The truth be told, I was so homesick I would stay in most nights, then one night I stumbled upon this fan fiction page. I went down the rabbit hole reading story after story. So much so that an idea popped in my head, so I opened a Word document and started at one. The one thing I was obsessed with was murder mysteries. I just couldn't get enough of them, and after watching all the murder mysteries on television, I was hooked.

So I created Lucinda Cartwether, a little small-town girl who lives in a little small town solving the mysteries. Until the CIA gets wind of how good she is and now she works for them going around the world solving mysteries.

It started as a joke really. I would post one every two weeks on the fan fiction board. The response blew me away, I had over seven hundred comments in two days. People would count down the days until another dropped. When I finished it, they were asking when the next one would come. There was no pressure, so after doing two books on the fan fiction site, I thought it would be even cooler to publish the books.

Since I was doing this in secret, and I still am, I had to google how to publish a book. I did everything in steps. First thing I did was get it edited by four people. Then I read the book over and over again. To the point where I hated it and doubted every single word.

I got a graphic designer I went to school with, who helped me create a cover. I uploaded the two books I had on two of the fan fiction sites first. Within a month of each other. I was shocked when everyone who read it on the free site went ahead and bought it. Then when the third one came out three weeks later, it became an overnight best seller. I was climbing the charts on all retailers; I was so fucking shocked.

Here I was at twenty-three, writing books in secret from my family. Until I hit *The New York Times* and had a semi freak-out and called my aunt and namesake Vivienne. I was a sobbing mess and she rushed over to see me. If anyone would understand me writing and keeping it a secret, it would be her. She had this dating blog for the longest time and no one knew who she was. Until she fell in love with Uncle Mark and it went from dating advice to parenting advice. I swore her to secrecy and showed her the paper. She had no idea what she was looking at since I didn't use Vivienne Grant. Instead, my pen name was Cooper Parker. The minute she saw the name, she knew. She pulled me into her and cried happy tears with me.

It was the week after that I got an email from the biggest publishing house out there. I was shocked when they wanted to speak with me. Of course, Aunt Vivienne stepped in and acted as my agent, she went soft on them for two books. The advance was not even five thousand dollars, but she knew what she was doing. Because the books blew the other three out of the water. They came back and asked for three more, but now Aunt Vivienne went in there and had demands. Six figures with higher royalties, she gave them a couple of days to think about it or she would take it to auction. I had no idea what any of this meant, nothing. Not one thing, all I knew is I loved writing this fictional world I was creating.

Needless to say, they called the next day and the rest is history. I've been with them for the last five years. I've hit *The New York Times* over two hundred weeks, which is insane because one of the books stayed on *The Times* list for over forty weeks. There were even weeks when four books ended up hitting the same list. My books were translated into fifteen foreign languages, with five more contracts that just came in. The best thing out of all of this is no one knew who I was. There was a small cartoon character of my face, which wasn't even me, it was who I thought Lucinda looked like. The only thing we had in common was the hair color, other than that she had a pixie cut with blue-rimmed glasses.

It was crazy how successful I was, and I would

celebrate in secret because the only thing my family knew about my job was that it was in writing. They knew it had to do with writing and the computer, since I traveled with them wherever I went. Once Franny caught me editing and asked me what I was doing. I told her I was freelance editing. She never asked me another question. My father sometimes tried to ask me what I did and all I said was I edit websites.

So now I was writing a book in which Lucinda was falling in love for the first time. I didn't know if it could happen. She was such a badass single person, who you knew had a love life off the pages, but now she was actually catching feelings and I was loving every single second of it. It was the first time there were two storylines going at the same time.

Finishing off the pie, I get up and walk to the bedroom. I hop into shorts and a tank top before sliding back into bed, this time with my laptop. I open my computer, checking my emails first, before opening the Word document and reading the last three chapters I wrote.

I put on my favorite classical music and start writing. I don't even know how long I write, when I'm in the zone, the only time I stop is to pee and grab water. When I finally look up, I see that it's now dark outside. "I should have written outside," I mumble when I get off the bed, going to the bathroom. My stomach rumbles and I walk over to the kitchen, opening the fridge and feeling suddenly exhausted. I grab the loaf of bread, fishing out a couple of pieces, and butter them on both sides. Taking out a frying pan, I start the burner, putting a piece of bread down in the pan, and then adding two slices of cheese, covering it with the other slice of bread. Making my way over, I take out the kettle and plug it in on the counter, filling it with water and then starting it. I grab a couple of strawberries and some bananas and make a fruit salad of sorts, and place it on the table. I flip the grilled cheese over, pressing down while I prepare my tea bag in the big mug.

I put the grilled cheese on the plate and carry it over to the table, where I sit down, turning on the big television. I'm scanning the channels while I eat my grilled cheese and fruit. When I finish, I grab my mug and open the sliding door, the breeze hits right away, so I grab my sweater before going outside. I put it on and then make my way up the stairs. I walk down the front steps, going past the sun pads, stepping over the skylight before hopping on the seat in the front. I walk over to the side of the boat and look over to see if the boat is still attached. Seeing it is, I smile to myself. "Would you look at that," I say proudly. Turning, I make my way over to the steps to go to the sun pads when I see Xavier sitting on the front of his boat. His sun pads are gorgeous as they take up the whole front of the boat, and Beatrice is next to him while he reads a book. "Hi," I greet, and he just looks over at me, not saying a word. "Did you see my loop de loops are still in place?"

"I saw," he mumbles, and I take a sip of my tea.

"How was your day?" I ask him, feeling awkward that we are the only ones outside.

"Good," he replies, his eyes never leaving the book.

I look ahead at the stars in the sky as I finish my tea, my eyes getting heavy. "Well, good talk," I say, getting up and walking back up the steps, not even bothering to look back. I also ignore the need to throw my mug at his head, instead I walk back inside and lock the door. I'm about to flip him the bird when my phone rings, and I rush to the bedroom where I forgot it.

Grabbing it, I see it's my father on FaceTime, so I press connect. The little circle goes around and around before his face fills the screen. "Oh, thank God," he says when he sees me. "I've been calling you for the past five minutes. I was about to send out someone for a welfare check." I shake my head and laugh.

"After five minutes? I could have been in the shower."

"Or sex trafficked," he counters, pushing his face even closer to the screen. "How would we know?"

"Dad." I look at him. "You have the location on my phone. You know where I am at all times."

"It could have been a ruse." He shakes his head. "There are crazy people out there."

"Oh, I know," I agree. "I might be looking at one." I laugh at my joke as he glares.

"Anyway, I'm calling to tell you that we are coming in tomorrow. My boat is going to be there the day after."

"I can't believe you bought a boat." I shake my head. When I told him I bought my boat, he freaked out, had a hissy fit, and one day later bought his own boat.

"Well, I can't believe that my daughter is living on a boat, but it is what it is." He shrugs. "This is how we live now."

"I can't wait. I even learned how to tie a loop de loop. I'll show you," I tell him and he laughs.

"Can't wait. Love you." He disconnects before I have a chance to ask him who else is coming.

I put the phone down and continue locking up before sliding into bed and falling fast asleep.

EIGHT

XAVIER

"GOOD TALK," SHE says, getting up and walking away. I can't help but laugh silently at her sarcasm.

"You see what I did there, Beatrice?" I point out to her. "I didn't talk to strangers." I pet her head as she huffs and closes her eyes. "Stranger danger."

I look over and see the boat next to me is now pitch black inside. Did I look over all day wondering where she was? Pfft, no. Did I watch the light in the middle of her sun pads? No. Did I smile when she said loop de loop? Silently. Did I want to look over and engage in talking to her? No. Yes. Maybe. I was just so curious, and it was secretly killing me even though I pretended I didn't care. Obviously, she was by herself, unless her boyfriend or girlfriend was in the boat and never coming out.

"You ready to go in?" I ask Beatrice, getting up from the sun pads and looking over at her boat. I go to the side of the boat, walking around to the front with Beatrice behind me. When I get onto the deck, I open the sliding doors and step in. Putting the book down on the middle of the coffee table, I lock up the boat. I head downstairs to my bedroom, going straight to the shower. Stepping in and hissing through while it goes from cold to warm, I turn it off when it gets hot. Stepping out and drying off before I slide into bed. "Night, Beatrice," I yell from my bed. She usually sleeps on the couch and then comes to join me during the night, but sometimes, she will sleep in the second bedroom. A queen bed all for her.

I turn on my side, and it takes me a while to fall asleep. When the alarm rings the next day, I actually groan out loud. I shut it off and look down at Beatrice, who is sleeping. "What do you think about sleeping in?" I ask her. She doesn't even answer me. Instead, her snores fill the room. "Good talk." I use Vivienne's snarky comment, laughing to myself and falling back asleep.

I feel Beatrice get off the bed and stretch, and my eyes open but then close back again. Rolling to my back and grabbing the phone, I press the button and see it's almost eight o'clock. "This is a first," I announce, throwing the covers off me. Walking to the bathroom, I grab a pair of boxers on the way. I walk up the steps and start my coffee when I hear the phone ringing from my bedroom.

I look down at the coffee cup and then back to where the phone is ringing, wondering if it's worth not drinking the coffee. It takes me two seconds to ignore the phone, opting for drinking the coffee instead of getting it. Beatrice comes to stand next to me, nudging my leg. "Yeah, we are going to go out. Let me get dressed."

I walk back to my bedroom, grabbing my black track pants and a sweater before reaching for the phone. I look down and see that it's Miles, my agent. I'm about to call him back when Beatrice barks, and I know I'm pushing it. So I put the phone in my pocket and walk back upstairs. "Now you are rushing me?" I ask her, grabbing the coffee cup as I make my way to the door where Beatrice is waiting for me. "This is what happens when you sleep in," I tell her as I open the door, and she steps out before me.

I have one foot out the door when Beatrice barks, and I look over to see Vivienne walking down her stairs. She's wearing gray, loose-fitting pants and a knitted sweater. Her hair is pinned on top of her head, and she holds her coffee cup in her hand. She looks over and smiles at Beatrice. "Good morning, Beatrice," she greets and then looks at me. "Have a good day, Beatrice," is the only thing she says before stepping inside.

"See what I did right there? Not saying anything," I explain to Beatrice as we walk down the dock. "It's what you should be doing. Since when do you bark at people?" I ask her as we walk out of the gate. "She didn't even say anything to me," I scoff, looking back over my shoulder at her boat, trying not to let it bother me. "This is what we want." I take a sip of my coffee. "To just not be bothered."

The walk is different at this time of the day. There is

more noise and definitely more people out and about. I have to leash Beatrice when we turn the corner and see a woman walking down the sidewalk with six dogs. The walk isn't as long as it is at sunrise, and when we get back to the boat, my phone rings. I take it out of my pocket and see it's Miles again. "Hello," I answer, putting him on speakerphone while I give Beatrice fresh water and food.

"Xavier," he huffs, "I was wondering if you would answer my phone call."

I chuckle as I wash my hands. "Why wouldn't I answer your calls?" I dry my hands and then open the fridge, grabbing the eggs.

"I called you twice last week and again this morning," he says.

"I was going to call you back," I lie to him. "It was on my list." It was, in fact, not on my list because I don't have a list.

"Liar." He calls me on it. He has been with me since I was drafted. He was the only one who was always in my corner. When I let him, that is. I buried things so much that it was hard to even be honest with him. "I'm going to be in New York next week." I go back to the fridge, grabbing peppers, an onion, spinach, and ham. "I want to sit down with you."

"Don't you have other clients you should be wining and dining?" I ask him as I start chopping.

"I do, including you." He laughs. "I think we need to sit down and look at things." I shake my head, not saying anything. "We should at least discuss a couple of things."

"I don't think there is anything to discuss." I open my cabinet to get the frying pan. "There hasn't been anything in the past two years."

"I think there could be," he informs me, and I roll my eyes. "Just hear me out."

"Send me your schedule, and I'll see if I can make it work," I say to him, turning the burner on.

"No," he snaps. "I'm going to schedule you in, and if you don't show up, I'm coming to your boat."

"Are you this pushy with all your clients?" I spray the pan before putting in the veggies.

"When they are acting like asses, yes. So I can come to the boat next Wednesday at two o'clock."

"I might be busy," I tell him, and he roars out laughing. "I think I have to wash the cat that day."

"You got a fucking cat?" he shrieks.

"No." I laugh at him. "It was a joke."

"Good, at least your sense of humor is still there. Text me where you want to meet," he tells me, and I'm about to hang up on him. "Don't make me chase you down."

"Bye." I press the red button, ending the call. "Can you believe that?" I look over at Beatrice, who sits at the entrance of the kitchen, waiting to see if I drop any food for her. "He wants to sit with me?" I add the spinach and then the eggs. "For what?" I shake my head.

I try not to think about the bad that happened two years ago, but no matter how many times I try to push it away, it just comes full force. "What could he want to talk about?" I put my omelet on the plate, walking over to the U-shaped table. "Does he want to talk about how for five fucking months I threw up every single day with dread?" I take a bite, getting up to get myself orange juice and water. Only when I sit back down do I continue, "Does he want to talk about how the press raked me over the coals every fucking game?" I shake my head, the tightness in my stomach making it harder to swallow.

"No matter how good I did, they always were there to kick me in my balls." I laugh bitterly. "I scored a goal in overtime, which clinched us to head to the playoffs, and what did they do?" I put my fork down and look over at Beatrice. "They happily reminded me that I went ten games with not one point, and I had a minus twelve like I didn't already know this." I close my eyes and put my head back. "It was fucking hell. Every single day was worse than the other." My heart starts to speed up a touch now. "I would sit in my hotel room when we were on the road, in the dark, and hope not to wake up the next day. Sitting in the dark every night as the anxiety would come and claim its place in my head." The tightness in my chest starts.

"I had no one to talk to, not one person." My hands start to tremble. "No one, and when I tried, I was basically told that I had to suck it up and ignore the press. They brushed it off, like always. No one even listened. Not one person listened to what I had to say." I laugh now, but the sting comes to my eyes. "Ignore it, they said." I swallow as the tightness gets even tighter, and a lump starts to form in my throat, making it hard to swallow. "Easy for them to say. They weren't the ones on the cover of the newspaper. After every game, a microphone was shoved in my face, asking me why I wasn't scoring goals." My back starts getting sweaty for a second, while my neck gets chills, and I know I'm two seconds away from a panic attack. I know the signs. I've always known the signs, but I've ignored them because that is what you did, apparently. I try to control my breathing, but I get up on unsteady feet and walk to the bathroom, not sure if I'm going to throw up or not.

I walk into the bathroom and sit in front of the toilet bowl with my back to the wall. Beatrice comes in and lies next to me, putting her head in my lap. "I can't do it." I pet her head, ignoring the tears leaking down my face. "Won't do it." I put my head back against the wall. "I survived once. I'm not sure I can survive again," I admit, trying to calm myself down. I close my eyes as I try to level out my breathing. "When I called Miles, it was the last phone call I thought I would make. I don't know what would have happened." Taking a deep breath in and then letting it out, I open my eyes to focus on Beatrice in my lap. "If this is how I react to even meeting with Miles, how the heck am I going to lace up my skates?" I pet Beatrice. "I would have to go on the road again," I tell her, "and whatever team thinks of taking me, there is going to be news coverage all over it." I try not to let it bother me. "One thing I know for sure," I say, once I know my heartbeat is calming down. "There is no way in hell I'm playing for another organization that doesn't support my mental health." She looks up at me. "Not going to do it."

I close my eyes once more with my head back. I don't even know how long I sit here before getting up. I walk back up the stairs and clean up the mess in the kitchen. I throw out the now cold omelet that I only ate half of, adding the plate to the sink. I plug the sink and turn on the water, adding soap to it. I look up while I wait for the sink to fill up, and I see her.

She is standing on her boat's back deck and holds one of the lines in her hand. "What the hell is she doing?" I mumble as I move my head to see better. "Is she practicing tying knots?" I ask as she looks at the table in front of her, her iPad tablet propped up. "She's on YouTube," I tell Beatrice, shaking my head. "How crazy is that?" Beatrice walks over to the back door and barks when she finally sees Vivienne. "What did we say?" I ask her. She just looks over her shoulder at me, and I can swear she tells me to shut up and to leave her alone.

NINE

VIVIENNE

"QUICK HITCH," THE guy says on the video as I sit on the side of the boat tying knots to the side tenders. I watch the video twice before doing it with him, and it usually takes me seven tries before I actually get it. I've been doing this all day long.

I started the day at sunrise, watching the sun come up. This time, it was uneventful. I intended to spend the day writing, knowing my parents are arriving tomorrow, but I just couldn't get anything done. I would sit down and just look at the screen. After an hour, I closed it down and decided to scroll YouTube for boat videos. Now it's almost dark, and I am still doing knots. I finish the knot and then get up, my stomach growling. "Time to eat," I announce, grabbing my iPad and walking on the side of the boat to the side steps.

Sliding the door open and stepping in, I put the iPad down on the counter before going to wash my hands. I whip up a salad for dinner, watching the news before taking a shower and falling into bed. The soft alarm wakes me up, and when I open my eyes, I see I haven't moved all night long. I have never slept better in my life. Getting out of bed, I start the coffee before going to the bathroom.

"It's today," I tell myself as I pour milk into the cup of coffee. "It's today." I open the sliding door and make my way up to the top deck, where I sit and have my coffee. I hear Xavier open his sliding door and look over and spot him coming out wearing shorts and a sweater.

"Ready to go, sleepyhead?" he speaks to Beatrice, who ignores him and walks off the boat. I take a sip of my coffee as I stalk them walking past my boat. He brings his coffee to his mouth as they walk up the dock. My eyes watch them until I can't see them anymore. "Jerkface," I mumble, turning back to look at the sky. Yesterday when I walked down the stairs and saw them coming out, I made it a point not to talk to him and only spoke to Beatrice, even though she can't talk back. It still made me feel better. I wait until the sun is fully in the sky before I get up and walk back inside.

I'm about to start breakfast when my phone rings. I grab the phone and see it's my father. "Hello," I answer him.

"I can't get in," he huffs, and I laugh.

"You can't get in where?"

"In the gate," he grumbles, and I can hear my mother

in the background telling him to be quiet. "I'm not going to be quiet. My child is in there."

"Dear God, your child is in her thirties." I hear Cooper in the background. "The word child doesn't really fit in here."

"Oh my God," I huff and open the sliding door, sticking my head out. I walk off the boat and onto the dock, and I take five steps before I see my parents at the gate with Cooper, Erika, Franny, Wilson, Chase, and Julia all behind them. "You said you were coming," I say into the phone as I walk down the dock. "You didn't say the whole family was coming."

I walk up the silver plank, pressing the button for them to come in. "I like this," my father says, opening the door. "It's safe."

"Glad you approve," I reply to him, and then I see Wilson, Cooper, and Chase lean down and pick up six massive bags. "What is all this?"

"We brought some stuff," my mother replies, coming in and holding the gate for Erika. "Just some food and, you know, stuff."

"It's not even eight o'clock," I inform them as my mother walks down the ramp to stand on the dock.

"I like this." She looks around. "Very nice."

My father then joins her and puts his hand around her shoulder. "It's nice."

"What are you guys doing here?" I ask Franny and then look at her outfit. "What are you wearing?"

"I was on Pinterest and I put in boat outfits and this came up." I eye her pants that look like a leopard print with a matching bikini top. A black button-down long shirt covers her shoulders.

"I'm sure you searched up safari," Chase says, walking in.

"I did not," she snarls and walks to join my parents.

"I tried to tell them that this was too much," Julia says. "Erika literally said this is too much." She points at Erika, who yawns.

"I don't have any kids and I'm waking up at the ass crack of dawn." She glares at Cooper. "Ridiculous."

"So where is the boat?" my father yells, and I have to shush him.

"Dad." I walk down the ramp toward him. "Can we be respectful of my neighbors?"

"Sorry, honey," he says. "Where is your boat?"

"This way," I direct, leading them to my boat.

"It's like its own village," my mother observes as she looks around at all the boats. "Are people friendly?"

"I have no idea, Mom. I haven't met any."

"That's my girl," my father says, beaming with pride, the smile across his face. "Make no eye contact."

I stop right next to my boat. "This is mine," I announce proudly, pointing at my boat.

"Now this is what I'm talking about," Julia says, pushing past me. "Permission to come aboard the vessel?" she asks.

"She isn't a captain," Chase fills in, walking past her. "Nor is she in the navy. I'm sure this boat is big enough for all of us."

"Go ahead," I tell her, and she claps her hands, "but

take off your shoes."

"Oh, yeah," Erika chimes in. "I saw that in *Below Deck*." She looks at me, slipping her Gucci flip-flops off. "This is so fancy," she adds, following Chase who puts the bags down and holds out his hand for Julia.

"Thank you." Julia kisses his lips, and then he's about to hold out his hand for Erika.

"If you touch her," Cooper growls. "I'm going to make you sleep with the fish." He pushes past me and onto the boat.

"Can we be normal for one day?" Franny asks me as she steps on the boat.

"You're dressed to go on a safari," Cooper tells her. "For one day, can you dress normal?"

I look over at my father, who is standing on the dock with his hands on his hips. He's wearing shorts and a white polo, a baseball hat on his head with the New York logo. "So what do you think?" I ask him as he looks at my boat. He puts his arm around my shoulder as I watch my mother step onto my boat.

"This reminds me of the boat we rented in Greece." She looks at my father.

"Can I go inside?" Erika asks and I nod my head.

"Make yourself at home," I tell them.

Wilson just shakes his head at Franny. "We can't buy a boat. Where are we going to dock it?"

I'm about to step onto the boat and follow everyone inside when I spot Beatrice coming for me out of the corner of my eye. She starts sniffing my father's shoes and then comes to me, licking my hand. "I see you made at least one friend." My father laughs and I lean down to rub her neck.

"This is Queen Beatrice," I introduce and then look up just in time to see Xavier walking down the dock. I think about not introducing them, but then my father is going to ask me why I spoke to the dog and not the human who owns the dog. Then I'm going to have to tell him that he's a jerkface, and well, it'll just spiral from there.

"Hi," I say to Xavier, who looks at me and then my father. "Dad," I say to my father, "this is my boat neighbor, Xavier, and Xavier, my father, Matthew."

He looks at my dad and I can tell that his face is a bit pale, as my father reaches out to shake his hand. I'm waiting for Xavier to reach out and he does, but it's a quick handshake. "Hello."

"Is that your boat?" my father asks Xavier, who nods his head again and I just stare at him.

"It is," he finally says. "Got her two years ago."

"Nice," my dad compliments. "Have you been at this dock for long?"

"About the same time as I bought the boat," he shares, and I can see he's uncomfortable. He heads to his boat.

"Let me ask you," my father says, and he stops walking, looking back at him. "How is the crime rate here?"

I groan, making Beatrice bark at my dad. "Yeah, tell him it's none of his business." I rub Beatrice's neck.

"I'm just asking," my father defends. "You're a single woman, living on a boat in the middle of nowhere." He puts his hands on his hips.

"Wow, I could not feel any more desperate than I do right now," I retort. "Dad, you couldn't even get into the gate. I'm safe." I ignore him and step on the boat, Beatrice following me.

"Beatrice." Xavier snaps her name. "Let's go." He motions with his head, and Beatrice looks at me and then back at Xavier, not sure she wants to go.

"I feel you on a whole different level," I mumble to Beatrice, who jumps off my boat and walks over to Xavier with her head down.

"Did I see a dog?" Cooper says, coming outside.

"My neighbor's dog." I point at Xavier, who just puts up his hand.

"You should get a dog," Cooper suggests and I shake my head.

"I don't have time for a dog," I tell him, shaking my head. "Dad, get over here and leave my neighbor alone," I hiss, walking into the boat.

Stepping inside, I see that Erika, Julia, and Franny are standing in the galley, while Chase and Wilson sit at the table watching television. "Where is your father?" my mother asks as she sticks her head out of my bedroom.

"I'm right here," he announces, walking in. "I was scoping out the neighborhood."

"It's crowded in here," Franny says. "Babe, come, let's go check the upstairs." She winks at him and he gets off the chair and they walk to the door.

"Do not have sex on my sun pads," I grit between clenched teeth.

"She didn't say anything about the captain's chair," Franny says, laughing, walking out of the galley.

"They aren't going to have sex, right?" I ask Chase, who just shrugs.

My father laughs. "They aren't going to have sex. We are right here, and it's daylight." He puts his hands on his hips before picking up his baseball hat and scratching his head. "Julia," he says. "Can you please go upstairs and tell them they are not allowed to have sex on this boat."

"I'll come with," Chase declares. "We can cuddle on the sun pads." He looks at me. "Cuddling is allowed, right?"

"As long as you are dressed, yes," I tell them, and Cooper and Erika go with them.

"What do you know about your neighbor?" my father asks me when Cooper closes the door.

"Matthew," my mother scolds, shaking her head. "Don't start, please."

"I'm not starting anything, Karrie." He shakes his head. "I'm just asking."

"I don't know anything about him," I admit. "I know he has a dog, and two days ago, he helped me tie my boat."

"He looks familiar," my father says, and I roll my eyes. "I've seen him before."

"You say that all the time. Literally, each time we go somewhere you think you know someone."

"And I usually do," he says, walking to the back door and I see Xavier get on the dock. "I know him or I've met him."

"Or you've seen him on *America's Most Wanted*." My mother laughs. "Or *Dateline*. Or *48 Hours*, or…"

The sound of Xavier's boat fills mine as he starts it. I look out, seeing him untie the lines before walking over and disconnecting the water and electricity. "I don't recognize him," my mother says, standing beside my father. "I mean, he looks nice."

"He isn't," I mumble, and my father turns back to look at me. "He is." I shake my head. "So what is in the bag?" I try to change the subject. "We should set up something for breakfast and eat outside."

My father never moves from the window. "Yup." He nods. "Definitely know him."

"Matthew," my mother chides, "can you please help?" He turns, coming toward us. "You go upstairs and entertain your guests."

I laugh at her. "You're my guest," I remind her as I walk to the door and slide it open. I take a step outside and up the stairs, just in time to see Xavier's boat pull out.

TEN

XAVIER

I CLOSE THE sliding door behind me. "What did I tell you about talking to strangers?" I ask Beatrice, who just looks at me. I look back out the big window, seeing the man on the dock again. "Is that who I think it is?" My head is spinning right now. When I opened the gate to walk in, I was hoping I wouldn't see Vivienne. What I wasn't expecting was to turn onto our dock row and see her there with a man. I slowed down my pace, and if it wasn't for Beatrice, I might have turned around and hightailed it out of there.

I was hoping to just walk by and nod politely before walking on my boat. But what happened? "You betrayed me." I look at Beatrice. "Not only did you talk to strangers, you went on her boat." Beatrice looks at me. "Not cool." She huffs and turns around, walking to her dog bowl, seeing it empty. She looks back at me. "That's what you get for not listening to me," I mutter, walking over to her dog bowl and picking up even the water bowl.

"I swear that is Matthew Grant. Even the guy who came outside after him looked so familiar," I recount, as I turn the sink water to cold. "It has to be Cooper Grant," I say to her. "He had a baseball cap on, so I couldn't really see his face, but it had to be. Which would make sense since Matthew Grant was there." She just sits there waiting for me to fill her bowl so she can eat and drink. "Matthew Grant." I shake my head. "You know, he was GM for the other New York team." Beatrice yawns as I tell my story. "He was huge." I look down. "He is huge."

I look up for a second, straight out the window in front of me to see a guy walking up to the top of the boat with a woman following him. She sits in the captain's chair as the guy looks down at her, smiling before kissing her. Someone says something because the guy looks over at the stairs. "Wait a fucking second." I squint to look at the guys. I gasp when I see the guy's face. "That's Brad Wilson," I say. Then a guy comes up the steps saying something to him, and they both laugh. He's followed by a girl who walks forward to the front of the boat. "Am I really spying on my neighbor?" I mumble and then see the guy from before coming up the steps, taking off his hat and I now know that it's Cooper Grant. "Why the fuck does she have the fucking Dallas roster on her boat?"

I look over at Beatrice as my heart starts to beat a touch faster. "Okay, it's time to ship out," I announce.

"You'll eat in a bit." Walking outside, I hope none of them look over at me. It is one thing for Matthew Grant not to really know who I was, but Wilson will know me for sure. We've gone toe-to-toe a couple of times. I walk to the back of the boat, undoing the electricity and water. I roll up both cords, walk into the cockpit, sliding open the back window so I can look out when I take off. I start the boat, turning before jumping back off and untying my lines. I rush back to the boat hoping that I don't attract attention. I get into the captain's seat and make sure everything is okay. I look at Beatrice. "Place," I command her and she walks over to her bed and sits down. "Here we go." I pull out of my slip before I start the thruster to turn. I look at the back seeing that all eyes are on me. It's a good thing I'm inside and they can't really see me. I make my way out of the marina, going slow until I reach the end and can open it up a bit. I sit down, looking straight out at the open water. Every single time is like the first time. Every single time the minute I look out into the horizon of nothing, I feel this calmness over me. "What do you think?" I look over at Beatrice, who sits looking out the back of the boat. "Want to anchor and spend the day on the water?"

She barks at me. "And we are going to have a little chat, me and you," I tell her as I make my way over to a spot I found last year. It's away from everything, in a little cove area. I stop the boat as it moves side to side, walking out to the side of the boat and going to the front. I press on the anchor button and then hear the clinking of the chain as the anchor reaches the bottom. I look over the railing before glancing around us to see if we are still drifting. "We are anchored down. Now do you want to eat?" I ask her and she barks at me. "Is that so?" I laugh as I fill her bowls with food and water. "Good to know we are on the same page."

I put down her food and water, stepping out onto the back deck and look up at the sky, seeing not a cloud in the sky. "Looks like it's going to be a beautiful day." I walk back in and start the generator so I can get something cooking. I whip up an omelet and then walk outside to eat it on the back table. Heading back inside, I grab some juice. "What are the odds?" I ask Beatrice, who lies down next to me on her side. "That the girl who buys the boat next to me is related to Matthew Grant?" I shake my head, almost in disbelief. I eat my omelet as my head is going around and around with all the questions. Even when I get up to wash dishes, I'm still thinking about it.

"Want to go lie in the sun?" I ask Beatrice, who just lies in the shade and doesn't even acknowledge me. I run down to my bedroom, grabbing my laptop before walking out and feeling the heat of the sun run through me. I sit on the massive sun pads, putting the laptop next to me.

I stare out into the horizon, seeing that it looks like the ocean never ends. "Peace," I say to myself, "this is peace." I grab my laptop and open it, waiting for it to connect. Beatrice comes over and lies next to me. "Are you here to find out who she is also?" I chuckle when I open the internet browser and type in Matthew Grant.

I press enter and the first thing that pops up are

his stats with the NHL. I look over to the side where there are six pictures and his Wikipedia page. I scroll down the list where they tell you where and when he was born. His height and then salary and I whistle out, "Definitely made a fuck ton of money." I laugh. "He's worth a fortune. I told you he is big time." My eyes roam down to siblings and then wife and kids. "He has four kids." I gasp when I see Vivienne's name third. "What the hell?" I click on her name and a picture of her pops up and she is fucking beautiful. I bring the laptop closer to my face to see it better. Her hair looks to be curled or something, the makeup around her eyes lets the green pop out. "Look at her." I click her picture and then my whole screen fills up with pictures of her. Pictures from when her father won the Cup to pictures of her when Cooper won the Cup with Dallas. "Holy shit!" I exclaim when I see her next to *the* Cooper Stone. "Cooper Stone is her grandfather." Beatrice just looks at me. "He's a hockey god. Like, think of Old Yeller." I put my hand up to the sky. "That's how big he is." I shake my head as I creep on all her pictures. "Look at her dressed up in this one." I turn the laptop to show her as she wears a long gown. "It was at a foundation dinner for Max Horton." I gasp, "Holy shit! She's also related to Michael Horton and Dylan Stone." I shake my head. "And the up-and-comer, Matthew Petrov."

I don't even bother looking at anyone else, my eyes are just for her. I put the laptop down and get up, going to get my cell phone. I walk back out to the sun deck. "Okay, Beatrice, let the creepy stalking begin." I pull up

Instagram. "Do you think she is on Instagram?" I ask Beatrice, and when I type in her name, I press it and see that she's private. "Hmm, she's private." I put my phone down. "It doesn't say what she does for a living." I look at Beatrice. "What the fuck am I doing?" I close the laptop. "It's a total invasion of privacy." I rub my hand over my face. "What the fuck is wrong with me?"

I get up, grabbing my laptop and my phone. "That was not cool," I huff and walk back inside. "Not fucking cool at all." I put down the laptop. Beatrice comes into the living room. "I'm going to be the first to tell you I was wrong in doing that." Beatrice looks at me. "You deserve a cookie," I tell her, walking over and grabbing her one of the cookies Vivienne bought her. "Okay, fine, maybe she's a nice person." She tilts her head to the side as I wave the cookie in front of her, not doing it on purpose. "If anyone would understand me wanting to keep my shit to myself, it would be her." I hold out the cookie for her. "This doesn't mean we have to be best friends with her," I inform her, holding on to the cookie from my end while Beatrice holds on to the cookie from her end. "We still don't talk to strangers, and I would really like you not to get all excited when you see her." Beatrice just looks at me, probably telling me to shut the fuck up and leave her cookie alone. "Heck, I don't even know if I'm going to be nice to her. Jesus, can you imagine if they recognized me today, how she would have all the questions the next time she saw me? They probably don't even know the real reason I left the league. I mean, come to think of it, even when I left and told the owners and the GM why I was leaving, none of them said, *what can we do to help*? Nope, they just looked at me and were kind of relieved that they didn't have to deal with me anymore." I groan inwardly, letting go of my end of the cookie. Beatrice turns around with the cookie in her mouth and walks over to her bed. "Thanks for the talk." I put my hands on my hips while she chews her cookie.

I take a deep inhale. "You know what today needs?" I walk over to the cabinet where I keep my books. "It's a good time for a great book." I look at the shelf in front of me. "Where should we go today?" I ask as I look through the long list of books. "This one." I pull out the book that I must have reread over fifty times. "This one is always a good one." Walking out to the sun pads, I sit down and open my book. "This is just what I need today." I look at the water and then back at the book in my hand. "Just what I need," I sigh, trying to make me forget about the girl who has not only moved in to the boat next to me but has now taken over space in my head. Space that needs to stay empty. Space that has no place for Vivienne Grant.

Eleven

Vivienne

"OKAY, I'M GOING to admit something," my brother, Cooper, says from one of the sun pads he's sitting up on. The same one I have my coffee on every morning. Erika is in the middle of his legs, leaning back on him. Franny and Wilson sit on the other sun pad in the same position. They all look forward to the water.

"I'm all ears," I say from the front of the boat, where I sit with my legs crossed. My parents went for a walk with Chase and Julia after the massive breakfast we had. It took way too long to prepare, but then we sat out on the back deck and ate at the small table I have. Most of us sat on the bench in front of the table and ate with the plate on our laps. It was just like camping, except better.

"This is relaxing," he admits, and I smile at him. "I get the hype now."

"You haven't seen anything yet," I tell them, looking over my shoulder. "Wait until we take her out into the water."

"When can we do that?" Franny asks me.

"How long are you in town for?" I ask her, and she looks at Wilson.

"We leave today at three."

"That's in like two hours." I laugh at her, and she sits up.

"I know, but I didn't want not to be here in case there was drama." She throws her hands up in the air. "This went a lot smoother than I thought it was going to go."

I laugh at her, picking up my cup of coffee beside me. "Of course it went smooth. Why wouldn't it go smooth?"

Erika holds up her hand. "I can give you one reason: Matthew Grant."

I laugh. "He was skeptical, but he turned around," I reply nervously, hoping that it's true. Cooper and Franny now both laugh.

"The only way he's going to be at ease is if he can park his boat next to yours," Cooper states.

"And then hire people to sit on it and watch you," Franny continues for him.

"Well, he can't take the spot." I shrug. "It's taken, and from what I heard, this yacht club is full for the year, and there is a waiting list." I drink another sip, my mouth becoming suddenly dry. "The only reason I got in was that the person who owned this boat before me had this dock slip for the last three years."

"I want a boat," Franny says, and Wilson groans.

"How about we just come here when you want a boat?" Wilson suggests.

"That's a no." I shake my head. "I don't want you two defacing my spare bedroom."

"We won't have sex in the bed," Franny says, smirking. "We can have sex in the captain's chair."

"Can we not, for the love of God, talk about the sex you have with my sister?" Cooper pleads. "I'm trying to enjoy my quiet time."

All I can do is laugh at him, then I look over and see my father walking back with Chase followed by my mom and Julia. "How do you think Dad feels being without Uncle Max?"

"Like he lost a limb," Cooper states. "I swear he wanted to FaceTime him this morning at like six when he woke up."

"He must have called me Max," Wilson says, "six times before I finally said, I'm Wilson."

We all laugh, and he looks up from the dock. "What are you guys laughing at?"

"You," I reply. He just glares, walks onto the boat, and comes up the stairs and then stands on the bridge looking out.

Chase walks past him and comes down to the front, sitting next to me. "How was the walk?"

"Do you want the good news or the bad news?" He looks at me, and I'm afraid to even answer him. Julia comes over and sits next to him. "The good news is he stopped every single person he saw out on their boat."

"He did not." I gasp, looking at Chase and then at my

father.

"Oh, but he did." Julia chuckles, tying her hair on top of her head.

"Bad news is that one guy told him he got something stolen off his boat five years ago." I roll my lips. "The guy went on and on about it for fifteen minutes. Ask me what they stole." I just shake my head. "A mop."

"You're kidding," I say, looking at my father who puts his hands on his hips.

"No." My father shakes his head. "If they are going to steal a mop from his boat, can you imagine what they will do with you?" he asks, and Chase next to me tries to keep from laughing. "They can sex traffic you, and then where would we be?"

"Sex traffic?" Franny says. "Dad, she's in her thirties and not a virgin, who is going to pay for that?" She then looks at me. "No offense."

"None taken. I agree I could maybe be sold for a goat or even a sheep depending on where they are sending me."

"You are definitely not going to no sheik," Franny huffs. "Now, as much fun as this was, I have to get home to my baby." She looks over at Erika and Cooper, who nod at her. "But we will come back next week with the baby."

"We should buy a boat," Erika pipes up. "We can be sister boats."

"Why is it that your family," Julia says, standing up, "talks about buying boats, cars, and houses like it's going to the store to pick up salt?"

"I've come to the point when we don't question anything," I say, getting up. "Let me walk you out."

"Is that to make sure we leave?" Chase laughs at me as he walks up the steps to the bridge. "How many times do you think we'll be stopped for pictures?"

"Can you not do that here?" I say. "This is where I live, and the last thing I need is people to point and be like, 'you know who she is?'"

"No one is going to point at you," my father assures me, "and if they do, it will be like, 'don't touch that girl because her father is going to cut your balls off and use them as bait.'"

"Look at you being clever with the boat talk," my mother says, kissing his lips.

"Come on, I have to return you to Max in one piece," Julia prods. "He gets cranky when he's without you for too long."

"Guy can't live without me," my father jokes.

"You literally called him ten times on our walk," Chase cuts in, getting off the boat and holding his hand out for Julia.

"That's because I forgot that I called," my father says as he gets off the boat. We walk down the dock to the front gate, people definitely staring at the nine of us. "Well, the good news is I get the boat inspected tomorrow, and then it's all ours."

"I can't wait," I reply sarcastically as we walk up the ramp. Cooper presses the button, and I'm about to walk out when my father stops me.

"You stay here so you're safe." Everyone laughs at

him. "Give me a hug." I hug him, and he kisses my head. "Love you, baby girl."

"Leave her alone." My mother pushes him. "Call us if you need something."

"Do you have the Ring cam on your boat?" my father asks, and they all laugh at him. Franny comes back to give me a hug.

"I miss you," she says softly. "Will you come visit soon?"

"You come visit me," I urge. "Big man isn't playing."

"We can rent a boat," Wilson says to her. "If you want, I'll look into it when we get home."

"You know what that means," Franny states, walking to him. "We're getting a boat."

I shake my head and wave at them as they drive off. I won't deny that I miss them the minute they leave. I won't deny that getting on the boat, I look over to the chair my dad was sitting in and even miss him. I walk back into the boat, grabbing my laptop and heading out to sit in the same chair my father sat in.

Opening the laptop, I check my emails before loading my Word document and starting to write. I turn on some music as I fall deep into the story. I don't even know how long I've been writing when I look over and see Xavier coming back. He is upstairs on the top bridge. The back of his boat is fully open, and I take a second to look inside it. It's very pretty. Beatrice sits on her bed, looking out and enjoying the view. I get up, looking at him. He sure took off fast after my family was here. He probably thought I was going to have a huge party.

I stand on the back deck of my boat and put my hand over my eyes to shield myself from the sun. He is coming in back first. He sits on the top with his sunglasses on as he slowly backs in. He looks right and left. I feel like I should do something. I get off my boat and go onto the dock. "Do you need help?" I shout at him, and he just laughs at me, which pisses me off.

"Can you catch ropes?" he shouts back at me.

"Only if you throw them directly at me." I cross my arms over my chest. "Do you think you can do that?" I ask him, and he laughs again, but this time, I smile at the sound. It's the first time I've really heard him laugh, and it sounds good on him. I walk down toward the side of his dock, where he ties his boat up. He looks down in front of him. "What are you looking at?"

"I have four cameras in the back," he tells me, and I look up, seeing said cameras. "I'm making sure I don't smash into your boat."

"Yeah, if you could not do that, I would appreciate that very much," I joke with him as he puts the boat in park. He walks down the stairs, coming over.

"Ready?" he asks me, and I want to flip him the bird. He picks up the black rope and tosses it to me. I catch it, smiling over at him like, "take that," and he tries not to smile but fails. "You need to tie that one to that cleat." He motions to the cleat in the front. I nod at him, and he walks into the boat, sitting in the captain's chair inside. I wait for him to back up the boat more. When he finally gets it backed, I squat down and tie the boat exactly how he taught me.

I get up, and he comes out. "Do you have to tie one more?" I ask him, and he tosses me the other rope, which I catch again. I pull it tight before making three loops. Once it's tied, I get up and dust off my hands. "I did it," I say more to myself than to him. I put my hands on my hips and look at my handiwork, feeling especially proud of myself. "Take that," I huff as he jumps on the dock and smirks at me before he hooks up his electricity and water. "You're welcome," I call to him as I walk past him, and I hear him laugh again. I want to ignore how I get goose bumps. Instead, I blame it on the nonexistent wind.

"Where are you going?" he asks me, standing up, and I turn around to look at him. He's in shorts and a white shirt. I can't see his eyes because of the sunglasses.

"I'm going to go and give myself a high five," I tell him honestly, and then he throws his head back and lets out the biggest laugh yet.

"Come on," he says, motioning with his head as he walks past me and onto his boat. "I owe you a drink."

I look at him, my eyebrows pinching together, and I wonder if I heard him right. "I'm sorry?" I ask, not sure what the hell is going on.

"You helped me out," he replies, standing on his back deck, "by tying my ropes." I tilt my head to the side as Beatrice comes over to me and circles my legs. "So for that, I owe you." He turns walking into the cabin and over to the side panel where he clicks switches on.

"Is this a ploy?" I ask Beatrice. "Is he for real?" All I can do is stand on the deck, watching him as he makes his way to the captain's chair inside and turns off the boat.

He then walks to the middle of the boat, looking out, putting his glasses on his head. "I'll grab you a beer."

Go home, my head yells out, but my feet are in control. Instead of just walking to my boat and ignoring him, just like he did me all those times, I walk over and step on his boat for the first time. "This should be fun," I mumble.

Twelve

Xavier

I WALK OUT to stand on my back deck. "You helped me out." I can hear the words coming out of my mouth at the same time as the ones in my head tell me to *shut up*. "By tying my ropes." I watch Beatrice walk over to her, and I shake my head. *Did we not just talk about this?* I think to myself, but instead, I look at Vivienne. "So for that, I owe you." I turn, walking to the side panel where I click on the electricity.

When I took up the anchor before, I was really hoping her family would be gone by the time I got back. I had wasted all day out there on the water and it was time to head back before high tide came in. I mean, technically, I could have stayed out all night, anchored there, but then what, was I never going to come back? So I started the boat and took my sweet time sailing back. The view and being on the water calmed me. My hands started to sweat a little when I knew I was getting closer, but I pushed through it. "It's going to be fine," I told Beatrice, who at this point was just lounging, living her best life. The yacht club got closer and closer, and I did a deep exhale when I pulled into my row. When I didn't see anyone on the top of the boat, I thought I had escaped. What I wasn't expecting was for her to look around the back of her boat at me. I focused on backing up my boat, and not hitting hers. I wasn't expecting her to walk off her boat and come onto the dock. I also wasn't expecting her to ask me if I needed help. I should have just told her no, but that is how we do it at the dock. Everyone helps out if they can. "Can I help?" she asked me, and I thought about telling her no, but the reality of it was I needed help securing the lines. She made me laugh when she asked me to throw it directly at her. The sound of my laughter was even foreign to my ears. When I went back in to park the boat, I thought about the last time I laughed. I couldn't even remember. I parked the boat, looking out at her, watching her hands tying the knots. She tied one and then moved on to the other. The smile on her face was contagious, making me smile. She gave herself props, dusting her hands off as she did it.

I walk back looking out, putting my sunglasses on the top of my head. "I'll grab you a beer." I motion with my head, even though everything in me tells me this is a bad idea. That I should leave well enough alone. I already dodged a bullet with her father and brother today. How many times was that going to happen?

From the looks of things, they might be here more this summer, the inevitable was going to happen. I just didn't want her to then turn around and tell them I was a dick to her. Not that it mattered, but I still didn't want to be that guy. I didn't want to be the man who I myself hated.

The walk over to the fridge is maybe ten steps, but it feels like it's shorter. Opening the other drawer and bringing out the bottle opener, I take the top off. "Do you want a glass?" I ask over my shoulder, finding her sitting at the back bench talking to Beatrice. That dog knows everyone's secrets. I laugh to myself. It's a good thing she can't tell any of mine.

"No." She looks up, and I see that her green eyes look almost blue in the sun. Grabbing myself a bottle of water, I walk back out to her.

"Here you go." I hand her the beer, her finger grazing mine as she grabs it. Her hair blows in her face from the breeze as she tucks it behind her ear.

"Thank you," she says as I turn around and grab a chair to sit at instead of going to sit next to her on the bench. I sit down facing her, giving me a full view of her.

I put my ankle on my knee, holding up my bottle of water. "To loop de loops." She throws her head back and laughs at that. She's wearing a loose white tank top, so I can see her whole neck. I have this image flashing in my head of me sitting next to her with my arm around her shoulders, leaning in and kissing her on her neck. I blink twice to make the image leave my brain.

"To loop de loops." She holds up her beer and takes a

sip. "Are you not having a beer?" she asks when she sees me take a sip of my water.

I shake my head. "I don't drink," I admit, and I wait for it. For the questions that always come after I declare I don't drink. *Why don't you drink? What happened? Are you in AA? You can have one drink? How come?* I brace myself for what comes next. Waiting. But instead of asking me the questions, she just nods her head at me, rendering me speechless and in shock. "Aren't you going to ask me why?"

Beatrice gets on the bench next to her and lies down, putting her head on Vivienne's leg. Vivienne's hand comes to rub Beatrice's head. "Why would I ask you why?" She tucks one of her legs under her other.

"Because it seems everyone does." For the first time, I'm honest about things. I never had the balls to say what I wanted to say. Always guarded in what I said. It took lots of therapy to make me be okay with speaking my mind. It took months of therapy to realize that what I wanted to say mattered. It also went against everything I had said to myself while I played hockey. Their motto: hide everything. At the end, I was even hiding myself.

"Well," she says, taking another sip of the cold beer. "I figured if you wanted me to know why you weren't drinking, you would have said, 'no, I don't drink because…' and then you would have given me your reason." She looks at me, her hair flying again in the wind. I can't help but wonder how her hair would feel between my fingers. Just the thought makes my stomach tighten and my heart speed up. "But you didn't, so it means that you aren't going to share. Which means it's none of my business."

"Just like that?" I ask her. This whole thing has put me on edge and pushed me out of the bubble I've created for myself in the last two years. A bubble that consisted of four people. Beatrice. Shelly, my therapist, Steven, my friend and co-captain, and Miles, my agent. A bubble that my therapist wanted me to expand. A bubble I wasn't ready to expand, or perhaps I was. Maybe this was a sign to make another friend. Or it could have also been the sign I didn't need another friend and was fine the way I was.

"Just like that," she confirms as she takes another sip of the beer. "How was the water today?" Her eyes light up just a touch more when she asks me.

"Calm. It was a gorgeous day."

I don't know what to say to her, and it looks like she's uncomfortable also. She puts the half-drunk bottle of beer down on the table and looks down at Beatrice. "I'm going to go now, pretty girl." She gets up, and Beatrice just looks at her. "Thank you for the beer." She points at the bottle on the table. "I'm going to head out. Spending the day with my family is exhausting," she says, and I wonder if I should get up and walk her to her boat, but my body feels like cement.

"They looked like they were having fun," I say of her family. I spent way too much time googling and then trying not to think about it.

"They did." She chuckles. "My father thought he recognized you." The minute she says the words, my whole body goes tight. The burning sensation starts to climb up the back of my neck. My stomach contracts, and then the lump starts to form in my throat. My ears suddenly fill with the sound of my heart beating ridiculously fast. My hands start to get clammy. "Don't worry, he thinks he knows everyone." She gets on her boat, giving me one last smile before she walks in and shuts the door.

I bring the bottle to my mouth, taking a sip of the cold water, hoping to everything I don't throw it up on the back deck. Swallowing down the lump in my throat, I get up and grab the bottle of beer before walking back into the boat. I pour the remainder of the beer down the drain and hang my head. "Do you think they knew who I was?" I look over at Beatrice, who has come to sit in the middle of the kitchen, probably waiting for her dinner.

I fill her bowl with food and then start closing the boat up. When I'm on the water, I always open the back sliding doors so I can see out the whole way. I go upstairs to the top, zipping up the curtains in case it rains. When I come down, I close up the back of the boat, securing the doors in place. "Want to go for a walk?" I ask Beatrice, who wags her tail.

I grab the leash, heading out, and I make the mistake of looking in her boat as I walk by. I see her silhouette sitting at the table as she talks on the phone. "Can I be more creepy?" I ask Beatrice as I quickly turn around to walk ahead. "All that is missing is me pressing my face to the glass looking in." I shake my head, walking out of the gate. I don't talk the whole time we walk and stay out as long as I can. Only going back when my stomach starts to growl.

When I walk back to the boat, I force myself not to look around. Getting onto the boat, I take off my shoes before walking in and going to grab one of the prepared meals I have made for myself, heating it up.

When I sit down, I look at Beatrice. "Her father recognized me," I tell Beatrice. "Do you think I should have told her who I was?"

She sniffs the table while I continue talking to her. "What do you think I should have done? Like, if I was going to tell her who I was, that was the perfect opportunity."

I take a bite of the chicken with some couscous. "I don't owe her anything." I try to convince myself. "She didn't even ask me why I wasn't drinking," I huff. "Not once did she pry. Even when I asked her if she was going to ask me why, she still said no." I shrug. "It's just as well."

Getting up, I walk over to the kitchen, washing up and tossing out my stuff. I grab my laptop, opening it when I sit on the couch, and come face-to-face with Matthew Grant staring at me. "Okay, got to erase my history," I say, going up and deleting all history and then shutting down the laptop. "It's going to be fine. I'll be cordial, and it ends there. If her father comes back and recognizes me, then so be it. I'll confirm who I am." I look at Beatrice who lies down in the middle of the room sideways. "You think she'd be pissed I didn't tell her?"

I rub my hands over my face. "I don't care. I've spent

way too much time even thinking about her," I gruff out, standing. "I'm going to take a shower." I walk down to my room, undressing on the way. The shower is quick, and when I get into bed, I reach for the book but not even that settles me. When I finally turn off the lights, I lie down on my pillow. "You need to either tell her or be okay that you didn't," I tell myself. "Which one is it going to be?"

THIRTEEN

VIVIENNE

THE SOFT ALARM fills the room, and I groan, reaching for my phone under the pillow where I always put it, but my hand comes up empty. I peek open one eye, but it's completely dark. My eyes try to get used to the dark, but instead, they just close again. My hand moves around the bed for the phone, but I can't find it. I sit up in bed, listening and finally realizing I left the phone on the table in the galley. "Great," I mumble, walking to the table and stepping on the step to get it. I turn off the alarm and look up to see Xavier walking by the boat with a cup of coffee in his hand and Beatrice next to him.

I watch him until I can't see him anymore before turning and wondering if I should go back to bed. Instead of climbing back into bed, I walk over and start my coffee before heading to the bathroom. I slip on a pair of shorts and walk back out to the coffee machine making my coffee. "Are you going to go outside and watch the sunrise?" I ask myself when I feel a ball of nervousness hit my stomach. "Are you going to go outside and maybe see him?"

I shake my head. Last night, sitting down with him at the table while I drank a beer had been the most nervous I'd ever been around a man before in my life. The minute he sat down and I looked at him finally, which was weird since I've seen him before but never that close. His hair is a bit lighter than brown, maybe because of the sun and the scruff on his face is longer than it looks. His eyes look brown from afar, but when you get close, you can see they aren't. I couldn't even tell you what color they were. It's so strange because they are brown in the center and blue gray around the pupil. Sometimes they looked gray, while other times, they looked brown. I tried not to stare too long, which made me even more self-conscious about not staring and that made me itch to leave. I must have sounded so rude when I just up and left in the middle of the conversation. I sit at the table, turning on the television as I enjoy my coffee.

The phone beeps, and I reach for it, seeing that it's Franny.

Franny: Are you up?

I laugh at her message, and instead, I press the FaceTime button. I look at the clock and see it's not even five her time. She answers right away. "Well, well," I say, looking at her sitting on her couch with Stella in the middle of her legs. "Look who it is, Stella Bella."

She just laughs at me as she waves her hands in the air. "Thanks for calling me right back last night," I tell Franny, who has a cup of coffee in her hand. "It's a good thing I wasn't in trouble."

Franny throws her head back and laughs at the top of her lungs. "If you were in trouble, why would you call me? I live in Dallas." I roll my eyes. "If anything, you would have called Auntie Vivi, who would have then called Stefano, who would have then bailed you out."

"Wow, so that's how it goes," I say, taking a sip of my own coffee.

"We got in later than we thought," she huffs. "Then I got home, and this girl just wanted her mama." She kisses Stella's head, hugging her. "I fell asleep before her in my bed. Anyway, I'm here now." She smiles. "So what was the big question you wanted to ask me?" Franny asks, and I tap my nails on the cup in my hand. "Oh my gosh." She sits up. "The nervous tap-tap-tap of nails." She looks into the phone. "Should I call Wilson to take Stella?" Her eyes go big. "Is this a sex question?" She puts down her cup of coffee and claps her hands, Stella copying her.

"It's not a sex question," I inform her. "It's not even that big of a deal—"

"You called me for advice," Franny cuts me off. "If that isn't a big deal, I don't know what is." She chuckles. "You never call me for advice. The only thing you call me for is to ask if you can stay with me when you come to Dallas."

It's my turn to laugh now. "I call you for more than that," I protest, and she shakes her head. "Anyway, so you know my neighbor?" I start to say. The lump forms in my throat, and I push it down.

"The one Dad spent half the day saying he knew but didn't?" Franny laughs. "Then it got Cooper saying, 'I think I know him, too.' You should have heard them the whole fucking flight. Mom finally snapped and shut them both up."

"Yeah, him." I ignore the fact they were talking about him, even when they left. "Well, he came back from wherever he went, and I helped tie his boat."

"Oh my God, you fucked him." She gasps and then puts her hands on Stella's ears. "Don't listen to this part. Your aunt Vivi is a dirty, dirty girl."

"Okay, well, one, her mother is dirtier than her aunt." I hold up one finger. "And two, why would you automatically go to me f—" I stop before I say the word. "Banging my neighbor?"

"Because everything is about banging," she says, and then I hear Wilson laugh in the background.

"Morning, Wilson," I greet him, and he mumbles.

"I'm going to take my pretty lady." He grabs Stella, who is so excited to see him that she grabs his face and leans in with her mouth open to give him a drooly kiss. "Now, you can't give anyone else kisses like that," he tells Stella. "Boys are gross."

"Oh, here we go," Franny says, and Wilson leans down and kisses her on the lips. "I'll join you guys when we finish here."

"Wait," I say. "Wilson, I want your opinion, too."

"Wow," Wilson replies, sitting on the floor, putting

Stella down so she can play. "You must be really desperate if you are asking for my advice."

"Okay, anyway, I swear having a conversation with you guys is like herding cats after giving them catnip," I grumble. "He invited me over for a drink after I helped tie his boat."

"Is that code"—Wilson looks back at Franny—"for a BJ?"

"Oh, good God." I throw my hands up and slap the table in front of me. "It's not always about that."

"But it is," they both say at the same time. The two of them slept together at my cousin Michael's wedding. Only to come face-to-face again a couple of months later, and Wilson didn't remember. It was funny watching them, and even funnier when their sex tape got leaked. I mean, funny for us, not for them. Most definitely not for my father, who at that point was foaming at the mouth.

"Okay, well, there is no sex on any table," I inform them as they are about to say something else. "There is no sex anywhere, not the table, not the chair, nowhere. He can barely say two words to me."

"But he invited you for a drink," Wilson says, picking up a toy and handing it to Stella. "So he said at least that."

"Yeah, and this is where the question comes in. He hands me a beer, and he doesn't drink anything."

"Maybe he's cleansing his system," Franny suggests. "People do that. It's like a huge reset." Wilson looks over at her, confused. "It's a thing, Wilson."

"When I asked him if he was having a drink, he said

he doesn't drink." I tap my fingers again.

"Okay." Franny ponders, not sure she understands even when I say the words. I'm not even getting my point.

"Should I have asked him why?" I ask them. "Should I have pried?"

Franny shrieks. "You don't pry ever," she reminds me. "Like if there is anyone in this whole family who actually minds their business, it's you."

"I know!" I shriek. "Last time the girls were together—"

Franny cuts me off. "Julia had to beg you to ask her for details."

"Why would I want to know her favorite sex position," I try to defend myself, "when she's doing it with my brother?" I fake vomit. "I wouldn't ask Erika either."

"But you're okay asking Franny?" Wilson asks me.

"I've pretty much seen what you two do in the bedroom," I remind him. "It's seared in my brain for the rest of my life."

"So dramatic." Franny rolls her eyes. "The question I think you need to be asking yourself is, do you want to know why he's not drinking?"

"What if you ask him, and he's a recovering alcoholic, and this is a sore subject for him?" Wilson puts in his two cents. "Like, how awkward is that?" He looks at Franny. "The girl who creeps on you wants to know why you aren't drinking."

"Hold on." I raise my hand. "I'm not creeping on him." I can't even say another word because my neck suddenly fills up with heat, and my heart starts to speed up, knowing that maybe I was creeping on him, but it was because he was a jerk and not because I liked him. "I'm done with you guys," I say, shaking my head. "Also, you both give horrible advice, and that is why I never ask either of you."

"Sure," Franny says, nodding her head sarcastically. "It's not because we just called you out."

"I have to go work," I tell them both. "Have a nice day." I don't even wait for them to tell me goodbye before I hang the phone up on both of them. "Creeping on him," I repeat the words and pfft out. "Like I would creep on him." I get off the bed. "I'm going to show them," I huff. "I'm not even going to go outside today." I grab my laptop and walk to the bed. "I'm going to work all day," I tell myself as I open the laptop. "Creeping on him." I shake my head. "I don't even like him." I check my email. "I like his dog better than I like him." My head yells *liar*. "I mean, fine, he's good looking," I admit as I switch my emails off, not even paying attention to anything. "And his laugh did make my stomach flip, but I was hungry." I open my Word document. "I'm going to focus on work."

I read back the chapters I wrote the other day to make sure that I'm where I want to be. I read my plot notes on what I want the next to be, and before you know it, it's almost six o'clock. My neck hurts, and my legs are cramped when I get out of bed. I walk to the back door, realizing it's almost sunset. I open the door, stepping out for the first time all day. I stretch as soon as I get on the back deck and stop mid-stretch when I hear a bark from beside me. "Hello, Beatrice," I greet her, and I'm shocked when she jumps off her boat and comes onto mine. She comes over to me, and I take a look back, seeing Xavier isn't anywhere in sight. I squat down in front of her. "How was your day?" I ask her as I pet her neck, and she licks my face. "Was it nice out today?"

"Oh." I hear Xavier from the side of me. "You're here."

I look over and see him walking out of his boat without a shirt on. I don't even try not to look down at his chest. "Dammit," I mumble under my breath, then stand and look over at him. "I'm here." I hold up my hand. "Why, did you miss me?" I look around now, seeing that the sun is setting. "I can't believe I worked the day away." Beatrice walks around my legs, and I put my hand out to pat her head.

"I'm about to throw some steaks on the grill," he says, and there it is, the little ting of nerves forming in my stomach. "Why don't you come on over?"

I fold my hands over my chest as I glare at him. "What is up with you?" I can't help the words that come out of my mouth. "Yesterday the drink, today dinner." I shake my head, and then I gasp. "Did my father threaten you?"

He laughs again, and there it is again, the little flutters. *I must be hungry,* I tell myself. "I met your father for five seconds," he reminds me, "and you were there." He shakes his head. "Why would he threaten me?"

"To be nicer to me." I can't even try to stop the words from coming out of my mouth. Even when I hear them, I want to cringe at how they sound.

He chuckles, thank God, thinking it was a joke. "Promise I'll be nice. Don't worry, I don't bite." He holds his hands up.

"That's usually what they say, right before they jump for your jugular," I say the words out loud.

"I have two steaks out and I'm not going to eat both, so would you like one?" He adds softly, "If you want, I can cook it and just hand it to you."

"No." I shake my head. "That sounds silly. I'll make a salad and come over." I look down at Beatrice. "Do you want to stay with me or go with that guy?" I point over at Xavier, who shakes his head laughing at me.

"Beatrice, come." He motions with his head. "I'll give you a special Vivienne cookie," he bribes her. "Come when you're ready," he invites me, and all I can do is nod at him before walking back into the boat.

"Why would you agree to that?" I ask myself as I walk to my bedroom. "What if he puts poison on your steak?" I stop walking. "You really need to get out of the book and"—I sniff, picking up my arm—"shower before you go anywhere."

Fourteen

Xavier

"NO." SHE SHAKES her head, and all I can do is look at her while my heart speeds up. "That sounds silly. I'll make a salad and come over." She looks down at Beatrice. "Do you want to stay with me or go with that guy?" She points at me, and I can't help but laugh at her again. Why does everything she say make me laugh?

"Beatrice, come." I motion with my head and see that she's trying to decide if she should stay with Vivienne or come to me. "I'll give you a special Vivienne cookie," I tell her, and Beatrice jumps off her boat and comes to me, sitting in front of me, waiting for the cookie I promised her. "Come when you're ready," I invite her, and she nods, walking back into her boat.

I look down at Beatrice. "Do we know what we did wrong over here?" I ask before turning and walking into the galley, going for the drawer that has the cookies. "Number one, you barked and left the boat." I hold up a finger. "Number two, you left the boat and didn't even come back to me." I add another finger to the one, and all Beatrice can do is look at my hand that has the cookie in it. "And number three, you made me ask her to come for dinner." She looks at me, tilting her head to the side, no doubt telling me I'm full of shit.

"Here is your cookie." I give it to her. "Under protest," I huff. "Seriously, you need to stop pushing yourself at her." Beatrice just eats the cookie, not giving a shit what I'm going to say. "Now I have to have dinner with her. Are you happy?" I ask her, and her tail flops around. "Yeah, whatever." I walk over to the kitchen and grab more veggies, slicing them and adding them to the foil pan. "Should I have done baked potatoes?" I look over at Beatrice. "Or maybe even some rice?" I walk over to the cabinet, opening it, and grab down the rice packet. "This I can do in the microwave," I say, looking back and wondering if I should open the package.

"Why the fuck am I so nervous?" I put the rice down and shake out my hands, hoping to shake out the nerves. "I've never been nervous around a girl before." I look at Beatrice, who I swear laughs at me. "I used to date before you." I glare at her. "Not religiously but occasionally." She puts her head down. "It's hard to date when I travel so much."

I shake my head. "I'm not having this conversation with you. Maybe I'm nervous because if I'm not nice to her"—I swallow down the lump—"her whole family is going to kick my ass." Beatrice just closes her eyes to sleep. "Thanks for the talk." I laugh nervously. "I'm going to put on a shirt," I tell her, walking down the steps and into my room.

Opening the top drawer, I put on a white T-shirt and take a second to look at myself in the mirror. "It's not a date, asshole," I tell my reflection before walking up the steps and back to the galley.

Looking straight out of the open back door, I see her walking over. She changed out of her shorts is the first thing that I notice. Her hair is blowing softly in the wind as she walks over with her head down. Thankfully, it gives me a second to take her in. She is wearing cutoffs, her legs bare with no shoes on them, her button-down short-sleeved gray-and-white-striped shirt tucked in the front. "Hi," she greets, stepping on the back deck, and I see she has a huge bowl in front of her. "I made salad," she tells me, holding out the wooden bowl.

I walk over to her. "Thank you." I grab it. "You look nice," I say, and if I could kick myself, I would.

"Thank you," she replies. "I figured after working all day, I should shower and change." She looks at me. "You look nice as well." She laughs nervously, and every nerve I had in me seems to settle in place. "I love this layout." She looks around the boat. "It's so spacious."

"Thanks," I say to her, turning around and putting the salad on the counter. "Would you like something to drink?" I ask, trying to keep my hands busy.

"I'll have what you're having," she says to me, not moving from the spot in the middle of the room.

"You can have a glass of wine if you like," I offer, walking to the wine fridge.

"I'll just have water, if that is okay." Now I'm suddenly feeling guilty that she is having water because of yesterday. "I work tomorrow, so I'll just stick to H2O."

I nod at her. "Make yourself at home." I point at the couch, and she walks over and sits down. Grabbing a bottle of water from the fridge, I turn and stop in my tracks when she picks up the book from the middle of the table. She turns it over and reads the back of the book. "Here you go," I say, handing her the bottle of water.

"Is this good?" she asks me of the book.

"Yes." I nod at her. "I've been hooked on that series for the last two years." She looks at the front of the book. "It's great if you like mysteries."

"I'll have to look him up." She puts the book down. "Can I do anything to help?"

"Not really. I'm going to throw the steaks on the grill." I turn, walking back to the fridge and taking out the steaks I marinated this afternoon. "How do you like your steak?"

"Medium is good." She gets up.

"Where would you like to eat?" I ask her as I step out onto the back deck, going to the grill. I pick up the cover, making sure it's hot enough before placing the steaks in the middle of the rack.

"Outside." She follows me outside. "If that's okay. I spent the day in bed."

I look over at her. "I thought you were working?" I question, confused now. Did I look outside a hundred times today? Maybe. Was it to make sure it was still sunny? Yes. Was I hoping to catch a glimpse of her? Yes. But only to make sure she was okay. She did leave my boat after having a drink. If something happened to her, I would be the prime suspect. Maybe I need to change up my reading preferences.

"I was working." She pulls the chair out at the table. "In bed."

I tilt my head to the side as I put the tray of veggies on the rack beside the steak. "I don't even know how to respond to that one," I admit, and she laughs.

"Wow, now that I think about what I said, I just realized it could mean so many things." She laughs as she takes a sip of her water while her stomach lets out a huge rumble. I can't help but laugh at her when she opens her mouth in shock and puts her hand to her stomach. "I guess I'm hungrier than I thought." She gets up. "Can I set the table while you cook?"

"Um, sure," I reply, and she looks at me.

"Just point me in the direction, and I'll only open certain cabinets," she tells me, laughing.

"You can open any cabinet you want, but to speed things along, they're in the bottom cabinet under the sink for the dishes," I direct her, laughing. "And the top drawer to the right for the utensils."

I watch her walk back into the boat, her shirt covering most of her ass. But my eyes stay glued to it anyway, that and her legs. She stops by Beatrice's bed, bending over, and I swear to Christ, my cock gets up and is ready to play. "Jesus," I mumble, looking down at the outline of my cock, pulling my shirt lower to make sure it's covered. "Can you take a chill pill, dude? She's like out of your league, and also, we don't like her like that." I look back and find her in the kitchen opening the drawers. She grabs two plates and then puts the utensils on top. She looks over at Beatrice as she talks to her. But because of the sound of the steaks, I can't hear what she's saying.

"I think Beatrice is hungry," Vivienne says as she walks out of the boat.

"Beatrice had her dinner and dessert," I inform her and look at Beatrice. "Did I not feed you?" I ask her. She ignores looking at me and instead lies down in the middle of the deck. "That is the sign of a guilty dog." I point at the dog before turning the steaks.

"Do you have a tablecloth?" she asks. "I don't want to get the table dirty." She's concerned about the small wooden table I have downstairs.

"We are going to eat on the top deck," I say, pointing upstairs. "There is a bigger table there." She nods at me, grabbing the plates and walking to the steps.

"I think I'm in love," she declares, looking back down at me. "Look at how pretty it is up here."

I laugh at her. "You have the same thing on your boat," I point out to her, and she looks down.

"Not as big as this. I want this." She puts the plates down on the table. "Like, I love this U-shaped sitting area. I just have a long bench." She talks to herself as I walk to grab an empty plate to put the steaks on.

After placing the steaks on the plate, I walk up the steps and see her standing looking out. I put the plate on the table, and she looks over. "I'll be back with the veggies." I turn around, and she's right at my back.

"I forgot the salad," she notes as she follows me down. "Do you want anything to drink?" she asks me over her shoulder. "I'll just grab two waters," she says, and I don't answer her. Instead, I walk upstairs and put the veggies next to the steak.

She comes up with the salad bowl in one hand and bottles of water in the other. "There is a fridge up here." I point at the side where there is a sink and a fridge.

"Of course there is," she huffs. "Tomorrow, I'm going to order a fridge for my upstairs and see if I can add things to it." I shake my head.

"Sit," I tell her as she slides onto the bench, and I walk over to slide onto the bench in front of her. "Grab the steak you want."

"Which one is bigger?" She grabs the plate of the steaks. "I mean, I know I'm hungry, but let's be honest, I'm not going to eat the bigger steak." She looks down and grabs the smaller steak, handing me the plate.

"Thank you," I say, putting the steak on my plate.

"This smells delicious," she praises, grabbing the veggies. "I mean, I did have coffee and a protein bar." She laughs as she cuts her steak.

"Do you not eat when you are working?" I ask her as she hands me the tray of veggies.

"I do," she answers, "but sometimes, I just get into the zone, and I don't realize the time."

I look down and cut a piece of my steak. "What do you do for work?" I ask her the question, and she looks down at her plate. My stomach sinks, thinking I asked her something I shouldn't. Her words yesterday replay in my head. "Forget I asked," I backpedal. "It's none of my business. If you wanted me to know, you would have told me." I smile at her, sticking to a completely neutral topic. "It's nice weather we are having."

FIFTEEN

VIVIENNE

"WHAT DO YOU do for work?" He asks me the question, and the minute he does, my stomach sinks, and I want to throw up the food he just made. Food that is the best thing I've eaten in a while. I look down, wondering how I can answer this question, knowing that in the end, what I tell him won't be the truth. "Forget I asked," he says, looking down at his food. If I didn't feel like an asshole before, I definitely feel like one when he says the next part. "It's none of my business. If you had wanted me to know, you would have told me." He smiles at me, and it's so fucking fake. I also hate it. "It's nice weather we are having."

I can't help but chuckle nervously. "It's okay to ask me what I do." When I walked in and saw he was reading one of my books, it was the first time I wanted to spill my secret. I couldn't help the giddiness inside me. I wanted to be like, "I wrote this," but instead, I pushed it down.

"No, it's not," he says, shaking his head while he cuts his steak and avoids looking at me. My stomach gets tight, knowing that I've ruined it.

"I work in the writing industry." I remain very vague. At least it's not a lie. Trying to figure out what to tell him and not spill the secret. I don't think I've ever come out and said I'm an author before, never. I mean, I've told my accountant and my lawyer, but I've never ever said my occupation to one person.

"I don't even know what that means." He laughs, and I can see he feels a bit more at ease and not that he's asked something he shouldn't.

"It's hard to explain." I cut a piece of steak. "But I edit stuff. Rewrite things." I put the piece of steak in my mouth to stop talking. Something inside me is not okay with lying to him, and I have no idea why. My family, who knows everything about me and has been there my whole life, doesn't know what I do. It's never bothered me once that they don't. But this guy, who I met, what, four days ago, maybe five? I have this guilt that I'm not telling him the truth. I stab a piece of salad on my fork, looking up at him and finding him staring at me. "What?" I ask him.

"You really aren't going to ask me what I do?" he quizzes, my eyes looking back down at my steak before lifting them to find him still staring at me from across the table. His head shakes, and I can't help but smile at him.

"Are we going to go over this again?" I joke as I cut

another piece of steak. I now realize I'm stuffing my face with all this food to shut my mouth from asking him everything. I've never wanted to ask questions in my life. I usually just sit back and wait, knowing that people share with you, whether you want to know or not. It's the human nature in us.

"Yeah, yeah," he says, and I wish the lights were on so I could see his eyes. "If I wanted you to know, I would have told you."

I point the fork at him. "Exactly, you are learning." I can't help the smile that fills my face when he just smirks and then looks down to cut his steak. Do I want to know what he does for a living? Yes. I mean, I haven't seen him leave to go to work all week. "You look like a stockbroker," I joke as he just stares at me while chewing. "You are definitely not in the medical field."

This makes him laugh. "Why do you say that?"

"You're grumpy," I tell him honestly. His eyes go into slits as he glares at me, making me laugh.

"I'm not grumpy," he defends right away. I smile at him and nod my head like, sure you're not.

"Okay, whatever you say," I tease him.

"I used to play hockey." The words that come out of his mouth do two things. One, they shock the shit out of me, and two, yup, still shocked. I blink for what feels like an eternity, the words replaying in my head.

I open my mouth to say something, but nothing comes out. He throws his head back, and all I can hear now is his deep booming laughter. "But." I shake my head. "But," I repeat, trying to let the words sink in. It's only then do I gasp. "That's why my father knew who you were." All he does is shrug and nod his head. "Great," I say, putting the fork down, "never going to hear the end of this." I shake my head. "Do you know how many times I'm going to hear, 'remember when I said I knew him?'" His laughter is even bigger now. "It's not funny. It's going to be for the rest of my life."

He chuckles. "Sorry about that."

I cut another piece of steak. "I mean, he did say you kind of looked familiar. But he says that all the time. We went to Greece one year, and he thought the sixty-five-year-old man making coffee looked familiar." I shake my head. "News flash, he didn't."

He cuts a piece of his own steak, chewing it before saying, "I didn't have the beard." He rubs his hand on his chin. Then runs his hands through his hair. "Or the long hair. That could be why he thought he recognized me but wasn't sure."

I tilt my head to the side and try to picture him without the beard. "Really?"

He nods his head, leaning back against the bench. "Oh, yeah, the team I played for was old school." He starts talking, and something in his voice makes me know that something deeper is going on. "I had to be clean cut. Hair was to be kept short and no facial hair whatsoever." I have to bite my tongue not to ask him what team he played for.

"Wow," I say, but I'm itching to ask him so many more questions. It's the first time that curiosity is killing me. It's the first time I want to pry and ask him all the freaking questions but I have to respect his space. "So you used to play?" I prod, not really invading his privacy since he mentioned that he used to play. So technically, I'm not intruding.

"Yup," he says, his tone tight, "walked away two years ago."

"What's your name?" I ask, and he laughs. "I mean, I could always google Xavier and hockey, and I'm sure I'll find you." I roll my lips to stop myself from laughing. "Don't worry, I would never google you." I chuckle. "But my sister, now she's another story."

He laughs out loud. "No need to go on Google." He stares at me. "Xavier Montgomery." I put my fork down. "So how about the weather?"

"Is that code for you don't want to talk about hockey?" I ask, swallowing down the lump.

"There is nothing to say." He sits up. "I used to play, and now I don't." He shrugs.

I pick my fork back up. "The weather has been amazing." I change the subject just like he wanted to. "Was it sunny today?"

"It was." He nods his head. "It's going to be sunny for the next four days."

I clap my hands in happiness. "Yes." I smile at him. "So how long have you had this boat?"

"Two years," he replies, and I can't help but try to piece together his past. "Hung up my skates and then bought the boat."

"See?" I fold my arms in front of me. "I didn't even have to ask you why you bought the boat."

"I see that. In case you are wondering what boat I had before." He gets up from the bench. "I didn't have one."

I gasp. "Did you know how to drive the boat?" I ask, his head going to the side.

"Are you asking me a question?" He smirks at me as he picks up his empty plate. "Is there something you want to know?"

"Oh, no." I shake my head. "Don't you even try it. I'm just saying you shit all over me when you asked what boat I had before." He looks down, trying to hide his smile. "You hypocrite." I get up laughing, grabbing my plate and the salad bowl. "Don't even." I shake my head, turning to walk down the steps and back into the kitchen. Beatrice gets up from her bed, stretching and then coming over to me. "Did you know he was a liar, liar, pants on fire?" I squat down and hold her neck. "You were there. You heard him, right?"

"Okay, fine," he huffs when he walks into the kitchen, two plates in one hand and the veggie tray in the other. "I could have been a bit nicer."

"Could have been?" I shake my head. "Could have been?" I fold my arms over my chest.

"Did you even drive a boat before you bought this one?" I ask, and he puts the plates in the sink before looking at me.

The smirk transforms into a huge smile when he leans against his counter. "Two questions?" He holds up one hand with two fingers while the other hand holds on to the counter. "Is this a record?"

I grit my teeth together and glare at him. "I called

you a jerkface," I inform him, "so you don't have to ask me that." The sound of his laughter is everything. "Also, FYI, I'll be calling you that again once I get back home." I have this sudden visual of me going over to him and wrapping my hands around his waist while I lean back and he kisses me. "I should go." I put my hand to my stomach, wondering if he put something in my food.

"What are you doing tomorrow?" he asks me and my eyebrows pinch together.

"Probably working," I answer him.

"What time do you finish working?" he questions me, and I wonder if he's doing this on purpose.

"Are you trying to get me to ask you why?" I put my hands on my hips.

"Are you wanting to ask me why?" he counters. Forget about me wanting to kiss him because now I'd love to throat punch him.

"No," I lie through my teeth. "Don't care."

"Now that's a lie." He laughs. "Do you want to go out tomorrow?"

"On a date?" My palms start getting sweaty.

"No." He shakes his head right away, and the air leaves my body. I should be happy he doesn't want to take me on a date. How awkward would it be to go on a date with him? Imagine it didn't work out, and we'd have to live side by side for the whole summer. "I'm asking you if you want to go out on the water."

I can't even contain myself when he says that. "Shut up." I put my hands in front of my mouth. "Don't tease me like that."

"I'm not teasing you. I'm serious. We can go out onto the water tomorrow."

"You aren't joking?" I ask him again, not sure if he's about to be like…psych.

"I'm not joking." He chuckles. "When you finish work, come over, and we will take the boat out."

"I can be finished by nine," I tell him, not even bothering to tell him that I don't have to work every day.

He laughs. "No rush. We can leave whenever." He pushes off from the counter.

"Deal." I hold out my hand, waiting for him to shake it. He takes five steps and puts his hand in mine.

"Deal." Our hands move up and down. "Scout's honor and all that jazz." He laughs at me, and again, I'm hit with a visual of him pulling me toward him. Taking his other hand and hugging me around my neck and then kissing my lips.

I let go of his hand as if you just poured ice-cold water on me. "I'm going to go now," I say, pointing over my shoulder, "before you change your mind and take it back."

"I won't take it back," he assures me, his hand falling to his side. "Come over tomorrow when you are ready."

I nod at him and walk out of the boat, turning around as soon as I step off the deck. I find him looking down at Beatrice saying something. His head comes up when he sees me. "I forgot to thank you…for dinner."

"It was my pleasure, Vivienne," he replies with his hands on his hips. "Have a nice night."

"You, too, Xavier." I ignore the way my heart speeds

up when he says my name. I walk over to the boat now. Not even bothering doing anything but going inside. I put my hand to my stomach. "Do you think he put some voodoo potion in my food?" I look over at his boat, seeing him coming out and going upstairs. "He played hockey." I walk to the bedroom where I tossed my computer.

I get onto the bed, bringing the laptop to me and opening Google. "What the hell are you doing?" I ask myself, shocked. "Are you out of your mind?" I close the lid of my laptop, appalled at myself. "That is so wrong on all the levels."

I get off the bed, taking the laptop to the kitchen and putting it on the table. "Yeah, it's better to visualize him kissing you than it is to google who he is," I tell the dark room. "Much better." I shake my head. "You need to shut up and go to bed, you have a big day tomorrow." I turn, walking to my bedroom and hoping that time flies by.

Sixteen

Xavier

"I WON'T TAKE it back," I tell her when she lets go of my hand and it falls to my side. "Come over tomorrow when you are ready." My hand still tingles from her touch. I move my fingers back and forth, hoping that maybe my hand is just asleep. Except it doesn't feel like the needles, it's like a tingle or a touch.

She nods at me and turns, walking out. "What was I supposed to do?" I ask Beatrice, who just looks at me. "Don't give me that look." I'm about to say something else when I look up and see her coming back. "Shit, she changed her mind," I mumble to Beatrice. My palms become sweaty, thinking that she is backing out. I'm so over my head that I don't even have a chance to think about what this means.

"I forgot to thank you," she says with a smile, "for

dinner."

"It was my pleasure, Vivienne." I put my hands on my hips before I decide it's a good idea to run my hands into her hair. My heart starts to beat even faster than it did before, the pressure starts to form on my chest. I try to steady my heartbeat, knowing I just need a couple of seconds to sit down and center myself. "Have a nice night." I hope she doesn't stay around, not knowing if she is going to be present for the full-on panic attack I feel inching its way to the surface.

"You, too, Xavier." She turns around and walks away. I look and make sure she goes on her boat before I walk out of the galley and upstairs to get some air. I sit down for a second, looking out at the horizon, knowing that it brings me peace. I inhale deeply and then exhale until the beating of my heart feels like it's normal. Until the pressure on my chest isn't so tight that it's going to make it harder for me to breathe.

I clean up the table before walking back downstairs and coming face-to-face with Beatrice. "I'm fine," I assure her as she comes to me and circles my legs, telling me that she's right here. "What the hell did I do?" I sit on the couch, and Beatrice follows, getting on the couch next to me. "It's like I was out of my body while the words came out of my mouth." She places her head on my lap. "She literally called me on my bullshit." I shake my head and rub my hands over my face. "She was right, I did the same thing she did, but I didn't have an asshole breathing down my neck." I rub the top of Beatrice's head. "We'll take her out tomorrow, and then my good deed will be done." I swallow down. "Good God, I even told her who I was," I hiss, and Beatrice's head comes up. "Yeah, I know, rule number two, don't go to the neighbor," I remind myself of the rule. "Rule number three, it's not my problem." I put my head back. "And rule number four, do not tell anyone who we are." I close my eyes. "That should be rule number one.

"Do you want to go for a walk?" I ask Beatrice, who doesn't move. Well, she moves. She just gets off the couch and makes her way down to her bedroom. "I take it that is you saying good night?"

Making my way to the kitchen, I wash the plates and put everything away before I lock up the doors. Looking next door, I see that all the lights are off. "It'll be fine," I mumble to myself. "What's the worst that can happen?" I close the curtains before walking to the table and picking up the book. "She googles and sees what a mess you are."

I laugh bitterly, walking down to my bedroom and tossing the book on the bed before going into the shower. I walk to the bed naked, slipping under the covers, and turning on the television, not because I'm going to watch it but just to have the background noise. Picking up the book, I turn on the soft light behind the headboard and I start to read. I read one page after another, and when my eyes start to burn, I put the book down. Shutting off the television, I shout, "Night," to Beatrice. Turning on my side, I close my eyes, and the only thing that flashes through my head is Vivienne. Her smile most of all, especially the one she does when she's really excited. It fills her whole face, making her cheeks a touch pink and her eyes crinkle. I turn on my back, trying to think about anything but her, but no matter how much I fight it, it all comes back to her. Turning on my other side, I replay our conversation at the dinner table. Her being shocked that I played hockey. Her not asking why I walked away. Usually, it's the first question someone will ask. Why did you stop? Fuck, even I would have asked the person why they walked away. I toss and turn five more times before throwing the covers off me and checking the time. "Three a.m." I shake my head, walking to the kitchen, grabbing a bottle of water and a cookie. Walking back to the bedroom, I fluff my pillows twice before trying to lie down again. I don't think I sleep for more than ten minutes when Beatrice jumps on the bed. I just look at her. "How did you sleep?" I ask her as the alarm starts to ring. "I bet you slept better than me." I get up, turning off the alarm as I walk over and slip on my boxers. Grabbing a pair of black gym shorts and a black sweater, I walk to the kitchen to start the coffee.

"I'm going to suffer today," I predict. Even though I didn't sleep, I feel so alive; it's the strangest thing. It's like my body is filled with adrenaline. "You ready?" I ask Beatrice, who sits by the door. "Baseball hat or no baseball hat?" I ask her as I open the door and step out.

I take two steps before I look over and see her outside. "Um." She looks over at me. "Baseball hat," she answers the question and laughs. She sits there with her hair on the top of her head, a blanket around her shoulders, and her laptop on her outstretched legs. A cup of coffee is in the middle of the table next to her phone.

I don't move from my spot for a good five seconds before Beatrice walks off the boat. "What are you doing out here?" The words finally come out. "Are you doing the writing thing?" I point at the laptop.

She stretches her arms over her head and laughs. "I am," she admits as I step off the boat and onto the dock. "I couldn't sleep, so I decided to get in the work early."

"Well, see you later." I walk down the dock, forcing myself not to look over my shoulder.

"You think she is as anxious as us?" I ask Beatrice as we walk out the gate. "She was sitting in the dark in the middle of the night." I look back at her boat, and all I see is the light from her keyboard. "That's not safe, is it?" I ask, walking down the sidewalk. I take a sip of coffee. "She's pretty, right?" I smile when I picture her. "Yeah, she's more than pretty." Beatrice walks beside me sniffing, not even paying attention to what I'm saying. "She's way out of my league." I shake my head, taking another sip of coffee. "Her brother will kick my ass if I even think about it. Who the hell would want their sister with a basket case?" I laugh. "No one, that's who."

The walk is longer than I want it to be, and I don't even know if I'm doing it on purpose or not. But when Beatrice starts to pant, I make our way back. She walks ahead of me down the ramp toward the dock. I walk down with the leash in one hand and the empty coffee cup in the other. The table where she was sitting when I left is empty, the coffee cup and phone both gone. Walking onto my boat, I slip off my shoes and walk inside.

Tossing the leash on the couch, I get Beatrice's bowl and walk over to the sink, turning on the cold water while I prepare her food. I'm pouring her food in her bowl when I hear a knock and look up to see it's Vivienne. Seeing her standing there with a plate in her hand, the smile just automatically fills my face. "Come in," I invite, and she opens the door, stepping in.

"Hi," she greets, smiling at me and then looking down at Beatrice. "I made breakfast. Nothing fancy, just some omelets." She looks down at the plate nervously. "And some fruit that I left outside."

"Is that for me?" I ask her as I fill the bowl with water.

"I mean, I made enough for two, but yes"—she offers me the plate—"it's for you."

"Will you be joining me?" I ask, trying not to make her feel even more anxious. I can't even imagine how she felt walking over here.

"If you don't mind, we can eat at my place."

I walk over to her after putting down the bowl. "Wherever you want to eat," I tell her as I stand in front of her. A soft little strand of hair has fallen out of her top bun, and my hand wants to come up and tuck it behind her ear.

"We can eat out on the deck right here." She turns and walks out to the little table. "So Beatrice isn't alone."

I laugh at her. "Like she would let me leave her anywhere." I shake my head. "I'll make coffee. What do you take in it?"

"Whatever you have," she tosses over her shoulder. "I'm going to go grab the fruit." I watch her walk away.

She's wearing yoga pants again, and they literally show her ass to perfection.

"Those should be illegal," I mumble, walking over to the coffee machine. I make two coffees, and when I walk outside, she is sitting down on the long bench with Beatrice next to her.

"I would have come to help, but"—she looks at Beatrice—"she needed some love." She rubs her head, and Beatrice turns on her side.

Sitting down in the chair, I hand her the cup of coffee. "So I have to ask," I say, grabbing a fork and cutting a piece of the omelet straight from the plate. "Did you google me last night?"

She throws her head back and laughs, the sound making my stomach feel like when you are on a roller coaster and you are going up the big first turn, as it slows down and you dangle there at the top, right when it drops you. That is what it feels like listening to her laughter. "I did not." She grabs her own fork and cuts a piece of omelet before she stabs a strawberry.

I gasp. "Wow, you really do respect boundaries."

It's her turn to gasp. "Oh my God," she says, grabbing a piece of watermelon from the bowl. "Did you google me?"

"No," I tell her. Technically, I'm not lying. I actually didn't do it last night. She's never asked about it before. I look over at Beatrice, who just looks at me, knowing I'm full of shit.

"Considering that there are no boundaries in my family," she states with a smile, and it's a real smile. "My family is always pushing their noses in other people's business, so I like to respect everyone else. I'm the last one to know anything because I don't ask." She shrugs. "Besides, Google can also be wrong sometimes."

"Really?" I respond, shocked. "I've found them to be pretty accurate."

"What was the last thing you googled?" she asks me.

"The weather." The words come out right away. "This morning." Fine, I did it on my walk, but it still counts. She eats a couple more bites of the omelet. "So when do you want to leave?"

"Whenever you are ready," she replies, putting down her cup of coffee. "I've finished my work, so I can go whenever."

I nod at her. "Well, let's clean up and we can head out."

She claps her hands in excitement. "Beatrice, I'm going on the water," she tells her. "Isn't that so much fun?" I swallow the rest of my coffee to keep my mouth busy before I tell her that I'll take her out every day.

Seventeen

Vivienne

"WHAT WAS THE last thing you googled?" I ask him, wondering if he googled me. I'm not sure if he would find anything or not. I haven't googled myself in a while. In the beginning, I used to google to see if someone figured out if I was Cooper Parker, but so far, my secret is safe.

But he answers right away without skipping a beat, so I know it has to be the truth. "The weather. This morning." I take a couple more bites of the omelet, the whole time my stomach is doing somersaults. I have to drink some coffee to calm myself down. "So when do you want to leave?"

"Whenever you are ready." I put down my cup, trying not to sound like a giddy teenager. "I've finished my work, so I can go whenever."

He nods at me, and I love the way his eyes look this

morning. They are on the gray side. "Well, let's clean up, and we can head out."

I can't contain myself after he says that, clapping my hands. "Beatrice, I'm going on the water." I hold her face in my hands. "Isn't that so much fun?" I kiss her on the nose, and she licks my face.

"I'm going to go clean up my boat." I stand. "Should I prepare lunch?" He shakes his head. "I'm going to anyway."

"I was going to head out to the bakery down the street and grab a couple of things," he informs me. "So how about you do what you need to do, and we meet here in about thirty minutes?"

"Sounds good," I say, getting off his boat. "Do you want me to keep Beatrice so you can go faster?"

He laughs as he gets up. "She could stay here by herself," he replies, and I just look at Beatrice, who is getting off the bench.

"Um." I look at Beatrice. "Want to come with me?" I motion with my head, and she comes to me.

"You know, she was an obedient dog before you got here," Xavier accuses, chuckling. "And we had rules."

"I don't know if you heard," I start to say, walking on my boat, "but rules are always meant to be broken." I open the door and wait for Beatrice to walk in. "See you in thirty." I smile, and I can't help the squeal that comes out of my mouth. "I'm so excited."

I walk in, closing the door behind me, and the sound of his laughter penetrates through my boat. "Make yourself at home," I tell Beatrice, who decides that she's going to lie down in front of the back door. "I have to wash the dishes," I inform her, walking over to the pans I made the omelets in.

The whole night I tossed and turned, I was so excited about today that I couldn't sleep. Finally, at four o'clock, I decided to get a start on the day, so I grabbed my laptop, my coffee, and my phone. It was cool outside, so I went back in, snatching a blanket. I didn't think I would get much done, but the words flowed. When he walked away from me, I decided it would be a good idea to make him breakfast. I obviously didn't think it through, and only when I was standing in the middle of his kitchen did it hit me. The back of my neck got so hot, I thought I was going to faint as I held the plate of food. I basically just threw myself at him. Luckily for me, it didn't backfire. I clean up in record time, even having time to dry and put things away.

Walking to my bedroom, I quickly make the bed and then walk over to the closet, opening it up. Grabbing a pink top off the hanger, I walk over to the front of the bed and open the drawer where my bikinis are. I grab the ivory bikini top with a black bottom. I step into the bathroom, pulling my shirt over my head. Putting the bikini top on, I see the middle has a peekaboo hole, showing the bottom of my boobs. Stepping out, I look at Beatrice. "Do you think this is too sexy?" She just yawns, making me laugh. "Fair enough." I don't give it a second thought before slipping on the cheeky bikini bottoms. "I should grab another suit in case," I mumble to myself. I'm fastening my jean shorts when my phone rings.

Jogging to the kitchen, I pick it up to see my delivery has arrived. "It's here," I tell Beatrice. "Come on." She gets up and walks off the boat with me. Both of us walk down the dock to the gate.

"Vivienne," the guy on the bike confirms, and I nod my head. He kicks the stand down before walking to the front of his bike and opening the basket. He takes two brown bags out, holding them by their handles. "Have a great day," he says while handing me the bags.

I'm about to turn around when I spot Xavier walking back. Beatrice barks at him, and he just smiles at her. He changed out of his sweat shorts and now is wearing beige khaki shorts with a blue sweater with white stripes over his chest. His sunglasses cover his eyes, and two canvas bags are in his one hand. "What is this?" he asks when he gets to the gate as I hold it open for him.

"I ordered something," I tell him. "Last night before I went to bed." We walk down the ramp and side by side to the boat, with Beatrice in the middle of us. "I just have to grab my bag, and I'm ready," I inform him and hand him the two brown bags in my hands. "These are for you."

He looks at the bags and then back at me. "It's a little something to thank you for today, and a little something for Ms. Queen B," I say quietly.

"Come on over when you're ready," he says to me, chuckling and walking away to his boat.

I get back on my boat, grabbing the bag and tucking my cell phone in my back pocket. I stop mid step before thinking if I should warn someone. I quickly pull up

Julia's contact because I know she will ask me the fewest questions. I press the phone button, and she answers after one ring, except it's Chase. "Hello."

"Hey." I close my eyes. "Why are you answering Julia's phone?"

"The question is why are you calling Julia's phone?" he counters, and I just groan.

"I'm about to head out, so I just wanted to give someone a heads-up," I say, omitting all key details. "I'll check in later tonight."

"Hold on a second," Chase replies, laughing. "You are going out and wanted to give someone a heads-up. Who are you going with?"

"You aren't my dad." I laugh. "And even if you were my dad, I wouldn't answer."

"You wouldn't have to answer because he had us all microchipped when we were young," Chase jokes, laughing. "Now, who, what, where, when, and why?"

"Me. On a boat, today, because I want to," I answer. "Signal is dying," I add, hanging up the phone.

The phone buzzes.

Julia: You better check in, don't make me activate the phone chain.

I groan out loud at the stupid phone chain that was started once when I said I was going to Alexis's house after school in sixth grade. I did go to Alexis's house, but then we went to the mall. When I got home, every family member I knew was in the living room with the police. From there, they put in place the family phone chain. It's only been activated once since then, and that was when

Franny's sex tape got leaked.

Putting my phone away, I make my way to his boat. His sunglasses now off, I can't help but smile when I see him. "Hi," I greet, waving nervously. I put my bag on the couch as he walks over to me. "What can I do to help?" I offer, looking at him and trying not to get lost in his eyes. "Keep in mind, I know absolutely nothing," I remind him, and he laughs.

"That's not true." He shakes his head. "You know loop de loops."

I laugh. "I do."

"How comfortable are you with untying the lines and then jumping on?" he asks me, and I follow him outside. I think about how hard it would be. Untying should be easy, but jumping on the boat, now that may be a problem.

"Well, worst case, I fall in the water," I say to his back, and he stops and looks over at me.

"No, worst case, you get tangled in the motor, and then we have bits and pieces of you in the ocean." He folds his arms over his chest.

I try not to laugh at him by rolling my lips. "I really think you need to stop reading those mysteries." He tries to keep a serious face, but he can't help the laughter that comes out of him. The sound settles me a bit, making me less nervous.

"I'll be fine, and if not…" I walk off the boat and stand in front of him. "Save yourself," I whisper softly. He turns, shaking his head as he disconnects the power and the water. My eyes follow him everywhere, taking mental notes about everything he is doing.

"I feel like I'm being watched," he declares as he rolls up the electrical wire.

I chuckle. "You are. I'm also judging you on your techniques," I joke with him.

"You're a trip." He walks past me and onto the boat.

"I've been called worse," I admit to him, and he stops walking to throw his head back and laugh.

"Okay, I'm going to start the boat," he informs me, walking into the cabin. The sound of the boat starting makes me bounce on the tips of my feet. The water starts to swirl around the back of the boat.

"You untie the front line first," he directs me as he opens up the two back doors. "Then you go to the back and throw it in and then jump in." He looks at me. "Are you okay?"

"I'm fine," I say, laughing as I walk to the front of the boat and untie the line, leaning in and putting it on the side of the boat. "Are you okay?"

He smirks at me and walks inside to the captain's chair. "I'll wait until you tell me you're untied!" he shouts, and I walk to the back of the boat and untie the rope, tossing it on the back of the boat before stepping onto the deck.

I look at him as he watches me over his shoulder. "Didn't die." I hold up my hands.

"Starting off on the right foot," he praises, turning now to face the front of the boat. "You going to come up here and watch?" I walk inside, seeing Beatrice sleeping on her bed, not even fazed that the boat is moving.

I walk to the captain's chair and look out at the horizon as he takes us slowly out of the dock space. "Try not to hit my boat," I joke. He just smiles at me, and my stomach flips.

Turning away from looking at him, I watch the water, wondering if maybe the eggs were bad. *Were they expired?* I think to myself as he finally clears the last dock and enters the open water.

"Come on." He motions with his head. "Let's get you driving."

I open my eyes wide. "Um, negative," I say, but his hand reaches out and grabs my hand.

His touch makes my arm tingle as he pulls me to him. "You'll be fine," he assures me as he puts me in front of him. My hands grip the stainless-steel steering wheel as I look ahead.

If I thought my stomach was a mess before, it's nothing compared to now. His front is pressed into my back. It's almost as if he's hugging me from behind. I focus on the water in front of me. I make the mistake of looking up at him and seeing him looking at me. "Xavier," I say softly, and I can almost feel his head coming down, his face coming closer and closer to mine. I can feel his breath on my face, my throat feeling like it's closing in. My heart's beating so fast, my breathing is coming out in pants. "I'm out of my comfort zone," I confess, waiting for his lips to fall on mine, but instead, he just throws his head back and laughs.

Eighteen

Xavier

WHAT THE FUCK are you doing? my head screams as I reach out and pull her to me. "You'll be fine," I assure her, putting her in front of me. I place her hands on the steering wheel. Once her hands grip the steering wheel, I can drop my hands, but I don't.

Instead, I push my chest closer to her back, suddenly wanting to be even nearer to her. *What the fuck are you doing?* my head screams again. My heart is beating so fast it's a wonder she doesn't feel it in her back. My chest starts to get just a bit of pressure and then she looks up at me. "Xavier." She says my name softly. It's the opposite of what I need right now. I need her to tell me to back the fuck up. I need her to tell me to get away from her. What I don't need is her to say my name softly. I don't need to get lost in the green of her eyes. I don't need to bend my head slowly, invading her space. I can almost taste her lips. "I'm out of my comfort zone," she says, her eyes looking at mine. I stare at the smile on her face, and all I can do is throw my head back and laugh.

"What do you feel uncomfortable about?" I ask her, my hands now moving off hers. I should step away from her, but I'm going to pretend I need to be close in case I have to take over the wheel. Even though there are two captain's chairs and I could easily swing into action.

"I don't know." She shrugs her shoulders. "Maybe this whole 'driving a boat' thing." I almost breathe a sigh of relief when she doesn't say it's me being too close to her.

"How are you going to learn if you don't practice?" I ask, and she rolls her eyes at me.

"I don't know. I just assumed it would be okay," she replies, taking her hands off the wheel to shake them.

"You are doing good," I reassure her. "You know what the colored buoys mean, right?"

"Yes, red buoys are left side," she says, and I'm about to correct her when she says, "Port." I smile at her, waiting for her to finish. "Green is the other side."

"Starboard," I remind her, and she nods.

"Yeah, that's what I meant." She stays looking ahead, making sure she is focusing on what is in front of her.

"It's open water." I try to calm her down. "I'm right here."

"Okay, tag," she says, looking at me. "Seriously, can you take over?"

I nod at her, and she steps away from the wheel, and I

sit on the chair looking out. "See, was that so bad?" I ask, and she leans down and puts her hands on her knees. Her breathing comes out in pants, and I wonder if I pushed her too fast.

"I thought I was going to have a heart attack," she declares, standing straight up. "How about I just be co-captain?"

"Do you know what a co-captain does?" I ask as she sits down in the chair next to me.

"I sit here and look pretty, making sure you have water when you need it." She smiles big, her eyes closing.

I chuckle. "Well, in that case, you're doing a great job."

"See, this I can do," she teases, watching the boat move through the water. I smile over at her, and neither of us says anything as I make my way over to the little cove I always go to.

"See, over there." I point at the empty water. "We are going to anchor there."

"That looks so pretty," she says, taking her phone out of her pocket and snapping a picture.

I reduce my speed as we approach the spot. "Can you just make sure nothing happens?" Her eyes go big, and I turn off the boat. "I'm going to go out and do the anchor."

I don't give her a chance to do anything before I walk out on the back deck and along the side toward the front, where I press the anchor button. I look over seeing the chain coming out before it stops. I look up for a couple of minutes, making sure we are anchored and not drifting. When the boat doesn't move, I look back into the cockpit and see her watching me. "You can move," I tell her, and her head falls forward, making me laugh.

Heading my way back into the boat, I look at her. "Do you want to sit on the top deck or the lower deck?"

She puts her finger to her mouth. "Decisions, decisions." She then smiles and looks over at Beatrice. "Which one does she like better?"

"The top one," I answer her, looking and wondering if she would have kissed me back.

"Then let's go to the top," she states, and I nod, turning around and walking out. She reaches down and picks up her pink T-shirt, and when I see her bikini top, my cock goes hard. Like rock hard. The side underboob peeking out makes me want to roll my eyes in the back of my head and groan out loud. It also makes me want to escape downstairs and jerk off. I turn around quickly before she can spot my dick and walk to the back. "What are you doing?" She follows me as I pull up the back bench seat.

"I'm going to roll out the carpet for Beatrice," I tell her, walking out to the back and snapping the rolled-up carpet before letting it open. "She sometimes likes to sit and sun."

"Well, now"—she puts her hand over her eyes—"she might have to share that with me."

I laugh, walking back and standing in front of her. "She doesn't like to share."

"Well, she will if she wants a c-o—" I put my hand up to stop her from talking. My eyes go to the top of her tits, but then try not to roam down, seeing the jean shorts falling on her hips.

"Don't say the word," I say, walking to the kitchen to grab a cold bottle of water. I might have to pour it over my head at this point.

"I forgot a towel," she states, and I look over, seeing her bend over, her ass cheeks peeking out. I close my eyes and look out the other window to the water.

"There are towels upstairs," I inform her, and she smiles.

"Are you coming?" she asks, walking to the stairs.

"Yeah." I nod. *In my pants right now*. The words almost slip out, but I bite them back. Putting the water bottle on the counter, I pull off the sweater I'm wearing, leaving me in my beige khaki shorts.

I walk out, Beatrice following me but stopping and lying down before I walk up the stairs. "We are going upstairs," I tell her, and she just stretches out in the shade.

When I get upstairs, I look out and see that she's gotten two towels, and she's laid them out, side by side, in the middle of the big day pad. She sits in the middle of one as she ties her hair on top of her head.

"Do you want anything to drink?" I stop at the fridge before walking to her.

"Just water," she throws over her shoulder as she stretches her legs in front of her. She puts her hands behind her, leaning back.

I grab a water bottle, walking to her and seeing her looking up at the sun. "Here you go." I hold out the bottle for her and she reaches up and grabs it from me. Our fingers graze each other for a second before I make my way over to the towel she set out for me.

"This," she says, opening her water bottle, "is what I call heaven."

I laugh. "Let's play a game." I'm not sure where the fuck this is coming from.

"Sure," she replies, folding her legs. "What do you want to play?"

Naked Twister, my head screams at the same time as I say, "Twenty-one questions."

She laughs. "So basically my worst nightmare." She takes a sip of water.

"I'll go first," I offer, and she rolls her eyes. "Why did you buy a boat?"

"Oh, that's an easy one." She smiles. "I went out on a boat with a couple of friends," she shares, and I want to ask her which friends, but instead, I just listen. "And I can't explain to you how at peace I felt sitting while anchored." I smile at her, knowing exactly how it feels. "I just pictured myself sitting on a boat in the middle of the ocean, anchored and having a coffee." She shrugs. "Next thing you know, I'm buying a boat." She taps her water bottle in her hand. "My turn." She fake vomits and looks up, trying to think of a question. "Okay, how is this one? If you could have dinner with a famous person, dead or alive, who would it be?"

I turn on my side, looking at her, crossing my legs at the ankle. "That's easy and weird both at the same time." I laugh. "It would be Cooper Stone."

She shakes her head and laughs. "I don't know why that surprises me. My brother-in-law, Wilson"—she looks at me—"he plays with—"

"Dallas, I know," I fill in for her.

"He almost cried when he met him." She laughs. "We still make fun of him."

"Almost cried. I would legit be a sobbing mess." I don't even try to be all calm, cool, and collected. "As someone who has always played hockey, you have no idea what that would mean." I look out on the water. "It would be like going to fucking Disneyland and eating with Mickey Mouse."

"Well, as someone who has done both." She laughs. "Both are equally good."

"My turn," I say, trying to think of a question. *Favorite sexual positions? Do you like to give head or receive it?* I shake my head to think clearer. "This is harder than I thought."

She laughs, and my cock gets hard again. "See? It's all fun and games until—"

"Yeah, yeah." I cut her off. "What's your dream destination trip?"

"So my family is a little bit extreme," she starts to explain. "Every single year, after the hockey season is over, we do this huge family vacation." I listen to her intently.

"Does Cooper Stone come?" I joke, and she laughs.

"He does." She nods her head. "It's just insane. One year, it was like seventy-five people, and we each had those huts on the beach. Every year is a different destination."

"So you've been to Bora Bora?" I ask, and she shakes her head.

"That is one the family has vetoed, only because it would take over twenty-four hours to get there, and there is no way in hell any of us are doing that. I think the farthest we've done is Hawaii."

"Okay, so what's your answer?" I laugh as she ponders.

"I would have to say Bora Bora. Or Fiji." She looks up, thinking. "Oh, oh." She holds up her finger. "Maybe taking the boat down to Florida."

"It's a nice route," I confirm, and she gasps. "I do that every winter."

"Jealous," she pouts. "Okay, my turn." She taps her bottle again. "What is your dream job?"

"I was doing it," I admit. I wait for the tightness to come when I talk about hockey. It starts to creep its way up. "Playing hockey was my dream job." I don't even try to deny it, nor do I try to push off how I feel about it. "Going into the arena every single day and lacing up my skates? Fuck, that was a dream come true." The lump starts to crawl up to my throat. "I would have done it until I was no longer able to."

She looks at me, her face filled with questions. Her eyes roam my face, her eyes focusing on mine when she asks me the question. "Why did you quit?" I've been asked by so many people. People who I didn't want to answer, people who wouldn't care either way. It just hits differently telling her, and I don't know why. Here, in the middle of the ocean, I'm finally going to be able to tell my side of the story.

NINETEEN

VIVIENNE

I LOOK AT him, not sure what he means by that. My eyes roam his face, focusing on his when I ask the next question. "Why did you quit?" He lies in front of me, looking at me. He brings the bottle of water to his mouth and takes a deep pull of it. He's on his side looking at me, his legs crossed over each other. His arm is propping him up, and I can see the muscle in full form. When he came up before, I wasn't expecting him to be shirtless. When I saw him up close, my mouth watered, which was dumb, since I'm around built guys all the time.

"That's a loaded question." He puts the bottle in front of him, his hand shaking a bit. Making me really anxious about his answer.

"That's a no." I shake my head, not willing to put him through this if it's going to be so hard on him. "You don't have to answer that. I take it back. Let me ask you something else, then." There is a reason I hate this game, and this is the top one. You ask something you shouldn't or something that the person doesn't want to share. My heart speeds up as I try to take it back.

He smiles at me, but it's sort of a sad smile. "Those aren't the rules," he tries to joke, but his voice is monotone. There is no feeling in it, no nothing, which makes me feel even fucking worse.

"I don't care," I say, my heart speeding up, suddenly feeling like an asshole for asking the question. "You see? This is why I hate this game." I throw my hands up. "It should never be played. Ever."

He chuckles. "It's fine," he assures me, looking straight at the water. "To be honest, I never really told anyone my side of the story." I swallow down the lump forming in my throat. "I don't even know how the media spun it." His eyes never leave the water. "I also didn't go out of my way to find it."

"Xavier." I say his name softly, silently begging him not to do this.

"I got drafted at eighteen." He smiles but like a real smile. "I thought I was a superstar even though I went like one hundred and ninety-three." He looks at me. "I mean, your family goes like one or two. I can't even wrap my head around that."

"They're all overachievers, so don't feel bad for yourself. You still got drafted and played in the NHL." I smile at him. "No one can take that away from you. There are kids out there who think you play in the NHL once you get drafted. The odds are not in their favor."

He nods his head. "I played on the farm team for a while, then I got called up. I played one game, got a goal, and then was sent back down. I was just waiting for the call-up again, except it never came. Still, I was playing hockey for a living. How much better did it get?

"It took five seasons for me to make the official team. I trained harder than I ever had in my life. I was working out seven days a week, pushing myself to the edge and then coming back." He stops talking. The sound of water hitting the boat makes it so peaceful, yet I know inside he's struggling. I know he is reliving this. I can see it in his eyes. "I was at the top of my game at that point. I was putting goals in, assists, on the power play, on the penalty kill. I was on fucking point." His voice trembles.

"I thought the team was behind me, but then I got traded." He looks back at the water. "That stung. But I was excited that at least another team wanted me." I don't say anything. I just listen, letting him take his time. Afraid to say one word to make him feel that his story isn't important. "The minute I got there, they gave me the ins and outs of the team. I had heard rumblings through the years. It was an old-school team run by old-fashioned guys. It took a week before they pulled me aside. In a friendly manner, of course." He laughs, and the laughter is of anger and bitterness. "They just let me know that this was a clean-cut team. No mustache, beards, nothing. It had to be clean cut every single day." He shrugs his shoulders and picks up his water bottle again. His hands shake less, but his lips quiver when he puts the bottle to his mouth.

"Honestly," I say, not sure I can stand the torture he is going through. "We really don't have to talk about this."

"According to my therapist, the more I talk about it, the better I will feel." He tries to make a joke about it, but my heart hurts knowing that just thinking and talking about this hurts him so much. "I didn't really care about the clean-cut thing, summer months though I refused to shave. But the day before training camp, I would buzz cut my hair and shave. Those first couple of years were some of the best hockey I've played. Until I got injured in a game against Toronto and had to have surgery."

"Eek," I say, "the dreaded S word."

That makes him laugh, and it's a real laugh because his head goes back as he booms out the sound. "Yeah, the dreaded S word. It was fine, but I was out for like three months, which, as you know"—he looks at me—"feels like eighty-four years." It's my turn to laugh at this. His tone is getting a bit lighter, so I'm hopeful that the worst is past, but something tells me it's not. "In reality, though, I missed about forty games. Not the worst, but it wasn't the best. Then it took time to get back into it."

"At least you got back on the horse," I tell him, trying to encourage him.

"Well, the next season, I came out swinging. I was at the top of my game. I had the best start to my season I ever had, and then one game, it just stopped. I don't really know how to explain it. I played the next twenty-seven games with two points."

"Everyone goes through slumps," I try to assure him,

and he just shakes his head.

"Yeah, but not only was I not performing, I had the lovely honor of being in the papers every single day. Every fucking day, the papers would let me know how much I was fucking up. Every single interview started with, so you haven't had one point in…" His eyes close, and his head hangs. My stomach rises to my throat, and I think I'm going to fucking throw up. "It would be during practices, after the games, on the street. It was constantly in my face. I was living in hell. My head was a mess. I would try to talk to the coach, who basically told me to grow a thicker skin."

I bite my teeth together now, hating this man who I've never even met. "What the fuck?" I hiss, not wanting to, and at least it makes him chuckle.

"Yeah, well, that wasn't the worst of it." He looks at me, swallowing. "When I went to the GM, he told me that I needed to basically just suck it up." I'm about to say something when he holds up his hand to stop me. "Actually, his exact words were, 'If you start producing, they'll leave you alone.'" He brings his water bottle to his lips, drinking the last drop of water. His hand shakes when he puts the bottle down.

"So that just tells you how much support I had. I tried talking to my captain. I tried talking to everyone, trying to get them to listen to me. Every day was such a struggle. I was lost. I didn't know what to do with myself. The harder I tried on the ice, the worse I was. I would suffer panic attacks as soon as I got home. I would have anxiety attacks when I was on the road. I went for seven days with one hour of sleep. I just couldn't shut off my brain. I couldn't not hear the whispers, and then it had crept into the locker room.

"It was such a toxic environment. I had all this going on with me. I needed so much help, but I got nothing. I was a ticking time bomb. One night, I was on the ice warming up for the game, and I just skated off the ice and refused to get back out there. That night, I got home and…" He looks up, taking a deep exhale. "It got so dark for me that one night I tried to end my life." The gasp escapes me, and my hand flies to my mouth. The tears form in my eyes as I listen to him. "I had a bottle of pills in one hand." He wipes the tear from the corner of his eye. "A bottle of Jack in the other, and there in my bathroom, I was going to just take it all away." I can't stop the tears from running down my face. "I was so sure that if I swallowed everything in the bottle, it would be over."

I can't even fathom how he must have felt, how desolate one must feel to think they don't matter. "Xavier," I say his name.

"My agent is the one who found me. I had sent him a message thanking him. He busted down my door and found me before…" His voice trails off. "He got me the help I needed. The team put out a stupid fucking statement saying I was taking an indefinite leave of absence from the team for personal reasons." The anger now fills my body. "They asked everyone to respect my privacy. I hung up the skates, sold my house, and never looked back. Got some therapy and then more therapy.

Adopted Beatrice, who is secretly my support dog," he says with a smile. "At this point, I'm convinced she knows how to speak and just doesn't talk to me, hoping I will stop talking to her."

"Would you ever go back?" I ask, and he smiles. "I can't not ask this."

"I don't know," he admits. "My agent thinks I should."

"What do you think?" I hug my legs to my chest, waiting for him to answer.

"I think that they failed me," he says without skipping a beat. "In more ways than one, they fucking failed me. They were supposed to be a family. They were supposed to have my back."

I get up and go over to his side of the sun pad and sit in front of him. He just looks at me, his gray eyes even more blue with the tears that came. "I don't know much about other teams but," I say softly, "I know my father treats every single player on his team as if they were his own. I know that my uncle Justin is doing that now. I know that Dylan, Michael, and Cooper feel it in Dallas. You got the shit end of the stick."

"Maybe. I just think more should be done for us. When you join the NHL, you think you are automatically king shit. There should be people there for you to talk to. People should be in place in case it gets to be too much. The whole thing needs to be more in your face. There should be so much more done for us."

"Maybe that person should be you," I urge him, and he laughs. "Maybe after all of this." I want to touch his face with my hand, but I don't. "The only person who can do it any justice would be you."

TWENTY

Xavier

"MAYBE," I TELL her, "I just think that there should be more done for us. When you join the NHL, you think you are automatically king shit. There should be people there for you to talk to. People should be in place in case it gets to be too much. The whole thing needs to be more in your face. There should be so much more done for us." I've never been this open about the struggle before. Sure, I told my therapist, but after her, I haven't even told Miles. Actually, scratch that, Beatrice also knows because I've told her little bits here and there. When Vivienne asked me the question, I wasn't sure I was ready or able to tell her. I didn't think I would tell her everything, but something about sharing it with her made it better.

Knowing she could google me and come up with the half-truth, the only thing I wanted was her to know my side of the story. I wanted her to know my truth, the whole truth. Reliving it was a lot less hurtful than the first time I told my therapist, maybe because it wasn't so raw. Maybe it was because I've grown past it. Perhaps it was because I knew, deep in my heart, I had done nothing wrong. At the end of the day, the system they preached about failed me. I can't even imagine how many other people it failed.

"Maybe that person should be you," she tells me, and I laugh. "Maybe after all of this." She sits right in front of me, and I can feel her heat on me. "The only person who can do it any justice would be you."

"You would be an amazing sponsor," I inform her, and she looks at me, her face not smiling. "If the whole editing thing doesn't work out for you." I can see the change in her right away.

"I need you to ask me what I do for a living," she tells me, and I can tell from her tone she's serious, which also confuses me.

"I thought we already went over this." I laugh at her, and her face doesn't even crack a smile. "Fine." I take a deep breath. "What do you do for a living?" I ask, knowing the answer she told me the other day.

"I'm an author," she shares nervously, looking down at her hands. "As in I write books."

"For other people?" I ask. "Like a ghostwriter?"

She shakes her head. "No, not like that." I can tell she's getting nervous because she looks down at her hands, and I can see she's tapping her fingers together. "When I was in college, I was a loner." She looks up.

"Unlike the rest of my family, I didn't have that big of a social calendar. If it was up to me, I would have gone to community college and lived at home. But the peer pressure was real." I chuckle now, seeing how nervous she is. I want to reach out and hold her hand to give her comfort, but she's too busy twirling her fingers. "Anyway, I went online to this fan fiction place." I open my mouth. "Yeah, I know, but then I started writing my own little story, and it just took off until…I would put out chapters every single week, and for the first time in a long time, I felt like I was in my own skin. I didn't get it because of my name because, well, my name was Miss Vicki's, so no one even knew who I was." She smiles shyly. "Also, because they are my favorite chip." I laugh, making a mental note to stock up on them. "It made me escape the reality that I was miserable at school. That I missed my family." She laughs, and I can see the tears in her eyes. "They drive me insane and crazy, but I was all alone for the first time in my whole life, and I didn't know how to feel about it." She brings up her hand. "But writing was my escape from my sad reality."

"Have you written a book?" I ask, shocked, and she nods at me.

"Yes, after I finished writing all the chapters on the fan fiction page. I scoured the internet to find out how to publish my book." I smile at her, thinking about how courageous that was for her to put herself out there for the whole world to see. I played hockey in front of a crowd, but what she did millions of people would be able to read. "I got a cover for it, and then quietly published it without thinking twice. I shut off the computer, took two sleeping pills, and the next thing you know, I wake up, and I'm number one on the charts. It was insane." She laughs through the tears. "And then I thought about telling my family, but then what if it was a one-time thing? A fluke."

"Was it?" I ask. "Did you write another book?"

"I've written more than one," she declares proudly. "I've written quite a few." She laughs. "I've never said that out loud before. I mean I've never said that out loud to anyone who doesn't work for or with me." She smiles even bigger than she did before and her eyes light up even more. "Oh, and my aunt Vivienne."

"Get out of here," I say, smiling at her. "I've never even met an author before." I can swear she blushes. "Are you in bookstores?"

"I am," she says, and I have so many questions. I've met doctors, lawyers, and politicians but never, not once, have I met an author. I've met reporters but never someone who wrote a book.

"That is so cool. What do you write? Is it romance?"

Her head goes back again as her laughter fills the quietness. "I do not write romance. I like to read romance but I don't write it." She looks down before looking back up again. "I write murder mystery books," she tells me, and I just stare at her as she lifts her eyebrows at me. "There is this main character." She looks at me. "I called her." Her eyes search mine, and it finally clicks into place. I sit up, gasping. "Lucinda."

"You are not Cooper Parker!" I shout, shaking my

head in disbelief, and she rolls her lips. "You're lying." I point at her.

"My grandfather is Cooper Stone, and my grandmother is named Parker," she explains to me, and my eyes just go wide. "Never, in one million years, did I think it would get so big."

I hold up my hand, sitting up in front of her. "Wait a second." I shake my head. "You saw your book when you came over?"

"I did," she admits, looking at me. "I was both shocked and surprised."

"But you didn't say anything." I tilt my head to the side.

"No one knows what I do for a living," she says softly.

"What do you mean?" I ask, my mind going in circles.

"I mean, I haven't told anyone, including my family, that I'm Cooper Parker. No one knows." Just when I think she can't shock me more.

"What do they think you do?" I wait for her to answer with bated breath.

"They just think I edit." I put my hands on my head. "To be honest, I wrote one book, never expecting it to come to a second, and then, well, two went into three." She shrugs. "Then it got to the point when I felt so weird coming out to them. Like, 'hey, can you pass me the potatoes, and in case you didn't hear, I just hit *The New York Times* and *Wall Street Journal*.'" I can't help but smile at that. "It was just easy to pretend it didn't happen."

"You have over thirty books!" I shout. "Trust me, I

know. I own them all."

"Actually, there are five more written and not published yet." She laughs at me, and I look up at the sky. "If you are nice, I can hook you up."

"You aren't just a regular author. You are like the real deal."

"Nah." She motions with her hands. "It's just me. The girl who annoyed you by trying to YouTube knots."

"Just me, my ass." I roll my eyes. "You're like an icon."

"No, I'm not." She shakes her head. "And this is making me a bit uncomfortable."

"Well, prepare yourself because I have a shitload of questions," I blurt, not even trying to contain my excitement, and it makes her laugh even more.

"Fire away," she invites, her eyes lighting up as she crosses her legs in front of me, and I'm so excited I mimic her, our knees touching

"So you write Lucinda?" I ask, and she nods.

"Correct." She puts her hands on her legs.

"And no one knows but you and now me." I point at myself.

"And my agent and my aunt Vivi, who helped me at the beginning, but then it got so big I needed an agent. Especially with the foreign contracts."

"Holy shit. I follow your fan page." Clapping my hands, I don't think I've ever been more excited about meeting someone in my life.

"I don't have a fan page," she informs me, and I shake my head. "My author name has a Twitter, Instagram, and

Facebook page, but those are run by my assistant."

"You're right, you have more than a fan page. You practically have one in every language," I tell her, and now she looks at me, shocked. "Are you saying you don't know?"

"I had no idea. I mean, I knew there were a couple of fan pages, and one day, I went in." Her face goes into a grimace. "Not everyone was a fan. So I'm never doing that again!"

"Aw, please, try taking a penalty shot in the opponent's building while they chant 'you suck.'" She throws her head back, and her laughter booms.

"Okay, that might be worse than what I read," she confirms to me and I just nod my head.

"How long does it take you to write a book?" I ask her, amazed.

"The last book took me a month because I was consumed by it," she admits. "And this book is taking me a bit longer because she's falling in love."

"Spoiler alert," I snap, and her laughter just fills the boat. "Okay, but like your next book comes out next month. You wrote it already?"

"I did." She nods, confirming it to me. "Two years ago." I put my hand over my mouth. Her hand comes out to grab my arm and bring it down. "If you want, I can get you all the books I've written that aren't published."

"Beatrice, do you know who this is?" I ask, and she just yawns. "It's *the* Cooper Parker."

She shakes her head. "I have so many questions, yet I don't know where to start."

"How did you start reading me?" she asks, and I shrug.

"I was scrolling Instagram one day, and then I saw this little clip of a story, and I got sucked into it."

"Um." I get up. "Wait here," I tell her and turn to run back into the cabin, going to my bedroom. I open the drawer and take out the special book that I don't touch. I walk back upstairs, and she's talking to Beatrice about something. "Okay, don't freak out."

"Never start a sentence with don't freak out," she teases me, and I sit back in front of her.

"I'm going to show you one of my prized possessions," I tell her, trying not to freak her out. "Your books, they just helped me in so many ways, I can't put it into words." I hold the book in my hand. "A couple of months ago, there was an auction for a signed copy."

She gasps. "The one that went for fifty-five thousand dollars? I donated it to the Max Horton Foundation."

I turn the book to her. "Try not to touch it. It's a first edition and it's signed." Only when the words are out of my mouth do I realize how stupid they sound since she signed the book. "I knew I had to get it." I look down at both our hands holding on to the book. "You see, this is the book I read after I forgave myself for asking for help."

"Xavier." She says my name in a whisper.

"I felt guilt for so long because I had them telling me that it was me and nothing to do with them." I smile as the tears run down her face.

Her hand leaves the book, and she puts it on my cheek. "You are so brave," she praises me as she leans in, and I watch her get closer and closer. The sun fades as she tilts her head to the side. Her eyes stare into mine, neither of us moving. I am the one who takes the final leap toward her, crushing my lips on hers.

Twenty-One

Vivienne

"I FELT GUILT for so long because I had them telling me that it was me and nothing to do with them." His voice quivers as he says this, and I can't even pretend I'm okay because I'm not. The tears are running down my face like a stream. His story cut me to the core. My head is still reeling as his words play over and over in my head, *I almost ended my life.* I can't even fathom feeling that lonely. My heart broke for him having no one. Not one person to fight for him. Not one person to hold his hand.

When he jumped up and ran down the stairs, I had no idea what he was going to do. To be honest, the only thing that went through my head was he was going to bring me his books to sign. But it was so much more than that. He came back and showed me the book I made my assistant send to the foundation, never thinking that it would go for the price it did. I even joked and put in a bid for it, but then it went above and beyond. I always wondered who bid on it.

My hand leaves the book, and I finally do what I've wanted to do since he told me his story. I cup his cheek in my hand, my fingers tingling with his scruff. "You are so brave." My thumb rubs the wetness of his cheek. My whole body screams at me to kiss him. My head, my body, my heart, they are all in sync. My head moves in closer to his, stopping midway. If this is going to happen, he's got to meet me halfway. I have to know I'm not the only one feeling this. My eyes stare into his, both of us not moving. My eyes plead with him to take that last step. My heart is pounding so hard and so fast I'm surprised it's not coming out of my chest. He is the one who takes the final leap toward me, crushing his lips on mine.

His hands drop the book between us as they go into my hair, the both of us closing the rest of the gap between us. My head moves to the side as my mouth opens for him, and his tongue slides in with mine. We moan as our tongues go around and around. I get up on my knees, and he follows my movement, neither of us breaking the kiss. My hand moves from his face to around his neck, trying to get us even closer to each other. I'm so lost in the kiss; I don't notice Beatrice trying to get between us before she barks. I can't help but laugh, breaking the kiss. "Does she not like to share her master?"

"I have no idea." He kisses my lips again softly. "I haven't kissed a girl." I pull back to look at him.

"Lie detector says that's a lie." I laugh.

"You." He kisses my lips. "Didn't." He repeats the kiss, his hand moving from my hair to my cheek as he holds my face in his hand. "Let." He rubs his nose with mine before kissing me again. "Me." He kisses me, his tongue sliding into my mouth. "Finish."

"I'm all for you finishing." I wink at him. "Beatrice, not so much." He throws his head back and he laughs. His hands fall off my face, and I want to grab his hands back to touch me. I lean in one more time to kiss his lips. "There, you can kiss him all you want," I tell Beatrice as I get up, and she lies down on the book.

"Hey," Xavier says, "my book." He pushes her to the side, grabbing the book and dusting it off. I can't help my laughter. "It's a first edition." He gawks at me.

"I have another one if that one gets messed up," I assure him. "Should we do lunch?"

"I guess." He gets up. "Since kissing is off the table."

"Kissing is definitely on the table," I tell him. "We can do the kissing after we make lunch."

He gets up with the book in one hand as he walks next to me, grabbing my hand in his. I look down at our hands, and I have this overwhelming sense that I've done this before. "What's wrong?" he asks, and I just shake my head. How does one explain that it feels like we've done this before without sounding like a crazy person?

"Just hungry," I lie to him because, truth be told, my stomach is still doing flip-flops from his kiss. We've shared one kiss, one amazing kiss. A kiss that, if I'm being honest, I want to do again and again and again.

He lets my hand go to walk in front of me, getting to the last step and then holding out his hand for me. "Thank you," I say, standing right in front of him. I smile up at him, and his eyes are a soft blue right now. "That was very chivalrous of you." He laughs at me, bending his head to kiss me. I can't even help myself from leaning into him. Wanting to feel his skin on me, he slips one arm around my waist, pulling me to him as I wrap my arms around his neck.

He bends his head, his lips touching mine just a touch before he looks at me. "What do you want to eat for lunch? If you like, I went and got some fresh bread and deli meat before we left."

"That sounds good. I can help."

"I need to put the book away." He holds up the book.

"Can I use the bathroom?" I ask, looking around.

"Oh, let me give you a tour of my home." He smiles at me, his eyes turning a bright blue. The sorrow from before forgotten, for a minute at least. "Down these stairs." He walks down the stairs, going to the left. "There is a big room here." He opens the door for me to see the queen-size bed. A white comforter is on the bed with a baby-blue blanket on the foot of the bed. "This is where Beatrice usually sleeps." He laughs. "And then over this way, to the right, is my bedroom."

"Ohh," I say, teasing him as he opens the door, and I see a king-size bed. "This room is massive." I look around as he walks over to the drawer beside his bed, opening it and placing the book down. "In there"—he points at the door—"is the bathroom."

"Can I?" I ask, looking at him, and he just laughs.

"Please, be my guest." He points at the door.

"I'm going to do one of those videos," I say, walking into the room, and he just looks at me. "You know the one where you go through the drawers and stuff of the guy you are hooking up with."

He claps his hands. "Hooking up with?" He tilts his head to the side toward the bed.

I throw my head back and laugh. "Good one," I say, walking into the bathroom. "Oh my God, you have two sinks and a huge shower." I look at the massive glass shower and the two glass sinks.

"You going to open the drawers?" Xavier asks from the doorway. He leans against the doorjamb, folding his legs at the ankles and his arms over his chest. He looks so fucking sexy right there, with his hair perfectly pushed back and the scruff on his face.

I turn and lean against the counter and look at him. "Is there something in them I shouldn't see?"

He just smirks, and I can't help but go to him. I stand in front of him, and with him leaning, he isn't that much taller than me. "You know, you are really, really hot when you smirk at me like that." Stepping even closer to him, I get on my tippy-toes and lean in to kiss him.

My lips are about to touch his when he says, "You know that you are really, really hot." He mumbles, "Like all the time." I laugh, now about to kiss him. "It's really annoying."

I can't help but throw my head back. "Especially when I didn't want to like you."

I'm about to say something when Beatrice comes down the steps and then walks between us. "Oh, look at that," I joke with him. "Saved by the bell." I tilt my head to the side. "Did you miss your dad?" I ask her, and she looks up at Xavier. "Or did you want something to eat?"

"When doesn't she want something to eat?" Xavier says to her. We both look down at her and then look back up at each other. "Thank you," he murmurs softly, "for coming with me today."

"Thank you"—I wrap my hands around his neck—"for bringing me to my happy place. Now, let's go eat."

He nods at me, and he stops next to another set of stairs as we walk back. "There are two bedrooms down there with bunk beds."

I shake my head. "This is a monster of a boat. Makes my three-bedroom two-bathroom look like it's a pool house."

We walk back into the kitchen; he goes to the fridge, taking stuff out. He grabs two bags of deli meat, placing them on the counter with lettuce. "Turkey or ham?" he asks, and I shrug, not really caring.

"I'm good with either." I lean against the counter. "What can I do to help?"

He shakes his head as he walks to the drawer, taking out a knife to cut the bread. "Nothing." I can't help myself and instead go to the fridge and grab a couple of types of fruit to make a fruit bowl. I work side by side with him as he goes about making our lunch. He chuckles and looks over at me.

"What?" I ask as I cut strawberries.

"I just." He shakes his head as he washes the lettuce and then grabs the paper towel to dry it. Placing a piece on each sandwich, he looks over at me. "Like, you are Cooper Parker."

I laugh, looking down at the fruit on the cutting board. "That I am."

"My mind is so blown right now," he says, and I look over at him. "Like out of anything you could have said." He shakes his head, looking back down at the sandwiches before walking past me. His hands grip my hips when he walks past me to the fridge, grabbing the cheese. "Nothing could have prepared me for that."

"I figured you told me your biggest secret." I put down the knife to look over at him. "You trusted me enough for that, so"—I shrug—"I trusted you with mine." I lean my hip on the counter as I cross my legs at the ankle. "You are the first person I've ever told who doesn't work for me."

He smiles shyly, turning to look at me. "I promise to guard it with my life." He holds up his fingers as if he's giving me a Scout's honor.

"I mean, if you're promising." I uncross my legs and take a step toward him, getting even closer to him. "I think we should seal it."

"Really?" He doesn't take a step to me to close the distance. Instead, he grabs my hips and pulls me to him. "Will sealing it with a kiss help?"

I wrap my arms around his neck. "I think we should at least try," is the last thing I say before his hands slide from my hips to my back, moving to the back of my neck.

His mouth closes in on mine, and there in the middle of his galley, he gives me the second-best kiss of my life.

Twenty-Two

Xavier

"I MEAN, IF you're promising." She uncrosses her legs and stands, taking two steps closer to me. "I think we should seal it."

"Really?" I smirk at her. All I need is to take two steps, and we'll be chest to chest again. But instead, I reach out, grabbing her hips and pulling her to me. "Will sealing it with a kiss help?" I've been dying to kiss her again since I last kissed her five minutes ago. When Beatrice interrupted us, I almost groaned and called her a cockblocker. I could have spent the day outside on the sun pad kissing her, and it would have been one of the best days of my life.

She wraps her arms around my neck. "I think we should at least try." I don't even wait for her to say another word before my hands move from her hips to the back of her neck. My hand buries in her hair as my mouth crashes down on hers. Her mouth opens, and my tongue slides in with hers, my cock going rock hard in less than two seconds. Our tongues move around and around in a circle. At first, the kiss is soft, but after a couple of seconds, the neediness is apparent. Our tongues get rougher, our heads moving side to side. I wrap an arm around her waist, picking her up, her long legs wrapping around my waist as I carry us to the couch. I sit down with her on top of me, straddling. The minute she feels my cock, her hips move up and down. I'm the one who breaks the kiss because I can't help but moan. I take a second to calm down, but the little daredevil moves from my lips to my neck, sucking in. My hands on her hips now have a mind of their own, and I slowly move them up to her tits. My thumb feels the skin on her underboob from that circle in her top.

"Xavier," she whispers out my name, throwing her head back as her hips grind onto my cock. Her hair swings left and right against my legs, and I swear my cock feels like it's suffocating.

"Yes," I reply, my thumb playing with her hard nipples through her bikini. Her head comes forward, her forehead on mine. Her hips move a touch faster. Her eyes find mine as she opens her mouth to say something, but instead, I slide my tongue into her mouth. My fingers pinch her nipples as her hips move up and down on my covered cock. The heat from her pussy comes through her shorts and my shorts and boxers.

"I want." She lets go of my lips, sitting up straight on

my cock. I can't help myself; I pull down her bikini top, and the nipple is right there calling me. My mouth sucks in her nipple as her hips press harder on my cock. I twirl my tongue around her nipple and then bite down just as she comes. "Oh my God," she moans, her hips moving up and down as she rides out the orgasm. Her head falls down onto my neck. "Holy shit." She hides her face. "Can a person die from embarrassment?" she mumbles, and I can't help but laugh at her. "It's not funny. I just had an orgasm from dry-humping your dick." I wrap my arms around her waist.

"I don't know about you." I kiss her shoulder. "But if that is how we are going to seal the deal, I'm all for it." I feel her chest laughing against mine.

"I'm going to need you to tell me Beatrice isn't watching us," she says, her head still in my neck.

I look around, not seeing Beatrice anywhere. "I think the coast is clear." She sits up, and I see her eyes are green as emeralds, her cheeks pink. She looks down, not showing me her eyes. "Hey." I put my finger under her chin and lift her face to look at me. "Why so shy all of a sudden?"

She groans, making me laugh. "I was a two-bit hussy. I mean, I've never gotten to the point in my whole life when I dry-humped a guy." She puts her hands in front of her face.

"You aren't a two-bit hussy," I reassure her, and she looks at me.

"Do you know what a two-bit hussy is?" she asks me, laughing.

"Not even for a second," I admit to her. "But I'm sure that you aren't one. Now, since we sealed the deal, how about we eat?" Her face goes white. "I mean, the sandwiches I made." I can't help but laugh when her eyes go big. "I mean, I could always eat that, but…"

"I'm going to need you to stop talking right about now." She gets up. "I'm going to go clean up." I roll my lips to stop laughing as she puts her boob back into the top. "I'll be back."

I watch her ass go as she walks down the stairs before turning back. "Which bathroom do I use?" she asks.

"Mine." I want her to share my space with me. I wait for the sound of the door closing before I put my head back on the couch. "Jesus fuck, that was..." I look down at my cock, which is still rock hard. "You are going to have to settle down." I get up and adjust myself at the same time Beatrice comes up and looks at me. "Oh, please, don't you start. Did you see how hot that girl is?" I ask her. "She's like a fifty out of ten."

She just yawns, ignoring me as she walks out to the back deck and smells the air. I walk over to the kitchen, finishing the sandwiches and plating them. I grab a bag of chips before walking to the back deck and placing the plates on the table with the chips. Going back, I grab two water bottles deciding also grab some cans of soda. I'm on my way back to the table when she walks up the stairs, and I stop. She took off her shorts, her black bikini bottom showing me everything. "Are you trying to kill my dick?" I say the words, making her laugh.

"No." She looks down at my dick and then back up at

me. "But the shorts were a bit wet." I close my eyes and groan when she says that. "Let me take this." She grabs the plate from my hands. "You can carry the cold water."

"I need to pour it on my dick," I mumble as I watch her walk away, which makes it worse since her ass is almost on full display.

She places the plate on the table as Beatrice walks to her and then strolls out to the carpet, jumping into the water. Vivienne laughs as she puts her knee on the bench, looking over, her ass on display now. "Is the water cold?" She looks over her shoulder and catches me watching her.

"I might have to jump in," I mumble, walking to her as she turns around and sits down, tucking her legs under her. "I brought your fruit," I tell her, and she smiles at me, her hair blowing in the wind. The smile on her lips is everything. It fills her whole face.

I sit down in front of her as she leans over and grabs a piece of sandwich, taking a bite. "Are we still playing twenty-one questions?"

I smirk at her as I grab a piece of sandwich. "Sure," I agree, taking a bite. "It's your turn."

She shakes her head as Beatrice comes back onto the boat and lies down in the sun. "I asked the last question. I asked you what you did for a living."

"That's not fair," she huffs as she opens the bag of chips.

"Fine," I say, taking another bite. "Have you ever slept overnight anchored?" she asks me, and I smile at her.

"Look at you growing and asking me questions."

"Not going to lie." She takes a bottle of water, twisting open the top. "I literally got heart palpitations when I knew I was going to ask that." All I can do is chuckle at her.

"Well, to answer your question. I have slept overnight." I look at her. "Would you want to do that?"

Her eyes go big. "Would you be able to?" she asks, and I just nod.

"I don't really have any warm clothes," she shares. I smirk, and she rolls her eyes.

"I can lend you some of mine," I tell her, and she claps her hands.

"Really?" She sits up. "Do we have enough food?"

"I have a couple of steaks I could take out," I inform her. "Even some chicken, if you want."

"Are we going to be okay with the power and stuff or like are we going to have to like pedal back?" she questions, and I can't help but laugh.

"We are going to be fine," I assure her. "The question is, which room are you going to choose?" I wink, and she just smirks.

"Time will tell." She brings the bottle of water to her lips. We finish lunch, and she helps me clean up, then we spend the day in the front of the boat on the sun pads. I lie down beside her, and it doesn't take long before the two of us are making out.

When the sun starts to go down, we make our way inside to cook dinner. I show her the little piece of fake grass I had made for Beatrice to go to the bathroom on. It amazes her, and finally, after dinner, she gets up. "I need to shower."

"Same." I get up. My cock has been hard for the last five hours at this point. She grabs her bag from the couch, and I slip my hand into hers.

She starts to go toward the spare bedroom, but I pull her into mine. "You shower first, and then I'll take a shower," I tell her as she puts her bag on the bed.

"Are you sure?" she asks, and I just nod.

"It'll give you a chance to do the whole 'what's in the bathroom' thing." I laugh at her as I pull open a drawer and hand her a black T-shirt and black gym shorts. "These should fit you if you roll them a hundred times." She grabs the clothes from me. "Of course, you'll look sexy in them, which will mean I'll never be able to wear these clothes again." She comes to me, kissing my lips.

"I'll try to look as unsexy as I can," she deadpans, and I pfft out as she turns and walks toward the bathroom. "If you want, you could come and wash my back."

I put my hands on my hips and look up at the ceiling. "I'm going to shower in the other bathroom." I walk out of the room before I change my mind and take her up on the offer.

TWENTY-THREE

VIVIENNE

"I'LL TRY TO look as unsexy as I can," I say to him with his clothes in my hand. I hear him go pfft, making me roll my lips and look over my shoulder at him. "If you want, you could come and wash my back." I try to tempt him, but all he does is put his hands on his hips and look up at the ceiling.

"I'm going to shower in the other bathroom." He practically storms out of the room, and I can't help but chuckle. Walking into his bathroom, I close the door, putting his clothes on the vanity before walking over and starting the shower. I take off my bikini top, seeing that I got just a touch of sun, even though he was practically covering me all day. There is making out, and then there is making out with Xavier. He's in a whole different atmosphere. Every single time he put his lips on mine, my stomach fluttered as if there was a family of butterflies. Every single time his fingers touched me or grazed me or I felt his body on mine, it was as if every single sense in my body had awoken.

After peeling my bikini bottoms off, I step into the shower and let the warm water run over me before I look around for some soap, and all I find is his body wash. Opening the top, I press it to take a whiff, and it smells just like him. My body wakes up immediately, my nipples getting hard, and my pussy getting wet. I don't spend long in the shower, getting out and drying myself off. Grabbing his T-shirt, I put it on and it falls to the middle of my legs. I don't even bother with the shorts, knowing that even if I roll them ten times, they still will fall off. I walk back into his room, going over to the little bag I packed this morning and grabbing the lacy thong I threw in there. Slipping it on and shimmying it up over my hips, I walk out of the bedroom and see Beatrice is on the bed in the other bedroom. She lies on her side stretched out. I stick my head in and see the bathroom door open. "Is he in the shower?" I ask Beatrice, who just looks up at me for a second before putting her head back down.

I laugh at her, walking up the steps to the galley and looking around, not seeing him anywhere. I walk out of the galley to the back deck, seeing that it's pitch black in the distance. I grab the railing, walking up the five steps to the top. He's lying in the middle of the sun pad with his head on a little pillow, his legs propped up, and I can see all he's wearing is shorts. I can't help the smile that comes to my face knowing I'm going to see him soon. I make my way to him. "Hey," I say, falling on my knees beside him, suddenly nervous, which is silly since we spent the day kissing.

"Hi," he replies, putting his arm around me and rubbing my back.

"I used your body wash," I tell him, and he leans over and smells my leg. "Hope you don't mind."

"I don't mind," he assures me, going back to lie on the pillow. "Although, I might get hard around guys now that smell like me." I throw my head back and laugh. "Lie down with me."

I get on my back, putting my head on his shoulder, looking up at the stars blinking in the sky. "It's so peaceful," I observe, listening to the water lap against the boat softly. "This is heaven." I put my arm across his stomach and look up at him.

He bends his head to kiss me, his tongue sliding into my mouth. It starts off slow like always, but then it goes from zero to a hundred. I throw my leg over him, making the T-shirt rise, and now the bottom of my ass is out. But I couldn't care less at this point. I just want his hands on me. I've never been this needy for a man before. I've never wanted someone so bad. His hand moves from my back down to my ass, and when his hand feels my bare ass, he stops kissing me. "Are you wearing?" he asks, his eyes searching mine.

"It's a thong," I tell him, my body on fire. My nipples almost pierce through his shirt at this point. The rubbing from the T-shirt makes them even harder, and my leg is now placed right over his hard cock. A cock that has been hard all day long, and it's taken a lot not to ask him to whip it out like a two-bit hussy. "Did you want me to take it off?"

He groans, "Vivienne, I'm trying really hard here."

My heart beats in my chest as I sit up and do the boldest thing I've ever done in my life. I reach down for the hem of the shirt and lift it over my head, tossing it to the side. "This should help, then." I don't even get a chance to say something else because he springs up, grabbing me around my waist, and twisting me so I'm on my back. My legs open for him as he puts his elbows beside my head.

"Dammit, Vivienne." He leans down and kisses me. "There is only so much I can handle."

"Xavier." I move his hair off his forehead and push myself up to a sitting position, making him go on his knees. "There is something I've been thinking about all day long." I put my hands on his hips. "Do you want me to tell you what it is?" I lean my face forward, rubbing my nose on his stomach. His stomach quivers under my touch, and I love that he's just as into this as I am. "I was wondering." My fingers go into the elastic of his shorts before pulling them down over his hard cock. His cock springs free, and I almost gasp because it's hard and thick. My mouth waters. My hand moves on its own to grip the shaft. "Yes," is the only thing I say before I lick the tip, tasting his precum.

"Fuck," he hisses, and I look up at him for a second before I turn my eyes back to his cock. I take the head in my mouth and twirl my tongue around it. "Oh my God," he mutters, and I can see him clenching his fist at his side. The fact that I'm the one making him feel so out of control makes me even bolder. I move my mouth over his cock, taking half of it in before letting him go. My tongue comes out to lick from his balls up his shaft toward the tip, where I twirl my tongue around it. My hand moves up and down on his shaft while my mouth takes his cock again, trying to get it deeper and deeper.

"Vivienne." He grits out my name. His hands go into my hair as his hips thrust forward slowly. "I'm not going to last," he admits between clenched teeth. I move my hand even faster, wanting to give him what he gave me before. His cock swells in my mouth before he says, "I'm going to come." But I don't let him go. Instead, my fist holds him tighter, and I suck his cock harder until I feel his cum shoot into my mouth. "Vivienne," he says. His hips thrust until the last drop, and when I let his cock go, he just stares down at me. "That was," he starts to say, and I lie back down on my back. "That was…"

"Amazing," I finish as my hand goes to the middle of my legs. I've never been this wet before. I'm at the point where if he doesn't take care of me, I'm just going to do it myself.

"You know what's amazing?" he asks, getting up and tossing his shorts to the side. His cock is still hard, and I want him to just slam it into me. "You."

"Show me," I tell him, putting one hand behind my head.

"Oh, you can bet your ass I will." He grabs the side

of my thong on both sides, and it's no match for him. "Fuck." His eyes look down as his finger comes to touch the landing patch I have in the middle. He lies on his stomach, his face right there, as his fingers move to my clit. "All day," he says, as his finger goes in a little circle, "I've wondered how you would taste." His tongue comes out to flick my clit, then his finger continues going around and around. My hips move up on their own. "You taste like heaven," he declares, his finger moving down through my slit. "Wet." He slips in two fingers without stopping. I can't help but moan and close my eyes, my legs spreading even more. "All day." He sucks my clit into his mouth while his fingers move in and out. "I thought about spreading you open and tasting you."

"Yes." I thrust up to meet his fingers.

"Sitting on the bench downstairs, I pictured pulling your suit to the side and just burying my face," he continues, his fingers moving faster.

"You should have. I was so wet." He nibbles on my clit, and one hand moves over my nipples. "In the shower," I admit to him, "I fingered myself thinking of you."

"Next time, I'm going to watch."

"Yes," I say before he bites down on my clit hard, making me yelp. "Harder," I say, needing to come again, knowing that it's right there. "Make me come, and then I'm going to need you to fuck me." I pinch my nipples, my whole body feeling like it's going to explode. I'm about to come when his fingers slip out of me, and I almost cry out.

"I'm going to fuck you on your back." He grabs hold of his cock in his hand and then rubs it through my slit. Slamming it into me until he is balls deep, we both moan. My pussy convulses around his cock, making him hiss out my name, "Vivienne."

"If you aren't going to move that cock in and out of me"—I move my hips up—"then lie back and let me ride it."

"Oh, you're going to ride it." He pulls his cock out of me and slams into me over and over again. "After I take you on your hands and knees." My eyes roll back in my head, his thrusts never fucking stopping. My toes curl as my stomach gets tight, and I can feel myself coming. "Pussy is getting tighter," he announces, and all I can hear now is the sound of our flesh slapping together. "Going to need you to…" He pulls out of me, and my eyes open in time to see him grab my hips and turn me over. He pulls my hips up as he slams into me. I arch my back and get lower on my arms, trying to get him to go even deeper.

"Harder," I throw over my shoulder as one of my hands finds my clit. "Faster," I urge as my finger strums my clit, and he pounds into me. Nothing about this is soft and slow. It's all about getting him deeper into me. His hands grip my hips as I finally come. "Yes," I moan. At the same time, he plants himself all the way in me, and I feel him getting bigger right before he comes.

I squeeze my pussy over his cock until his chest collapses on my back, turning us both on our side, his cock still buried inside me. "Holy shit," he swears as he tries to get his breathing back. His chest is pressed against my back, and both of us have a sheen of sweat on us. "Are you okay?" he asks, and I look over my shoulder at him.

I push my back onto his front, making him fall from his side to his back. "I'm not okay," I reply as I lie on top of him, and my hand goes to grab his cock so I can ride it. "I want to come a couple more times." I put my feet on the sides of his hips, moving up and down on his cock. His hands grab my hips, and I look over at him. "Can you help me?" I ask before I slide my tongue into his mouth. I ride him as one of his hands pinches my nipple while the other hand moves to play with my clit. "Yes," I call out, coming in a matter of seconds. By the time I'm finished riding him, I've come three times before he comes in me again.

I finally roll off him, and even if I wanted to, I don't think I would be able to move. "Where are you going?" he asks. "I'm not done with you yet." I look over my shoulder and see his cock is still hard. "Time to fuck you under the stars."

Instead of asking him for a minute, I turn on my back and open my legs for him. "This time, do it nice and slow."

Twenty-Four

Xavier

SITTING ON THE bench watching the sunrise while she rides my cock is the best thing I've ever done. We spent half the night fucking outside and the other half fucking inside until the alarm rang. I was going to sleep through it, but her mouth was on my cock, so I was up and ready to go. We walked outside after I came in her mouth with a cup of coffee in our hands.

She was wearing just one of my T-shirts while I was wearing a pair of shorts. She sat next to me in the front of the boat. One thing led to another, and she was sitting on the table while I ate her out, right before she sank onto my cock where she rides me now. The T-shirt is pulled off over her head as I suck her nipple. I let her do the work and only come when she's come twice. "I think I'm addicted," she declares as she tries to get her breathing under control.

I kiss her shoulder. "To what?"

"Your dick." She laughs as she pulls herself off me. "I'll be right back." She puts the shirt back on her, walking away from me.

I tuck myself in as she walks away and comes back two minutes later, bringing the apple pie with her. "You okay?" I ask as she sits next to me, nodding her head.

"Figured you needed some sugar." She kisses under my jaw.

"I got my sugar," I inform her, "right on this table." She laughs.

"Um, we had sex," I say, grabbing a piece of apple pie.

"Was that what we did?" she jokes with me.

"We didn't really use protection," I remind her, and a burning forms in my stomach, thinking how irresponsible I was. "I should have stopped it." I shake my head, not ready to look into her eyes.

"Hey." She nudges me and puts her finger under my chin. "I could have stopped it also." She smirks. "I have an IUD, and I haven't had sex in a while."

"I'm clean also," I tell her, "but still, I should have made sure you were okay."

"Um…" She laughs, grabbing a piece of the pie. "Did it not show that I was okay?" She feeds me a bite of pie. "I was okay last night." She kisses my lips and avoids looking at me, grabbing her cup of coffee. "And I was more than okay this morning. Now if you don't trust I have an IUD, I can get something from the doctor." She takes a sip.

The pit of my stomach goes to my throat. "No." I shake my head. "It was for me to make sure you were okay. That you were protected."

She looks at me. "That's the nicest thing someone has ever said to me." She leans back and crosses her legs. "Now, can we not talk about this anymore?"

"Works for me," I agree, putting an arm around her shoulder and pulling her to me, kissing her head.

The two of us drink our coffee and eat some more pie before she gets up. "We should head back." I look at her and hold her finger with a thumbs-down. "We can come back tomorrow if you want."

"Fine," she huffs, "let me go get dressed." I follow her downstairs, and we have another round because she bent over to grab something, and my cock fell into her.

We sit side by side as we make our way back to the dock. Only when I turn into our row do I see her father on the dock with his phone in his hand. "Is that my father?" She gets up, and then I see more people joining him. "Oh my God, my uncle is here and my cousins." She shakes her head. "What the fuck?" she says, and I get nervous.

"I'm going to back in," I tell her, "and you can get off the boat."

"To tie the ropes." I shake my head.

"Why don't you go deal with your family?" I suggest, feeling my hands shake, wondering if the last two days meant anything to her. Wondering if it changes things now that we are back at the marina?

"No way. I'm going to tie the ropes." She walks

toward the back of the boat, turning and coming back to me. Her hands are on her head. "Shit, what do I tell them?"

"You do not tell them we had sex." That is the only thing that comes out of my mouth, and she laughs.

"Not that, like who do I say you are?" she asks me and I laugh. "Like how do I introduce you?" She looks so worried. "Like, we could give you a code name."

"No." I shake my head. "Just introduce me as me."

She nods her head, walking away from me. When I'm close enough to the dock, she yells at someone to grab the ropes.

Wilson steps forward, grabbing one while her cousin Dylan Stone grabs the other. When I'm in place, she gets onto the dock tying the ropes by herself, and when they are all secure, I turn off the boat.

"Where the hell were you?" I hear her father shouting. Beatrice jumps off the boat in front of her and barks at him, making all the girls laugh.

"Okay, well, for one," Vivienne says, "what the hell are you guys doing here?"

"You said you would check in," her father barks. "Chase said."

"I said she was fine. You were the one who went off the deep end yet again," Chase corrects, stepping forward.

"How would you feel if you went on your child's location and saw that they were in the middle of the fucking ocean?"

"You done fucked up on this one," Max Horton adds, and my mouth hangs open when it dawns on me that he's *the* Max Horton.

"It's my fault," I finally say, coming off the boat. "I took her out yesterday, and we anchored overnight."

"Dad," Vivienne says. "This is Xavier."

"Wait," Wilson says. "Monty?" He uses the nickname I went by.

"Hey." I hold up my hand, and now her father looks at me.

"Nice to meet you, sir," I say, holding out my hand.

"I wouldn't shake that hand," one of the girls says, and she walks over to Wilson and puts her arms around his waist. "You don't know where it's been or if, you know, they did the dirty."

"Francis," a woman hisses out. "Ignore her. I'm Karrie, Vivienne's mother."

"Xavier," I introduce myself.

"You know my brother Cooper," Vivienne says. "That's my sister-in-law, Erika." She points at the woman who sits on her boat. "My brother Chase, who is a snitch." She points at him, and he glares at her. "And his wife, Julia." I nod and then look at the woman who sits next to her. "That's her twin sister, Jillian, who is married to Michael. You might know him and my cousin Dylan and his wife and my cousin, Alex." I look at her.

"We played against each other a couple of times," I state.

"I'm Uncle Max," Max says, coming to me. "We met a couple of times." I nod at him. "Nice to see you."

"Okay, now that all that is out of the way," Vivienne says, "what are you guys doing here?"

"Emergency phone chain," everyone says at the same time. I don't even know what to say.

"I'm fine," she assures them. "Why didn't you call me?"

"We did," Matthew scolds, turning his phone to her, "one hundred and fifty-six times."

"Your father was calling a helicopter to take him out," Max adds, shaking his head.

"You were the one who gave me the idea," Matthew defends.

"It took all of you to come out and make sure I was okay?" Vivienne folds her arms. "You flew all the way in from Dallas?"

"Hey, kids-free weekend," Alex explains. "Now, how do we fire this boat up and take her out?"

"Um," Vivienne deflects.

"If you guys want to go out on the water, we can take my boat out. It's bigger and can fit everyone," I invite.

"Yes," Michael says, clapping his hands. "Not going to say he has a nicer boat, but damn." I roll my lips when Vivienne glares at him.

"We just need to get some food," I finally suggest, and Julia steps up.

"There are fifteen bags here filled with food." My eyes go over and look at the whole back of her boat, and it's full.

"We each brought stuff," Jillian offers.

"Well, then let's go," I urge and look over at Vivienne. "If it's okay with you?"

"It's fine with her," Cooper says. "Can I go on your

boat?" I just nod my head.

"How big is this boat?" Max asks as he steps on the back deck.

"Four bedrooms, three bathrooms," Vivienne answers.

"It sleeps twenty," I finally say, and they all gasp.

"Now, this is what I call a boat," Franny declares, coming on the boat. It takes thirty minutes before everyone loads back up. I have time to take Beatrice for a walk, and Vivienne changes. When I get back, the girls have made themselves at home upstairs while the guys sit on the back deck.

"This is the boat I want." Franny looks over at Wilson from the top, and he just shakes his head.

"What can we do to help?" Matthew asks, and I look over at Vivienne, who nods as she goes to untie the ropes.

"We got it," I say, walking to the captain's chair. All the men follow me, and I laugh. "You know what? Why don't we leave from upstairs? It's a better view."

The men make their way upstairs as I wait for Vivienne. When she jumps back into the boat, she kisses my lips. "I'm sorry for whatever is going to happen," she mumbles, walking up the stairs toward everyone. I follow her up as the guys stand near the captain's chair while the ladies just lounge.

I start the boat and make my way out toward the ocean; I'm waiting for someone to ask me a question. I take them for a tour of the island, pointing out things. The girls now have made their way down to the sun pads in the front, where we had sex last night.

Every single time one of them says something, I'm

expecting it to be about the game. I'm expecting her father to ask me what happened. I'm expecting Wilson to bring it up. I literally have my heart beating a mile a minute for a good straight hour.

They talk about everything except the game, and only after the first hour do I let go a bit. We anchor down for lunch, and I let go a bit more each time. The only questions they have are about the boat. Then they ask how far I've taken it. We spend the day on the water with her family, and when the sun goes down, I finally make it back to the dock.

"Beatrice is tuckered out," Vivienne observes, coming to me as I drive us back. The guys are now sitting in the back of the boat. She steps closer to me. "You okay?"

I nod my head. "Yeah, I thought for sure they would ask me questions," I answer her honestly. "But it's like I was just one of them."

"You mean a human," she jokes, and I lean in and kiss her lips, and then I fly back.

"Sorry, I shouldn't have done that," I apologize. "Anyone could have seen."

"I'm going to go out on a limb and say my family knows we've spent the night together," she states, and my eyes go even bigger.

"Why do you say that?" I ask, pulling into our row. "There are four bedrooms on this boat."

"Well, it could be when Franny asked if we slept together, and I told her that I don't kiss and tell," she starts, "and then she said it probably wasn't good. So I had to do it for your honor." I laugh at her as she kisses me one more time before walking off toward the back. Wilson gets off with her. Dylan and Michael both throw the ropes, arguing about who threw it better.

"Thank you," Matthew says when I turn the boat off, "for taking us out today."

"Anytime," I say to him, and he smirks.

"I'll be around," he informs me as he gets off the boat. It takes about twenty minutes for them to leave. Beatrice and Vivienne walk them out while I hook the water and electricity up.

I turn my head, seeing her walk to me, and my chest gets tight for a whole different reason. She has something in her hand as she walks to me. "They all gone?" I ask her when she gets closer.

"Yup," she confirms, "finally."

She hands me the box that is in her hand. "This was delivered today," she says, and I look at her, confused.

"What is it?" I ask, looking down and seeing that it's addressed to her.

"You are going to have to open it to find out." She smirks at me. I walk onto the boat and into the galley, grabbing a knife and slicing through the tape. I open the flaps and gasp. "What is this?" I look at her.

"Those are top secret," she whispers, leaning against the counter. "They are my next five books."

My hands shake as I pick up the books. "Holy shit!" I exclaim as I look at the unseen covers and books. "Oh my God." I turn them over to look at the back and read the blurbs.

"Looks like I've been replaced," she gripes to Beatrice. "Fucking Lucinda."

TWENTY-FIVE

VIVIENNE

THE ALARM GOES off at the same time he slides into me. "Hmm," I murmur as he slowly fucks me from behind. One hand plays with my nipple, and my eyes are still closed as he fucks me. "Yes," I pant out when I'm coming. He grunts out right after me.

Kissing my shoulder, he whispers, "Good morning."

"Morning." I lean back and turn off the alarm. I'm about to ask him if we are really getting up when Beatrice jumps on the bed, coming to us and sniffing us.

"Morning," I greet her as she lies on her side before rolling on her back, wanting me to scratch her belly. "Does someone want to go out?" I ask, feeling Xavier get out of bed. I watch him walk to the bathroom, and I want him again. "He's all that and a bag of chips," I share with Beatrice.

Xavier comes out of the bathroom with his shorts on and a T-shirt. "You look better naked," I tell him, and he laughs at me.

"You, too." He laughs. "You getting up or staying in?"

"I'm going to get up and work." I toss the covers off me, going to the bathroom. I wash, slipping on a pair of pants and a sweater. I walk out smelling coffee, and when I walk up the stairs, he's pouring two cups of it. I walk up to him and hug him from the back, kissing his shoulder.

He hands me a cup, kissing my neck as we walk out of the boat. "It's going to be a nice day," I observe as I slip my shoes on.

"Where are you going?" he asks me, slipping on his shoes.

"I figured I'd join you on the walk." He smiles. "If that is okay?"

"More than okay," he confirms, the two of us walking down the dock with his arm over my shoulder. We don't really talk as we walk with Beatrice in front of us. We get back when the sun rises, and I stop at my boat, getting on it. Beatrice follows me.

"You go work," he urges me. "I'll make breakfast."

I nod at him, walking into my galley with Beatrice behind me. I put the coffee cup in the sink before grabbing my laptop and charger. "Should I work here?" I ask Beatrice. "Or should I go next door?" I look over and see if I can see him. "Is it too needy?" I ask her. "I mean, should I give him space?" She tilts her head to the side. "I don't want to give him space." I think about it, jumping when I hear a knock on the back door.

He opens the door. "What is taking you so long?" He sticks his head into the galley. "Is everything okay?" He looks at me, his eyes roaming my face. "What's wrong?"

"Nothing is wrong," I assure him, and he steps into my cabin. "It's just that I thought maybe you wanted space."

He puts his hands on his hips. "You are going to work." He tilts his head. "You can write, and I can read." He smiles, and I shake my head, laughing.

"Fine." He opens the door and steps outside, waiting for me. "I just thought maybe you would want alone time."

He bends to kiss my lips. "That was sweet of you," he says, slapping my ass before he walks away. "Don't do that again."

"Wow," I note, walking off the boat. "For the record, if you are going to slap my ass"—I look up at him—"it would feel better with your cock in me." He snorts as I walk onto the boat, going to the couch and sitting down. He comes in, making us omelets and cleaning up while I open my computer. He sits next to me, reading the book with my feet in his lap.

His phone rings, and I look over at him, waiting to see if he's going to get it. He doesn't move a muscle. "Are you not even going to check who it is?"

"It's probably my agent, Miles," he replies, his eyes never leaving the book. "I think I'm supposed to have dinner with him." He puts the book down and looks over at me.

"That's nice," I tell him, and he shrugs.

"He wants to talk to me about going back," he shares, rubbing my legs. I just look at him, wanting to ask him how he feels about it, but not sure if I should. He looks at me, smirking.

"Ugh," I say, knowing he's waiting for me to ask him the question. "Do you think you would ever go back?"

"I would have to sit down with the team's GM to even consider it. All the cards have to be on the table."

"If you want," I start nervously, "you can talk to my dad about it."

"I don't need him to think I'm unstable while I'm dating his daughter," he says, and it makes my chest contract. I put my computer down on the table, then grab the book out of his hand and place it down next to the computer before climbing into his lap.

His hands go to my hips while my hands go to his face. "You are not unstable," I correct him, my eyes searching his. "If anything, you are the most courageous out of everyone."

"You're just saying that because you like me." He rolls his eyes.

"No." I shake my head. "I really like your dick," I try to joke with him, "and the rest of you is growing on me." He laughs right before I kiss his lips. "But with my father, or even my uncle Max, you can look at things you can do to help other players who are in your shoes but don't know what to do or who to talk to about it." My thumbs rub over his cheeks. "You can do so much good." I kiss his lips. "But first, call your agent and see what he has to say."

"Fine," he huffs, wrapping his hand around my waist and picking me up with him. I wrap my legs and my arms around him as he walks over to the counter, grabs the phone, and goes back to the couch.

"You could have just asked me to move." I laugh when he sits back down.

"But then I wouldn't have you all wrapped up on me." He kisses my neck. "Here we go," he says. Looking down at the phone, he presses the call button. I literally feel like my heart is going to come out of my chest. I put my hand on his chest, feeling his heart is beating faster than mine.

"It's going to be fine," I assure him, but he doesn't say anything because the guy answers the phone.

"Miles." Xavier says his name.

"I was wondering if you were avoiding me," the man says, laughing and makes Xavier chuckle.

"Who, me? Never," Xavier replies. "What's up?"

"I was supposed to be in town, but something came up," Miles explains. "But I have news."

"Do I want to know?" he asks, his heart beating even faster.

"A couple of GMs are interested," Miles reports, and my eyes never leave Xavier's.

I can see the way his eyes go a darker shade of gray. "Okay," he says.

"Set up the meetings," he finally adds. My eyes go big as I have to keep my lips sealed shut before I cheer for him. I know that it took a lot for him to take that step.

"Then just message me back the dates, and I'll set up things on my end."

"I'm almost afraid to ask what changed," Miles states. "So let me set shit up before you change your mind." He just disconnects, and I wait for Xavier to say something.

"How are you feeling?" I can't help but ask him, my hands trying not to shake while I wait for him to answer.

"Not the worst I've felt." He looks down at my hands on his chest. "Will you come with me?"

"Yes." I don't even have to think twice about it. "Wherever it is." He pulls me to him. His hands circle me as I lay my head on his shoulder, not saying a word, hoping he can feel my strength and energy go to him.

I don't know how long we sit here before he kisses my neck. But it goes from bright and sunny to a bit darker.

"Let's go watch the sunset," he urges, and I think he means going up on deck, but instead, he means taking me out to watch the sunset. He unplugs everything, and in a matter of fifteen minutes, I'm walking back onto the boat.

"Look at you," he throws over his shoulder at me, "a perfect yachtie." He puts his arm over my shoulders when I stand next to him as I wrap my arms around his waist. He takes us to our spot, and I walk up to press the anchor button, the way he showed me when we were with my family.

"It's good," I tell him, and he turns off the boat before joining me on the sun pad. He props up the sun pad to lean back on it. He sits down and opens his legs for me to sit between them. I press my back to his chest, moving to the side so my face touches his. We both watch the sunset, neither of us saying anything. "Do you want to stay here for the night?"

He looks at me and smiles. "With you, I'll stay anywhere." He kisses me on the lips. I turn in his lap, and in a matter of minutes, we are both naked. He slides into me at the same time our mouths fall on each other's. I cling to him as we both come, and we walk inside a couple of hours later. We munch on a couple of things, and his phone beeps. He looks at me, not sure of what to do.

"You can answer it tomorrow," I tell him, and he just looks down at his hands starting to shake.

I slip my hand in his, the tears threatening to come, but I stay strong for him. "You are the one who controls this narrative," I reassure him. "You. No one else."

He kisses me softly before letting my hand go and walking over to his phone. I swear I'm holding my breath, waiting for him to tell me what is on the text. I hate that I'm itching to ask him what it says. Hoping he tells me before I ask him, I keep it neutral. "Everything okay?" I ask as the lump forms in my throat.

"Yeah." He looks down. "Can you leave tomorrow?"

Even if I hadn't been able, I would make it so I could. "Yes," I tell him. "Just one little thing." I hold up my hand. "I need to stop by my place and pack. The only thing I have on the boat is boat attire."

He chuckles. "We can go by your place before we leave," he assures me, and I look over at Beatrice.

"What about Beatrice?" I ask, and he smiles from ear

to ear. I even think about taking her with us, or we can get a dog sitter to come and walk her.

"She's going to stay with her favorite human in the whole world," he says, looking at her. "Steven, my co-captain, is going to take her."

I nod at him. "Then it's settled." I take a deep breath and smile to make sure he knows I'm okay, but deep down inside, I've never been more nervous.

Twenty-Six

Xavier

"DON'T LOOK AT me like that," I tell Beatrice when I turn to pack some of my T-shirts in the luggage on my bed. She is sitting in the middle of the bed, just watching me. "You think I want to do this?" I shake my head, walking to the closet and grabbing the three suits I have. "It's complicated." I place the suits in the middle of the garment bag. "You'll be fine." She yawns in my face. "You think I'm not freaking out?" I shake my head, my heart speeding up when I think about it. My chest gets just a touch tighter, but I breathe through it. "Steven is going to come and take care of you." Her head perks up, and she looks over at the door, listening to see if he's here. When I called him last night to ask him to watch Beatrice, he jumped at it. It also helped that he wanted to come and stay on the boat. Out of everyone she's met, she loves Steven. It helps he's always bringing her some treat or another.

I look back into the bag, wondering if I am packing enough or if I am packing too much. It's been such a long time since I had to dress up in suits. "Do you think I should pack another suit, or is three enough?" I put my hands on my hips, settling for the three suits. "Three is good enough." Beatrice just yawns at me. "Toiletries." I turn, walking to the bathroom and seeing the towels from this morning are still on the floor. After our walk this morning, Vivienne was going to go to her boat to shower since all her stuff was on her boat. But I persuaded her that we should conserve water by showering together. So now her stuff is in my shower. Picking up the wet towels, I hang them up on the hooks. When Miles called me, I was going to say no, but something just said yes. I grab the black leather bag, throwing my toothbrush in there with my toothpaste, along with my deodorant and aftershave. I zip it up at the exact moment I hear Steven call out my name.

I walk out of the bathroom seeing Beatrice look over at the door, not sure she heard him or not. "Who's that?" I ask her, and then she hears him.

"Where is my pretty, pretty girl?" he calls, and she's off like a bat out of hell. I can hear her tail hitting the walls as she runs up the stairs. "There she is." I hear Steven, then I hear him laughing. "I guess you missed me."

I shake my head, tossing my toiletry bag in the luggage and zipping it up. I take a deep inhale and exhale. "Here we go." I grab the bag and walk up the stairs. Steven is sitting in the middle of the living room playing with Beatrice, who is on her back, waiting for him to scratch her stomach. He wears shorts and a T-shirt with a baseball cap. "Look who it is."

He looks up at me and smiles. "Who the fuck are you, and what have you done with Xavier?" He laughs, and I shake my head and look down at my outfit. Gone are the boat clothes, and in their place is my other look. I'm wearing blue pants with a white shirt tucked in and white leather sneakers on my feet.

"I don't look that different," I say, walking to the door and putting down my bag. "Just more put together."

He shakes his head. "Still rough around the edges."

I laugh at him. "Thanks for doing this for me."

"Thank you," he says. "It's been too long since I've been on the water."

I nod at him. "I should be back in about a week, maybe before."

"Take your time," he urges. "If you miss her, you can always FaceTime me."

I walk over to Beatrice and squat down in front of her. "I'm going to be gone for a bit, but I'll bring you back something." I rub her head, and she looks at me. "Try not to miss me." My chest contracts a bit less than it did before. "Call me if you need anything."

He just laughs at me. "Go away." He shoos me with his hand. I pick up my bag and walk off the boat, leaving the bag on the dock when I walk onto her boat and see her bag there on the deck. I knock before opening the door and spot her sitting at the table on her computer.

"You ready?" she asks, closing the laptop and sliding out. She's wearing black jeans with a white tank top.

"As ready as I'll ever be," I deadpan, and she comes to me.

"It's going to be amazing." She looks up at me smiling, and somehow, I believe her. "And if it's not, then fuck it, you come back here and keep doing what you're doing." I rub her arms. "Let's go," she says, and I just nod. "What time is the flight?" she asks as she locks her boat.

"I need to give them an hour's notice," I tell her, and she just nods. I pick up her bag, joining her on the dock when I see her look over at my boat. "Where are you going?" I ask her, and she just looks over at me.

"I didn't say goodbye to Beatrice," she explains, walking inside the boat. I pick up both bags and wait for her to come back. She walks out of the cabin, wiping her face off. "I gave her a cookie, and she licked me from my shoulder to my forehead."

We walk to her SUV, taking her keys out and pressing the hatch button. I place our bags in the back and sit in the passenger seat. "It's weird," she says beside me when she pulls out of the parking lot. "Usually, you are the one driving."

I laugh at her, looking out the window, my heart in my throat. She puts her hand on my leg. "Don't worry, I'm a good driver." I smile over at her. "I've only hit one cyclist my whole life, and she didn't do her stop." I can't help but laugh at that. "Cyclist stop signs are a thing."

She glares when my laughter gets louder.

I bring her hand to my lips as she makes her way to her house. "This is me," she states, pointing to the beautiful brownstone. I follow her out of the car and up the steps, looking around at all the trees that line the street. It's a quiet neighborhood, which you would never think exists in New York. The big black door opens when she turns the key, and she steps in.

She places her keys on the marble table in the hall, stepping up one step to the foyer. "This is your house?" I ask, shocked, looking around.

"Well, technically, my grandfather bought it for my mother when she started working for him. Then my parents lived here for a bit, then my aunt Allison moved in here. Then my aunt Zara," she explains as I take in all the detail. "But for now, I live here." She smiles. "Do you want something to drink?" I shake my head. "Okay, I'm going to show you something, but you can't freak out." She grabs my hand, dragging me to the stairs, where we walk up to the second level. I look over and see a bedroom, but instead of stopping, she walks up another level of stairs. When we get to the landing, there are three doors that are all closed. "Now, you promise not to make a big deal out of this?"

"Do you have a sex room?" I ask, my eyes going big, and she rolls her eyes.

"Yeah, that's exactly what this is," she snorts as she places her finger on the door, and it unlocks. I don't know what I expect is behind that door, but it's definitely not what shows up.

"This is my office," she announces, and I take a step in. There are frames all over the walls from *The New York Times* list, along with frames of all her book covers.

"I've died and gone to heaven," I say, walking and looking at all the little trinkets she has. "This is all Lucinda stuff." I look around and see little things that Lucinda had mentioned in the books. "This is…" I look around, spotting sweaters on the chair, and I can't help but walk over.

"Those are from the publisher," she shares. I pick up one of the sweatshirts and hold it open to see what is printed in the middle of it. Her pen name is on the front with the tagline, *Lucinda Cartwether Solves Them All.*

"I want one," I say, looking down at the different colors. "I want them all."

She shakes her head. "I'm going to go and pack. You can stay here for as long as you want."

"I might ask to live in here," I declare to her, not even joking. My heart that was so tight in my chest before is now beating normally, well, not that normal since I'm in this room. But the anxiousness is gone and in its place is a happy beating. She walks out of the room, leaving me alone in her treasure trove. "This is better than a sex room!" I shout out loud, and all I can hear is her laughter as she walks down the stairs.

I take three sweatshirts, and I'm almost tempted to take a couple other things, but I restrain myself. I smile when I walk from frame to frame, seeing her name on there. I walk out, closing the door behind me before walking down the steps. "Vivienne," I call out her name.

"In here!" she yells from one of the rooms I saw walking up. I walk into her room and take a look around. "In the closet." I look at the luggage in the middle of the bed and walk over to sit next to it.

She walks out of the closet with a hanger in each hand. "Okay, I'm trying to pack and, well, I don't know where we are going."

I laugh because she didn't even ask me where these meetings were. She was just automatically ready to come with me, no matter what. "Vegas, Phoenix, and San Jose."

"So…fucking warm." She laughs, walking back into her closet. "Should I pack something fancy?" She sticks her head out.

"I guess, I can take you out on a real date," I say, smirking.

"Ohhh, there is this club in Vegas I read about." I tilt my head to the side. "I think they have like special rooms, and you can have sex."

My mouth opens in shock. "Are you out of your mind? I'm not asking you to a sex club on a first date."

"SO, on a sex-ond date, then." She laughs at her joke. "Get it? Sex and then ond."

I can't help but laugh at her. She's nervous about how I'm feeling and trying to do whatever she can in order for the focus to be on her. "Clever," I muse, grabbing my phone and texting the lady for the plane. The text comes back that the plane will be ready in forty-five minutes. She comes back out, folding things into the luggage and then putting in the sexiest pair of shoes I've ever seen.

"Definitely going to get you to wear these." I pick up one in my hand when she comes back out of the closet.

She has changed into a white tank dress, and my mouth waters. Her legs are tanned and on display in caramel sandals. This woman could wear anything and still be the most beautiful person in the room. "I'm almost done." She walks over and grabs a jean jacket, slipping it on. She comes over and zips up her luggage and tries to take it off the bed, but I put my hand on it.

"Don't you even think about it," I warn her, and she comes over to me.

Stepping in the middle of my legs, she brushes the hair back away from my forehead, my hand running up the back of her leg. "Are you okay?" Her eyes search mine.

"Surprisingly, I'm not doing as bad as I thought I would be." I am and forever will be one thousand percent transparent with her.

"Well, if it helps"—she bends to kiss my lips—"we can join the mile-high club." I can't help but laugh at that. I grab the bag and place it in the hatch next to the other two bags.

Putting the address into the GPS, she makes our way over there. Grabbing her smaller bag to help me, I wait for her to walk up the steps of the plane before joining her.

She sits down in the chair and looks over at me, smiling. I bend down to kiss her lips before I sit in the chair across from her, the table in the middle of us, looking out the window. My mind is racing for a whole different reason now.

Everything with her is easy. There is no forcing conversations. If we have nothing to say, we say nothing, and it's okay. The last two weeks with her have been a dream, which makes going out west something to think about. What is going to happen between us? How the fuck are we going to make this work?

Twenty-Seven

Vivienne

I FASTEN MY seat belt and open the shade of the plane window, looking out. My heart beats faster than I want it to be. *I need to be his rock this week*, is the only thing on my mind. He has to know he can lean on me. "Good afternoon." I look up seeing the flight attendant standing there. "I'm Kalie, and I'll be with you on this flight." She smiles at both of us. "The flight time to Vegas is five and a half hours. We should be arriving at six p.m. local time. They are just closing everything up, and we should be taking off in the next thirty minutes. As soon as we are in the air, I'll bring you something to drink. What can I get you?"

"I'll have a soda water with lime, please." I smile at her and then look at Xavier. He literally takes my breath away. He's sexy in everything he wears. Shorts that fall on his hips, showing me that side V I love, mouthwatering. In the morning wearing shorts and a shirt with a cup of coffee in his hand, he makes my stomach flutter. Him naked is in a whole different world. Just thinking about him naked makes my toes curl. But seeing him dressed up a little, well, that just made his whole package even better.

"I'll have the same," he tells Kalie, who nods her head and walks away from us. I unbuckle my seat belt, and his eyes open wide. "Are you okay?"

I walk over and sit in the empty seat beside him. "Everything is fine." I smile up at him. "I just wanted to sit next to you." I fasten the seat belt and cross my legs. His arm leans over my legs as he bends to kiss my lips.

"You look beautiful," he compliments me softly me, and my hand comes up to cup his cheek, my fingers feeling the tickle from his scruff.

"You don't look too bad yourself." I smile before I lean over and kiss him. The plane takes off, and when we are finally in the air, Kalie brings over our waters, placing them on the table in front of us.

I grab my cup, bringing it to my lips, the bubbly water bursting in my mouth. "What's going through your mind?" Xavier asks from beside me.

"Is it that obvious?" I reply, not sure how to even start this conversation.

"Pretty much since yesterday," he says, and I can't help but laugh.

"And here I was thinking I was doing an amazing job hiding it." I laugh nervously. The last thing I want is for him to be worried about me.

"It's just," I start to say, and I try to find the words without sounding so needy. But knowing I have to be one hundred percent honest with him. "This thing." My mouth suddenly gets dry, and I have to take another sip of water. "That we're doing. What is it?" I swallow down the lump as the back of my neck tingles. "Like, it's fine if it's a fling."

"It's not a fling." He shakes his head. "Fuck, this is not a fling." He unbuckles his seat belt. "Let's go sit on the couch." He motions with his head toward the couch on the other side of the plane. I get up, walking over to the couch and sitting down. He sits down beside me, putting his arm around me. He lifts my legs so they are draped over his. "Before the plane took off, I was thinking the same thing," he admits to me, and I feel a lightness leave, and the heaviness start to come over me. "Like, if we do this whole West Coast thing." I don't say anything. Instead, I wait for him to continue. "You have a whole life in New York."

"I do," I agree. "Do you have a home office?" I ask, and he shakes his head.

"I had a house in Long Island," he says, and I'm shocked.

"I lived in Long Island for most of my life," I tell him, and he looks just as shocked.

"Sold the house two years ago."

"Do you miss it?" I look into his eyes, seeing them get darker as he shakes his head.

"Almost took my life in my master bathroom. I never

wanted to go back there again," he confesses, looking at me. I lay my head on his shoulder, not even thinking how it would be if he wasn't here. Just the thought makes me want to vomit. "But to answer your question." I look up at him. "It's more than a fling."

I can't help the smile that fills my face. "Are you saying I'm your girlfriend?" He just rolls his eyes and I throw my head back and laugh.

"That sound," he says when I stop laughing, "your laughter is the second-best sound I've ever heard."

"What's the first?" I ask him, and he looks around to make sure we are alone.

Leaning into me, he whispers in my ear, "When you moan out my name right before you come." Just the way he says it makes my whole body go hot. I don't even think before I move to straddle his lap. He makes sure that my dress is covering my ass. I shrug off my jacket to make sure I'm covered also.

I lean into his chest. "Xavier," I say his name in a whisper. "Unbuckle your pants."

"Fuck no." He shakes his head. "There is no way I'm letting anyone see you like that." He grabs my face and slides his tongue into my mouth. "It's for me and only me."

"Ugh, you are so getting laid when we get in the hotel room," I promise, not moving from his lap. He wraps his arms around me as I lay my head on his shoulder for as long as he lets me. Kalie comes and asks us if we would like to eat, and I finally get off him.

She only brings out some things to snack on since we

are getting into Vegas at dinnertime. We spend the flight playing cards, and when we land, he carries my bag off the plane for me. The black Escalade is there to greet us. "Welcome to Vegas, Mr. and Mrs. Montgomery," the man welcomes us as he opens the back door. I step in first, ignoring the fact that neither of us corrected him.

It takes less than five minutes before we are driving away from the airport. When we pull up to the hotel curb, there are two men waiting for us. The door opens, and Xavier steps out first, turning to help me out. "Thank you," I say to him, and he bends to kiss my lips.

"I'm Devon, your concierge," one of the men tells us while the other one grabs our bags. "Right this way." Xavier slips his fingers into mine as we follow him into the side entrance. "Welcome to the Cosmopolitan Hotel."

I smile at him as he shows us around the suite, my whole body itching to get Xavier alone. I walk over to the floor-to-ceiling wall of windows facing the Bellagio. "Please call me if you need anything. We are available twenty-four hours a day." When he walks out of the room, I turn to Xavier, who just stares at me.

"Why are you so quiet?" He puts his hands on his hips.

I shrug my jacket off, tossing it onto the couch that is against the wall. "I was waiting for him to leave." The next thing I do is take off the one-piece tank dress I'm wearing, and he hisses. "So I could show you my new set." I stand in front of him wearing a lace bra and matching thong.

He walks over to me, his eyes a dark gray. He reaches

behind him to take his shirt off while my hands go to his pants. I don't even wait before I sink to my knees and take him down my throat. He lets me suck his cock for a couple of minutes before pulling me off and up. He turns me around, pressing his chest to my back. "Lean forward," he instructs me, and I push my ass back onto his dick.

He grabs my hip with one hand as he squats down behind me. I feel his fingers move the string to the side and then feel him stick his tongue into me. I moan out his name, "Xavier."

"Hmm," he responds, getting back up and sliding his cock into me. His hands are on my hips as he pushes his whole cock into me. I get on my tippy-toes as I arch my back for him, getting him even deeper. He pulls my hips higher, and my feet are barely touching the floor as he pounds into me harder and harder. It doesn't take us long before we both jump off the edge.

"Well then," I say when he slides out of me. "Now, that is a welcome to Vegas." I kiss under his chin, walking to the bedroom, past the king-size bed, and toward the bathroom.

He's right behind me as he turns on the water in the bathtub. I look over at him. "Never fucked you in a tub before. Got to scratch that off the bucket list."

We take a bath together, but I'm the one who does the fucking. Not even caring when the water splashes over the rim, it takes four towels to mop up all the water.

The next morning, he gets up, and I watch him from bed getting dressed. He slides into his black dress pants and puts on his white dress shirt. "Fuck, you're hot." I can't help the words that escape my mouth.

He chuckles as he finishes getting dressed. "What are you going to do while I'm gone?"

"Well, I'll probably have to take care of needs." I fan myself as I sit up, holding the sheet to cover my naked chest.

He just stares at me, licking his lips. "I still have to watch you do that." I can't help but blush because I've never done that before.

He comes over to the bed, sitting down beside me. "I won't be long." He kisses my lips.

"I'll be working," I tell him, and when there is a knock at the door, he gets up.

"That's my ride," he huffs.

I get up, settling on my knees. "You are going to be amazing, and they are lucky to have you." I kiss his lips as we hear the knock again.

He gets up and looks down at his cock. "I hope he doesn't think this is for him," he jokes, laughing while he walks out of the room.

Only when I hear the door close do I let out the breath I was holding. "He's going to be fine," I state when my phone rings from beside the bed.

I pick it up, thinking it's Xavier, but instead see my father's name and say, laughing, "Hello, Daddio."

"Where are you?" is the first thing he asks me. "Your location is showing me Vegas."

"Then it's not broken," I tease him, getting up and grabbing the robe.

"What the hell are you doing in Vegas?" he shouts, and I roll my lips. "You better not be eloping!"

"Do it!" I hear my uncle Max yell. "Best thing I ever did."

"Would you mind your business and go away?" my father hisses at him. "Vivienne Allison Grant." He uses my full name

"I'm not getting married, Dad." I let him off the hook. "Xavier is here for business." I stick to the minimum of why we are here.

"Is he meeting Bernie?" he asks me.

"Who?" The name is not ringing any bells.

"The GM of Vegas," he informs me who Bernie is.

"I have no idea," I tell him the truth.

"Only you would go with someone and not ask any questions." He laughs. "I didn't know he was looking to get back into it."

"I think he's just weighing his options." I won't go into any other details because it's his story to tell and not mine.

"Well, how will it work if he does pick Vegas?" my father asks me the loaded question I was asking myself for the last two days.

"We are not there yet, so I have no idea." My mouth goes dry. "Is that what you called me for?"

"No, I'm reminding you about the gala next week," he says.

I close my eyes and hiss, "Shit."

"Yup, so it's next Saturday night," he reminds me of what I already know but forgot. "Are you staying with us?"

"Negative," I reply. "Remember the last time?" He just laughs.

"I take it you are bringing Xavier?" he asks, and I look at the phone in my hand.

"Who are you?" I ask him. "Where is my father, with the whole no one touches my kid?"

He laughs. "What can I say? The other three wore me down. He's a good guy," he says softly, and I have to wonder what he knows. I also know that I don't want to know what he knows because I'm afraid I'll tell him the truth. "That doesn't mean that I am not going to have a sit-down with him when he comes here."

"There he is," I declare, shaking my head.

"I want to know what his intentions are with my daughter." He says the words, and I groan.

"Dad, it's not the eighteen hundreds." I laugh. "We are dating. Leave it at that."

"Negative," he replies. "Call me tomorrow to just let me know you are okay."

"I'll be fine. Love you," I tell him and disconnect the call. I'm about to put my phone down when it rings again. I pick it up expecting it to be my father again just to make sure I'm okay but it's my aunt Vivienne.

"Bonjour," I say in French as soon as her face fills the screen.

"Bonjour, ma petite poulette." She uses the nickname she gave me when I was little. "How are you doing? It feels like I haven't spoken or seen you in years." I roll my eyes at her.

"It's been almost a month," I tell her and she just stares at me.

"Something is different about you." She pushes her face even deeper into the screen. "You look a bit different. Your smile is a bit brighter." She taps her finger on her chin. "Could it be a penis smile?" I laugh at her. "I know that smile. I wear it often."

"Eew," I say, trying not to picture my aunt and uncle naked.

"C'est la vie." That's life, she shrugs. "Now tell me why you look so happy."

"Do I really look that different?" I ask as my heart speeds up. "Could be I met someone." I know the minute I say those words it'll be like opening Pandora's box. There is no way she is just going to let me drop this little hint and not expand on it.

"Define you met someone?" she asks me seriously. "Like, you met someone and took him home for a roll in the hay or you met someone like you saw him more than twice?"

"Like, I met someone that I really, really like," I say to her.

"What?" She holds up her finger. "This sounds a little serious."

I shrug. "I think so," I admit out loud for the first time. "I told him," I say the three words, "I told him what I do for real."

She gasps, looking around her, making sure she is alone when she says, "Like, about Cooper Parker?"

I nod my head. "Mon Dieu." My God. "This is so

much more than getting good sex." She puts her hand on her lips. "This is like slip a ring on my finger and marry me."

I hold up my hand showing her no ring. "We can relax about that but I told him everything." I smile. "And get this, he's a huge fan."

"Who isn't." She rolls her eyes. "Maybe now you can perhaps tell your family so I don't feel like I'm keeping a secret from my best friend." I laugh at that. "You don't know what it feels like."

"Well, perhaps I just might," I tell her and I hear someone calling her from the background.

"Okay, I have to run, but I want you to FaceTime me with the man who has captured your heart," she says, blowing me a kiss. "J'taime, poulette."

"J'taime, ma tant preferee," I tell her and she winks at me before hanging up.

I put the phone down as I hear her words play over in my head, he has captured your heart. Said heart now starts to speed up even faster as I get up and walk over to look out the window, the sun filling the sky with not one single cloud in sight. "Good luck, Xavier," I whisper, hoping he can feel my energy.

Twenty-Eight

Xavier

I SIT IN the back seat of the SUV, looking out the window. My leg moves up and down with the nerves that are soaring through my body. My heart's beating so fast it's the only thing I can hear in my ears, and my hands become clammy. My stomach is in full knots, making it so hard to swallow. I grab the little bottle of water that is in the cupholder in the middle of the seat, my hands shaking as I unscrew the top. I bring the bottle to my lips, taking a sip. My throat feels like it's tightening even tighter. Screwing the cover back on, I put my head back on the headrest, closing my eyes. I start to control my breathing just like I had practiced. I think back to my happy place, but I'm a little shocked and surprised that now it's with Vivienne sitting in the middle of my legs as we watch the sun setting. I don't have time to think about what it means because the SUV comes to a stop. The door opens right away. "Mr. Montgomery." The man nods at me as I put one foot out, hoping my knees don't buckle, making me fall flat on my ass.

"There he is," I hear from the side and see Bernie, the GM, walking toward me with a smile on his face. He extends his hand to me when he gets close enough. I have enough time to wipe my hand on my pants before shaking his hand.

"Bernie," I greet him as he lets go of my hand.

"Thank you for meeting with me." He smiles. "Shall I show you around?"

"Sure," I agree. It's the first time in my whole career that I'm doing this. When I was traded, it was done with my agent, and I was just told where to go. Now I feel like I'm being courted. He takes me around the training facility, the whole time telling me the best of it. It's a state-of-the-art facility for sure, and because it's the off-season, there really isn't anyone here. The walls are filled with iconic plays through the years as he tells me about the way the club works. I really don't say much. Just listening at this point.

We visit the dressing room, and then he takes me to his office. "Have a seat," he offers, pointing to the empty chair in front of his desk as he walks around his desk to sit behind it. I take a seat in front of him. "So, do you have any questions for me?" He pushes back in his chair, rocking.

"Why me?" I ask the obvious question, and he just looks at me. "You must have heard some of the gossip that has been going around." I chuckle nervously.

"From where I sit, there are always three sides to every story," he answers. "Everything in the middle is muddled."

I nod at his honesty. "How would you handle a player who comes to you, telling you the pressure with the press is overwhelming him?"

"There are always things we can do on our end," he starts. "The press can be one way when you are winning and another when you are losing. I think it's important for both sides to be respectful of that." I take in the words he's saying. "But I also know I have to have my players' backs. If they come to me and are like, 'I can't do it anymore.' I have to take them out of the press lineup." He puts his hands on the desk. "But you have to know, doing that will just put more press on their back."

"It can be," I agree with him. "But if I tell you I can't deal with it anymore, and I need help." I watch his face when I say the next words. "I just don't want to be ignored and then thrown to the wolves with no one at my back."

His eyes find mine as he gets the full extent of my words. "There is nothing I won't do as a GM to protect my guys. I don't know what happened in Long Island." His eyes go down, and then he makes sure he's looking me straight in the eyes when he finishes the next part. "But I know that we win as a team, and we lose as a team." The rest of the conversation is about what he wants to achieve as GM, and like everyone out there, his main goal is to get a Cup into his hands.

The meeting lasts maybe two hours, and when he walks me back to the waiting SUV, I turn to him. "I want to thank you for taking the time to meet with me." He extends his hand again.

"Thank you"—I put my hand in his, shaking it—"for wanting to meet with me. I will get back to you soon."

"I look forward to hearing from you." He slaps my shoulder. "You look good," he says, and I can't help but smile.

"I feel good," is the last thing I say before I get into the SUV, closing the door behind me. I finally let out the breath I must have been holding the whole time, the stress pouring out of my body. When I finally get control of my breathing, I pull out my phone as soon as we drive away, texting Miles.

Me: Met with Bernie. Wasn't as hard as I thought it would be. He has a great mindset.

I press send, and it takes him three seconds to reply.

Miles: I wouldn't have set it up if I didn't think you guys were a good fit. One down, two to go.

I laugh at that text, not having the time to respond to him before I look up and see we are pulling up to the hotel. I thank the driver before stopping to talk to the concierge. "How may I help you?" I smile at him and tell him of the plans I want to make.

When I open the door to the hotel suite, my whole body goes on alert for her. I look at the couch, seeing she isn't there. "Hello," I call, walking back to the bedroom. Stepping around the corner, I see her sitting in the middle of the bed with her laptop on her lap. Her eyes fly up to mine, and it takes me a minute to catch my breath. She is, without a shadow of a doubt, the most beautiful woman I've ever met, inside and out. Just the thought that she means so much to me makes my stomach go tight. *What the actual fuck is going on?* is the only thing my head is thinking. Is this really happening to me? My feet move to her as I sit on the bed beside her.

"Hi," she greets me, moving her computer off her lap and turning to me. Her eyes light up, and I can't wait to kiss her. I make the distance between us nonexistent when I pull her to me. My lips fall on hers, making all the questions that I've had answered.

I've gone and fallen in love with her.

She moves around me to straddle my lap. "I missed you," she says to me, wrapping her arms around my neck as I wrap mine around her waist. She lays her head on my shoulder, burying her face in my neck as she gives me soft kisses.

"How much longer do you have to work?" I ask her softly.

"I'm done," she states, and I turn to kiss her head.

"Good, because I have a surprise for you," I tell her, and she moves her head out of my neck.

Her eyes widen. "Is it a big surprise?" She wiggles her eyebrows at me, and I can't help but throw my head back and laugh. "Because after three rounds last night, I've already seen that surprise."

"It's not that," I confirm, "but the car will be here in thirty minutes." As soon as I say that, she jumps off my lap.

"What do I dress in?" She walks over to the walk-in closet. She gasps. "Oh my God, are we going to the sex club?"

I shake my head. "We are not." I shrug off my jacket and toss it on the bed.

"It could be fun." She turns and walks into the closet. I watch her in her little shorts and tank top, my cock thinking about how much fun it really would be.

"It could be," I admit to her, pulling my shirt out of my pants and unbuttoning the buttons. I make my way into the closet with her. "But it's still a no."

"Buzzkill." She smirks at me. "So we aren't going to a sex club. What should I wear?" She turns to me.

"Anything," I tell her, kicking off my dress shoes.

"What are you going to wear?" she asks, watching me unbuckle my Tom Ford belt, her eyes roaming down and then up to me again.

"I'm wearing jeans and a shirt," I inform her as I walk over to my dark blue jeans. She grabs a pair of blue jeans and a top before turning and walking to the bathroom.

"I'm going to shower quickly," she declares as I finish getting dressed. I slip on the white sneakers and go into the bathroom, spotting her coming out of the shower and wrapping herself with a towel. "How long do I have?"

"About fifteen," I tell her, and she nods, drying herself off. She looks at me.

"You're distracting me," she scolds as she slips on a pair of baby-blue panties, grabbing the matching bra. "Stop looking at me like that."

"I can look at you any way I want," I retort, leaning

against the counter behind me, and she just laughs.

"Is that so?" she shoots back at me, grabbing the blue jeans and putting them on. They mold her every fucking curve.

"It is so." I fold my arms over my chest and my legs at my ankles.

"Why is that?" she asks, grabbing the baby-blue top and slipping her arms in the holes where they go. The thick spaghetti straps sit over the bra straps as she buttons down the front, tucking it in when she's done.

"Because you're mine." I push off from the counter and kiss her bare neck. "And I can watch you all night long if I want."

She laughs as she puts her head back for me to kiss her. I bend and kiss her lips softly. "How can I argue with that logic?" She grabs the hairbrush and brushes her hair. "I need my shoes, and I'm ready," she announces, walking to the closet and slipping her feet in a pair of Gucci flip-flops. "Okay, where are we going?" She smiles.

"It's a surprise." I slip my hand in hers. "Grab your phone," I remind her of her cell phone that is on the side table. "And I would text your dad. Tell him you might be out of service for the next couple of hours."

She looks at me, trying to figure out where we are going. Instead of texting her father, what she does is call him, and he answers right away. "Twice in one day." He laughs.

"Yeah, don't get used to it," she jokes. "Listen, I'm calling you to tell you that I'll be out of range for a couple of hours." She looks at me, rolling her lips.

"What does that mean?" he snaps, and I can imagine his face.

"Xavier is taking me on a date," she starts to say, and I close my eyes, thinking maybe calling her father wasn't a good idea.

"Oh, if you are with Xavier, it's fine," he backpedals. "Have fun and be careful. Gotta go. Your mother is calling me." He hangs up, and she looks down at the phone in shock.

"What the fuck?" she mumbles, but I don't have time to tell her anything when there is a knock at the door.

"Ride's here," I say, grabbing her hand again and pulling her with me. She puts the phone in her back pocket. We make our way down to the SUV that drove me this morning.

The man has the door open for her, and I hold her hand as she gets in. I'm expecting him to close the door, but instead, she lets go of my hand and moves over to the other side, so I can get in with her. I sit down, looking over at her as she slides closer to me. I put my arm around her as the driver gets into the car. "So are you going to give me any clues?" She bends her arm, slipping her fingers into mine.

"No." I smile and then bend my head to kiss her lips. Every single time my lips touch hers, it's like a piece of me is put back together. Every single time my lips touch hers, it's like breathing becomes that much easier. Every single time my lips touch hers, it's like I've finally found my home.

"Fine," she huffs. "As long as you hold my hand." I

pick up her free hand and bring it to my lips.

"Always," I tell her, looking in her eyes and wondering if she feels the same way I do.

TWENTY-NINE

VIVIENNE

"ALWAYS." HE KISSES my fingers, looking into my eyes. The flutters in my stomach feel so much different this time. It's a tightness that comes with it. When he walked into the room before, I was so anxious for him, I had no idea what to do. So instead, I just straddled him and hoped he could feel my strength. As my eyes stare into his, the lump in my throat stops me from saying what I really want to say.

"Look," he says, pointing to something out the window. I turn my head to the side and see the helicopter. My mouth opens in shock as I look over at him. "Surprise!"

"Oh my God!" I exclaim as the SUV comes to a stop. "Is that a helicopter?" I ask him with excitement as the driver opens the door for me.

I step out, feeling Xavier next to me. He puts his hands

on my shoulders. "I can't tell, is this a good surprise or a bad surprise?"

I look up at him behind me. "This is a good surprise," I confirm, the smile permanently on my face when it comes to him. He slips his fingers in mine as we walk over to the helicopter. The pilot is there to open the door for us. I get in first as he tells me how to buckle up. He then hands me a headset with a mic in front of it. I put it on as Xavier gets in and buckles in, placing his headset on his ears. "Hello," I say, and he looks over at me. "I guess you hear me."

"I do," he says as the pilot gets in the front.

He puts on his headset. "Testing," he speaks into his own mic. "Can you hear me?"

"I can," we both say at the same time.

"Perfect," he replies, turning on the helicopter. "My name is Micro, and I'll be your pilot today." He starts flicking switches on. "We are going to be going over the Strip," he relays. "And then making our way over the Grand Canyon."

I squeal in surprise. "Shut up." I hit his arm. "Oh my." I look out my window as he pulls up. I can't help but be amazed by the Strip from the sky. "Look." I point over to the Bellagio fountains. "The Vegas sign." I point down to the line of people waiting to take pictures before we leave the Strip.

"Have you ever done this before?" Xavier's voice comes out, and when I shake my head, his smile fills his face more. The sun comes into the helicopter, making his eyes even brighter. I watch in amazement as we fly toward the mountains. The scenery is the most beautiful I've ever seen. The pilot takes us toward the Grand Canyon as we fly low until he pulls up again toward a cliff on the side. "You see that?" Xavier points to what looks like a trailer. I strain my eyes to see it more, and now it looks like there is a seating area outside the silver trailer. "That is where we are going to stay," he says, and I look over at him.

"What?" I say, turning back to see that one side of the silver trailer is filled with windows overlooking the edge of the cliff.

The helicopter lands next to the trailer. The pilot turns off everything, then looks over at us. "I'll open the door," he says to us, taking off his headset and then opening his door. I take off my headset, putting it down in front of me as I unbuckle my seat belt. The door opens, and then Micro holds out his hand for me. I grab his hand. "Watch the step," he tells me of the step under the helicopter. I step onto the dirt landing, turning and watching Xavier step down. "Here are the keys." He hands Xavier the keys. "I'll wait until you are in the trailer before I take off." He smiles at us. "Call us when you are ready." He nods over at Xavier, who just nods back at him.

"Shall we?" He slips his hand in mine as we walk down the dirt path toward the silver trailer.

"This is insane," I say as I step up two wooden steps to what can only be a porch. A sitting area right in front of the door with four poles holding up an awning. Two double couches face each other with a round, brown glass table in the middle of them. Off to the other side are two wooden chairs with plush cushions facing the edge of the cliff. The sun and heat off in the distance feel like we are on top of a cloud. It's so magical even if I wanted to snap a picture of it, I don't think it would do it justice. It's the most romantic place I've ever seen, and all I can see in my head is the two of us sitting out here with me in his arms.

"Let's go inside, and then we can sit outside," he suggests, and I can't say anything because the words are stuck in my throat. He puts the key inside the glass door, turning it and opening it.

He steps in first, and I follow him. "This is our home for the night." He steps out of the way, and I see a long counter against the wall facing us, with a set of stainless-steel drawers. A wooden counter with a sink and stove right next to each other. A bookcase at the end of the counter separates the four-poster king-size bed. Big plush pillows are on the bed with two long body pillows on each side. The back of the bed has a big window with potted plants in front of the ledge. I hear the door close at the same time the helicopter starts. We walk over to the glass door, and I wrap my arms around his waist. His arms come out to circle around me as we watch the helicopter fly away from us.

"So"—he looks down at me—"is this better than a sex club?" I can't help but laugh at him.

"I'm going to agree." I turn in his arms as his hands grab my face, the heat from his hands going right down to my bones. "This is most definitely better than a sex club." I smile as he leans down and softly kisses my lips. His tongue slides into my mouth, and my tongue fights with his. The kiss starts off slow but quickly goes to hot and heavy. He picks me up, and I wrap my legs around his waist. My shoes fall off and onto the floor with a clatter before he puts a knee on the bed. He places me down on my back, his lips never leaving mine. Our hands work in a frenzy to get our clothes off of us, our mouths only letting each other go when we have to peel off his T-shirt. He slides into me, our mouths drowning our moans.

We've been together before, many, many, many times, but this time, it feels different. This time I feel different. "Xavier." I finally let his lips go to whisper out his name. His eyes look into mine as our hips thrust to meet each other. I put my hand on his face as he puts his forehead on mine. The words at the tip of my tongue make my heart speed up even more.

"Vivienne," he says my name in a whisper, and I close my eyes when I jump over the ledge. He buries his face in my neck as he follows me. My legs wrap around his waist, my arms wrapping around his neck, pulling him even closer to me. He tries to get me to roll over, but I tighten my grip on him. "I don't want to hurt you," he says softly.

The lump forms in my throat because the only way he can hurt me is if he walked away from me. Just the thought makes me want to throw up. "I'm fine." I'm finally able to say without my voice cracking. I don't know how long we lie here together, but when he slips out of me, I want to call him back. He holds out his hand for me to scoot forward. He grabs a white robe, holding it out for me. "What is this?"

"The bathroom is outside," he explains, and I can't help but gawk at him. His laughter fills the trailer. "It's an outhouse."

"What does that mean?" I ask him, slipping my hand into the arms of the robe.

"I have no idea, but we'll find out together." He grabs his own robe and puts it on. He snags my hand, slipping his fingers in mine.

"I'm going to just say this," I tell him as he slides the glass door open. "Not a fan of outhouses." He just chuckles as he walks to the side of the trailer, and we see a wooden door. I hide behind him as he opens the door. A sink, toilet, and standing shower fill the room. "This is smaller than the bathroom on airplanes," I mumble as he walks inside.

"I don't think I've ever laughed as much before I met you," he states, bending and kissing my neck.

"You're welcome," I return as he turns on the shower.

"This is going to be a tight squeeze," he tells me, and I can't help but roll my lips. It is not only a tight squeeze; we have to turn at the same time. I have never laughed so much in my whole life. My stomach and cheeks hurt from laughing. After getting dressed again, we sit outside facing the mountains.

The smell of coffee fills the trailer, and my eyes flicker open. I stretch my arms before mumbling, "Good morning."

"Good morning to you," Xavier says, and I turn to

watch him make my coffee naked. I grab a couple of pillows from the side, putting them behind me as I sit up in bed. My back's against the trailer, the sun streaming in through all the windows. He walks back over, holding two cups of coffee, putting one knee on the bed. I sit up, holding the white sheet to my naked body.

"Thank you." I smile at him as he gets back into the bed. He kisses my lips before taking his place on the bed next to me.

"Did you sleep okay?" he asks me, and I just smile at him, nodding.

"Surprisingly well," I tell him as I take another sip of the hot coffee.

"You know," he starts to say, "you never asked me how yesterday went." The coffee now feels like it's about to climb back up my throat.

I avoid looking into his eyes. "I didn't want to pry," I answer honestly, leaving out that I wasn't ready for him to tell me he's moving to Vegas. I wasn't ready to be the needy person who asked him, what about me? I didn't want to put any more pressure on him than he had.

"It's one of the things I love about you," he says softly, and my eyes fly up to his when I hear the love word.

"Um," I start to say nervously.

"I want you to pry," he informs me, not even making a big deal about what he just said.

"Okay." I push it to the back of my head. "How did it go?" I try not to dwell on it.

"It went really well," he says, nodding and looking down at the cup in his hand. I don't know why, but it feels like I'm holding my breath underwater, fighting to get to the surface. "He answered all my questions." He shrugs. "I still have to meet another two GMs."

"Keep your options open," I say what I think he needs to hear. I say what I think I should say. "I think you'll know when it's the right fit." The tightness in my chest gets even tighter. "With that said." He looks at me. "I have this thing in Dallas that I need to do. Do you want to come with me?"

He smiles at me, the same smile that gives me all the butterflies in my stomach. "Are you asking me out on a date?"

I close my eyes, laughing. "I guess so." I bring the coffee to my lips. "I guess I am." I look up at him as he leans down and kisses my lips.

"It would be my honor," he accepts softly, right before he takes my mug from my hand, turning and putting both mugs on the ledge above our heads. "I think we should seal the deal." He rolls on top of me. "Just for good measure."

Thirty

Xavier

THE PLANE LANDS, and I look over at Vivienne, who is staring out the window. The last days have been a roller coaster of emotions. Meeting with the other GMs just confused me even more. I thought I would know when it was right, and now, I'm not sure.

I want to tell myself it's because they all had the right answers to my questions, but the reality of the situation is I was putting Vivienne into my equation. "Are you ready?" She smiles at me when the plane stops, getting up. "Meeting a couple of my family members is one thing." She tucks her hair behind her ear. "But the whole family is something else."

I chuckle, getting up and standing in front of her, wrapping my arms around her waist. "How bad can it be?" She just rolls her lips at that statement, putting her hand on my chest and tapping it.

"That is a good attitude to go into this with." She kisses my jaw before turning and walking out of the plane. I follow her down the four stairs, seeing her father standing there next to a black SUV.

"Hey, you two," he greets us, putting his sunglasses on his head. "Surprise."

"I want to say I'm surprised to see you here," Vivienne says, going over to him and hugging him. "But then again, I'd be more surprised if you weren't here."

He laughs at her, turns to me, and holds out his hand for me to shake. "Xavier," he says, and when I put my hand in his, he brings me in for a hug. "Looking good."

"Um. Thank you," I reply, unsure of what the fuck is going on. I've never been in this kind of a relationship where my girlfriend's father picks me up from the airport. To be honest, the longest relationship I had was one week, and then it just fizzled out. I didn't have time, and she wanted more.

The porter brings over the bags, placing them in the trunk. "So," Matthew says, "how are things?"

"Dad," Vivienne scolds. "Remember we spoke about this, boundaries."

He throws his hands up in the air. "I didn't ask him anything." I look over at Vivienne, who rolls her lips and shakes her head, looking at me.

"I didn't tell him anything, but he knows we were in Vegas for you," she informs me, and I just nod my head. I never for a minute thought she would tell him anything about me.

"It's okay." I put my arm around her shoulder.

"See," Matthew says, "it's fine."

We get into the SUV, and I have the pleasure, or actually displeasure, of sitting in the front next to him. "Are you staying with us?" Matthew asks, and I look over at Vivienne, trying to keep my cool. There is no way in fuck I'll be staying with Matthew, and it's not because I don't like him, but because I'm not going to not sleep with Vivienne in his house. I also know I respect him enough not to do it under his roof.

"Nope," she says. "Erika said we can stay at the condo since it's downtown and next to the venue."

"Okay, but we have Sunday lunch," he tells her while looking in the rearview mirror, then turns to me. "You'll love it."

"Or not," Vivienne murmurs to me as she looks out the window.

"We have dinner tonight at five," Matthew says to us both. "Your grandparents are coming in tomorrow and are excited to meet your man."

I look over at Vivienne and then back at Matthew. "Are you talking about Cooper Stone?" I ask him, my heart beating a bit faster than normal. "Like, *the* Cooper Stone?"

Matthew just chuckles. "Not another one." He looks over at me. "When Wilson met him, he cried." He stops the SUV, putting it in park.

Vivienne opens her door, and her father follows her out of the SUV, giving me a chance to wrap my head around all of this. I get out in time to grab the last of the luggage out of the trunk. "Thank you, Dad," she says, kissing his cheek. "Send me the details for tonight."

"Will do. Xavier." He turns to me. "I'd like to sit down with you while you're here." My hands start to tingle with nerves. "Get to know you a little better."

"If that is code for threatening him." Vivienne puts her hands on her hips. "The answer is no."

"I'm not going to threaten him," he says, but his tone doesn't give me a warm fuzzy feeling. I also know that eventually, I'm going to want to sit down with him to give him my side of the story.

"I think that will be a good idea," I agree, my hand gripping the handle to the suitcase so tight my knuckles turn white. He nods at me and gets back in the SUV, leaving me to follow Vivienne all the way up to the penthouse.

She punches the code into the door, and it clicks open. I wheel both suitcases into the bedroom before she turns and looks at me, her eyes bright as the sun. "I didn't tell my father anything."

"I know that," I reassure her. "I never thought you did."

"Good," she says. "Now, are you sure you are okay with all this?" She uses her hand to do a circle in the air. "It's a lot, and there will be a lot of people there."

"Are you going to be there?" I ask her, and she nods her head. "Then I'm going to be there."

"Okay." She smiles as she comes to me. "And if it becomes too much for you, all you have to do is say the word."

That night when we walk into the restaurant, I don't know what I'm expecting, but it's definitely not all these people. I'm introduced to her aunts, who are identical, and then their husbands, who also played. She introduced me to her namesake, whose first question was if my penis was the reason she was smiling. I just about choked on my drink. I met her cousins who are up-and-coming, especially Matthew Petrov, who should go one or two at the draft pick next year.

She doesn't move from my side the whole night, making sure I feel okay. Making me love her even more. That night, when we slide into bed, and I take her in my arms, I wait for her to sleep before I whisper, "I love you."

She walks into the bedroom the next evening as I slip on my black jacket. "Are you almost ready?" she asks, and I stop midway. I've seen her looking beautiful the whole time, but this, right here, in this white gown she is wearing, she is quite literally a masterpiece. Her hair is split in the middle and pulled back into a ponytail. The only jewelry she is wearing is silver earrings. The dress is what I can't stop looking at, every step she makes toward me, her leg comes out of the slit on the right side. It's a one-shoulder long dress, with a slit in the front and in the back. A big, white fabric flower sits on one shoulder as it ruffles down. "You look so handsome." She sits down on the bench, slipping her feet into sparkly silver high heels with red bottoms. She stands up and smooths down her dress. "Is this okay?"

"It's." I try to find the words. "It's." I shake my head as

she puts her hands on my chest. "You look so beautiful." I lean down and kiss her lips, not even caring that she just had her makeup done.

She wipes the gloss off my lips when I let her go. "Shall we go?" she suggests, and I think about it for a second. "The sooner we go, the sooner we can come back here, and you can see what I'm wearing under this."

I groan as my cock stirs to attention. "That doesn't help anything." She slips her hand in mine as she grabs a small silver purse and ushers us out to the waiting car. "This is a big deal, right?" I look over at her. It has just dawned on me that this is going to be a huge night.

"It's the annual Brad Wilson event," she explains. "He runs a hockey school for underprivileged children in the summertime. During the regular year, he has training programs for kids. He's working with three different schools, trying to bring in a sports program."

I nod at her. "There may be press there." She says the words that usually would push me over the edge. But there isn't anything they can say to hurt me. Does it make me less anxious? Not even a bit. I look out the window, ignoring the way my chest tightens as we get closer and closer. The car pulls up, and I spot the red carpet right away. When the driver opens up the door, I put one foot out and then the other, trying to not look around. But I can't help it when I hear the clicks of the flashes. I hold out my hand for her. She slips her hand in mine, and my heart goes back to a normal beat. The minute she is out, she looks up at me, smiling. "You got this," she reassures me softly, and for the first time, I actually believe I do.

We walk down the carpet with her by my side, posing for pictures. The roar of the people goes up when her cousins, Michael and Dylan, arrive at the same time. "That was intense," I say as we make our way inside.

"If it makes you feel better"—she leans in—"you've never looked better." I laugh as a server holding a silver tray with champagne flutes stops in front of us. I grab a glass for her, handing it to her, and she looks at me. "It's fine."

"I don't want to make you uncomfortable," she says, and I lean and kiss her lips.

"It's more than okay," I assure her, and she grabs the champagne glass from my hand. We spot her parents, going over and saying hello to them.

"You look so handsome," Karrie compliments me as she kisses my cheeks.

"You already have a woman." Matthew pulls her away from me. "Stop flirting with mine."

"Don't worry about him," Max says, chuckling, "his bark is worse than his bite."

"What are you two bickering about now?" I turn to see Cooper Stone coming toward us, his hand in his wife's hand.

"He started it," Matthew accuses, pointing to me. "Dad," he says, looking at Cooper. "This is Xavier." He says something to me, and I literally am too stunned to speak. I am too stunned to even move.

"Another one." I look at Parker as she comes to me. "Don't worry, dear," she reassures me, and I bend to kiss her cheek. "He's harmless."

"I'm sorry." I finally clear my throat. "It's a pleasure and an honor to meet you."

"Jesus," Cooper says. "I feel like I'm in the military every time someone says that." He shakes my hand and brings me in for a hug before going to Vivienne, who he boops on the nose before he kisses her cheek.

"At least he didn't cry like Wilson," Max teases, and just like that, I feel like I've known them forever.

She stands by my side all night until Franny comes to see her and needs help in the bathroom.

She kisses me on my lips, telling me she is going to be right back. I stand here with my hands in my pockets, looking around, when I hear someone say my name. "Xavier." I look over to my left and see Nico, the owner of the Dallas Oilers. "I thought it was you," he greets, extending his hand for me to shake. My hand comes out to shake his. "How have you been?"

"Good," I lie to him. "Better now."

"I have to say"—he looks around for a second, making sure there isn't anyone close by—"I think you got the short end of the stick when it came to Long Island." I swallow down the lump that has now moved from the pit of my stomach to the top of my throat. "Word on the street is that you are meeting with a couple of teams."

"I did," I say the two words, nodding. "It's been two years, so I'm weighing my options. Plus, my agent thought it would be a good idea."

"Well, if you are throwing your hat in the ring again," he offers while he looks at me, "I would love to sit down with you."

The hands in my pockets get super clammy. "Are you kidding?" I ask him, shocked.

"There are two things I don't kid about. One is my wife and kids," he says with a smile, "the other is my hockey team." He smirks now. "Plus, it'll piss Matthew off a bit." I can't help but laugh at that.

I don't know why I thought the past was behind me at that moment. I don't know why I let my guard down. I don't know why I thought I deserved the good I was getting, but the next morning when I wake up, I see that I can run from my past, but eventually, it catches up to me.

Miles: Thought you would want to see this.

I click the link and see a picture of Vivienne and me from last night walking down the red carpet. It's on page six of the New York paper, but it's the headline that says it all.

Hockey Princess with Hockey Washed-up Has-been.

Thirty-One

Vivienne

I OPEN MY eyes and look over, smiling at Xavier but find the bed empty. I sit up in bed, listening for the water from the bathroom, only to hear nothing. I slip out of bed, picking up one shoe that he threw over his shoulder. "Xavier," I call his name, expecting him to answer me right away. But all I get is radio silence. "Xavier," I call him again. This time, I pick up his dress shirt from last night, slipping it on. I button down the front as I walk out of the bedroom, seeing the kitchen empty. "Xavier?" I look around, trying not to panic, when I see him sitting outside on the patio.

I walk over and slide open the door. "Hey." I smile at him, and he looks up at me. I can tell right away something is wrong. His eyes are darker than they have ever been, and his face doesn't go into a smile. "I was looking for you." Usually, he would open his arms for me to sit on his lap, but this time he just looks ahead.

"I was just sitting here thinking," he replies. His voice is very monotone.

"I'm going to go make myself a coffee." I try not to panic. "Do you want one?" He shakes his head, his eyes never leaving the horizon. I walk back into the house and shake out the jitters that are in my hands now. My heart, which was so full all last night, is now feeling like it's being crushed. "It's all in your head," I tell myself as my hands shake, putting the pod in the coffee machine. "It was just a busy day yesterday." I look over to the window, seeing him sitting there in the same position he was before. "Maybe it was too much for him." I walk over to the fridge, taking the milk out. I grab my cup of coffee, trying not to let the stinging of tears win out. "Maybe this is the beginning of the end." I close my eyes and take a deep inhale before exhaling. A single tear escapes and I brush it away as fast as it came.

I walk out into the warm air and sit in the chair beside him. "I think it's going to be a nice day," I say, trying to get him to talk to me, but all I can feel is he's not even here. "How long have you been up?"

"Maybe a couple of hours," he answers, not once looking at me, and my leg starts to move up and down. I don't say anything, waiting for him to talk to me, but he says nothing. The two of us sit side by side as he looks out into the distance. Every single minute that goes by makes my chest get tighter and tighter. Every single minute that goes by makes me feel more and more like

I'm losing him.

"It's going to be a nice day," I repeat, trying to get him to say something, but instead, he just nods. It takes me back to the beginning when we met. "What's going on?" I can't not ask him, and he looks at me. I can see the turmoil that he's going through. I have no idea if this is going to be the last day we wake up together. I have no idea if this is going to be the last time I get to sit with him and share this. I have no idea what the fuck is going on. However, I know the only man I have ever wanted in my life might walk away from me without knowing how I feel about him. "I have no idea what is wrong with you." I try not to let my voice quiver, and I have this feeling I'm going to be sick all over the patio. "But I thought you should know." I swallow down the big lump in my throat. "I'm in love with you." His head whips to look at me. I can't help the tears now. "I'm so in love with you, and I'm here for you." I wipe the tears off my face with the back of my hand. "But I don't know how to be all up in your business. But if you give me a chance, I can try to learn. So I'm going to need you to meet me halfway." I can't believe I just laid it all out for him like this. In my head, it was going to be romantic with us on the boat watching the sunset. Or when we were in bed with each other. What I didn't think would happen would be us sitting on a patio, with me wearing his shirt from last night and my face probably with makeup still lingering under my eyes.

He looks down at his hands, shaking his head before reaching over and pulling my chair closer to his. "The only woman in the world who wants to try to be in my business." He looks down at the floor. "This morning, I got a link from my agent," he finally says, his voice cracking a bit as he tries to clear his throat. "It pretty much sums us up." I look at him confused, as he hands me his phone.

I open the phone and see the article on page six, my eyes going to the headline. I can't help but roll my eyes. "Please." I don't even bother reading the article. Instead, I just turn it off and hand him back his phone.

His face is filled with shock when his hand comes out to grab his phone. "It doesn't bother you that you are with someone who is washed up?" he asks me, and I lean over, putting my cup of coffee on the floor beside my chair.

"No," I say right away. "There is nothing in that article that bothers me because it's full of shit." I couldn't be angrier than I am right now. I also know I can't show him how angry I am because he'll think it's for a whole different reason. "Actually, I'm angry because it's bullshit. Just the headline is pure fiction, to say the very least." I look over at him, hoping that he sees me. "I'm not angry because of the words on the page. I'm angry that they took up space in your head. I'm angry that you sat out here thinking about it. I'm angry more so that I put you in this situation."

He just stares at me, and I'm pretty sure he has no idea what to think right now. "But they—" He starts to talk, and I hold up my hand.

"There is so much wrong with just the title that I'm

pissed we even have to address it."

"How so?" His tone is low, and I wonder if he regrets coming with me. I wonder if he regrets it all.

"Well, there were a couple things wrong with that title." I turn to look at him. "For one, since when am I a hockey princess?" I shake my head. "And two, you walked away from the game when you could still play. That's not washed up. Washed up is someone who can't even get on a team, not someone who has GMs vying for them." I get up from my chair and go in front of him, getting on my knees and holding my hand up to grab his face. "No one, and I mean no one, especially me, cares what people write in the newspaper." I try to be strong, but knowing that in the blink of an eye, I can lose him is just too much for me. The tears run down my face. "What do you want?" I ask him, holding my breath, waiting for him to answer. "Deep down inside of your heart." I search his eyes with mine, seeing the light is slowly coming back to them. "What do you want?"

"I want a team that has my back," he finally says. "I want a team that will be okay with me talking about not being okay. I want a team that is willing to be open about mental health and all its struggles." His voice trails off. "I want a team that I can be proud to be a part of." He puts his hand on top of mine. "I want to help people who are suffering the same things I'm suffering but are afraid to speak out."

"So let's make it happen," I tell him, smiling.

"Just like that," he says, and all I can do is nod at him.

"Just like that," I repeat, moving my head close to

him, closing the distance as I kiss his lips. "If anyone can do this, it's you," I reassure him.

He shakes his head. "It's amazing how much faith you have in me."

"I wish you could see how amazing you are through my eyes." I smile at him.

I stare into his eyes when he says the words. "I love you, Vivienne," he says softly, his forehead touching mine. "I am in love with you." My heart that I thought was beating a mile a minute before picks up even more. "This is not the way I wanted to tell you how I feel." He kisses my lips softly. "Although I must have told you about fifty times that I love you without you knowing." I chuckle, the nerves from not long ago gone.

"That doesn't count." I laugh finally without the pressure on my chest. "The only thing that counts is I said it first." He pulls me up and turns me to sit on his lap. My arms go around his neck as my head rests on his shoulder. His arms hug me tight around my waist.

"I'm sorry," he says softly as I kiss his neck, "for being a dick."

"You weren't a dick," I reply, then laugh. "I mean, you were a little bit of a dick, and you scared the hell out of me." His hand rubs my back. "But it's fine."

"Nico wants me to meet with him," he shares, and I sit up right away, looking at him. "He came up to me last night, wondered if the rumors were true about me looking to get back into the game."

"And?" I question, and he smiles at me.

"Look at you prying into my business," he jokes while

I glare at him. "He wants to sit down with me tomorrow."

"Are you going to do it?" I can't even try not to ask the question.

"I am," he confirms. "I would like to talk to your dad about it."

"Well." I tap his shoulder with one hand. "No time like the present." I kiss his lips. "Family lunch is in one hour." I get up off his lap. "Which means makeup sex has to last no more than ten minutes since it takes forty minutes to get there." I hold out my hand to him, and he gets up, holding my hand.

"I think you need to text your father and tell him we are going to be late," he suggests at the same time he throws me over his shoulder and slaps my ass. "We might be really, really late."

Thirty-Two

Xavier

"WITH A MINUTE to spare," Vivienne says from the passenger seat as I pull up to her parents' house and shut off the car. "And you thought we would be late." She laughs, putting her hand on the door handle.

"Nothing says get off my daughter like your father calling you while I'm in you." I shake my head, getting out of the car. Taking a deep breath, I walk over to the sidewalk and slip my hand into hers. "You look beautiful." I bend to kiss her lips.

"You aren't so bad yourself." She gets on her tippy-toes and kisses my lips.

"Dad!" we hear Cooper yelling from the open door of her parents' house. "Vivienne is making out with Xavier in the middle of the sidewalk. The neighbors are watching." I can't help but laugh at him teasing Vivienne, who flips him the bird.

"There are so many cars here," I note, seeing both sides of the street are lined with cars, and even the driveway is packed.

"Everyone is in town, so that means chaos with the family," she states as we walk toward the door where Cooper stands.

"I could hear the voices from the street," Vivienne says when we walk into the house. I look up, seeing a couple of kids running through the rooms and then disappearing.

"If you think it's loud from the front of the house, you should hear the backyard," Cooper says to us before he turns and walks back into the house.

"Here we go," Vivienne encourages from beside me. "Don't forget you love me." She smiles up at me. "You can't take it back."

"Never," I tell her, feeling the flutter in my stomach as we walk into the kitchen, and she was not fucking kidding. Every single corner is filled with people. I follow her as we make our way through the crowd saying hello to everyone as if we didn't see them yesterday.

"This," she coos when she gets to Franny, who holds her daughter in her arms, "is Stella Bella." Vivienne grabs Stella from Franny. "And she loves me the most."

The little girl squirms in her arms and throws herself back at her mother. "Traitor," Vivienne mumbles. "Wait until you're five and want candy."

"Stop threatening my daughter," Wilson warns, coming over with a bottle of water in his hand for Franny.

"There you are," Michael says, coming over to us with Dylan following him. The two of them are two peas in a pod. "I wanted to ask you, Xavier, did you cry when you met my grandfather?"

"Ugh," Wilson groans, "whatever." Making both of them laugh.

"If you would go golfing with my grandfather, do you think you can handle it?" Dylan asks me, trying to roll his lip.

"Fuck you both," Wilson says, then looks at me. "Last year, he asked me to go golfing. I thought it was all the guys, I show up, and it's just the two of us."

"And it made him so nervous," Michael says, holding his stomach while he laughs, "he barfed in the bushes the whole time."

"It wasn't the whole time." Wilson rolls his eyes. "It was the first six holes."

"It's okay," Franny says to him, trying not to laugh. "It's sweet."

"Aren't you glad you didn't cry?" Vivienne leans over and mumbles. "Let's go get food."

She slips her hand in mine as she steps outside into the yard. A big white tent covers half the yard with round white tables everywhere. Most of them are filled with people, a long table toward the back of the tent is filled with silver food trays and people in line getting food. "There you are," a woman with strawberry-blond hair says, coming toward us, and Vivienne shrieks. "I was wondering if I was going to meet the man everyone is talking about." She smiles at me as Vivienne takes her in her arms. They rock back and forth as they hug.

"Xavier," Vivienne introduces, going to the woman's side and side-hugging her, "this is Dylan's sister and my cousin, Abigail."

I nod my head at her. "Pleasure to meet you," I say. "We didn't meet last night, right?"

She throws her head back and laughs. "We did not. I got in this morning."

"Abigail is in her last year of nursing school," Vivienne tells me proudly.

Abigail smiles. "That would be me."

"Oh, cool, where are you studying?" I ask her, and she looks down shyly.

"I'm doing my master's in nursing at Johns Hopkins," she replies, and I whistle.

"Damn," I say, "that's impressive."

She shrugs her shoulders. "I guess so." We turn and say hello to a couple more people before finally making our way to the food, only stopping six times to say hello to people we met yesterday.

"So," Vivienne says when she hands me a white plate. "Do you remember who everyone is?"

I shake my head. "I know the hockey guys," I answer honestly. "The rest are a blur."

"Next time, we'll do cue cards," she teases me as she fills her plate with food. I follow her as she makes her way to an almost empty table. Erika is sitting down and eating with Cooper beside her.

I pull out the chair for Vivienne, who smiles at me before she sits down. I sit in the chair next to her. "How are you holding up?" Erika smirks from in front of me when the chair next to her is pulled out, and Julia sits down, followed by Jillian. "It can be overwhelming."

"That's an understatement," Jillian adds. "I wanted a low-key baby shower." She shakes her head while she grabs a piece of salad. "They invited a hundred people." She shrugs. "You learn to just go with it."

"If you can't beat them, you join them," Julia advises as Chase comes over looking for her. He grabs a chair from another table, cramming himself onto ours.

"You can sit at another table," Cooper tells him. "She's right there."

"This coming from the man who has a heart attack if he doesn't see Erika after three point one seconds," Chase fires back at him.

"That's because they have five kids, and he's scared he's going to be stuck with them alone," Vivienne says to Chase.

All I can do is sit back and listen to their banter, trying to keep up with the conversations about who is who. I lean back in my chair, putting my arm around Vivienne's chair as my thumb slowly rubs her back. I look around the yard, searching for Matthew, and when I find him, I get up. Vivienne looks up at me. "I'll be back." I lean down and kiss her lips.

"Venturing off on your own," Alex says from beside Julia, "that's ballsy."

I chuckle as I zigzag through tables, doing my best not to make eye contact but then stopping at the table where Matthew sits with Max, Evan, Viktor, Justin, and

Mark. "Hey," I say, and Matthew looks at me. "I was wondering if you had a moment."

"Oh my God," Max says. "He's going to ask for her hand in marriage." He pushes Matthew's shoulder. "The last one out the door. You know what that means." Matthew looks over at him. "You're that much closer to the grave."

"You keep forgetting that you are older than me." Matthew gets up, and Max follows him.

"Oh, I didn't," I start to say, and the rest of the guys just shake their heads.

"It's a package deal," Evan explains. "M&M for life."

"I can't believe that nickname took." Viktor laughs at them. "One year for Christmas, we got them the blue and red shirts."

I look over at Matthew and Max, who just glare at them. "This is a lot of fun," Max says, "but let's go inside." I nod at them and follow them into the house. Matthew walks toward the stairs, going to the front door and then down a hallway to an open door. I step inside and see that this is probably his home office. There are pictures of all the men in the family in their hockey gear, most of them action shots. I take a second to look around before seeing him and Max sitting on the leather couch in the corner. "Take a seat."

"Wow." I shake my hands, walking to the couch in front of them. "I feel like I've been summoned to the principal's office." I laugh nervously when the door opens, and Vivienne comes in.

"You were going to have a meeting without me here?"

She folds her arms over her chest. "Rude."

"He might be asking for your hand in marriage," Max offers. "Why would you be here? Unless." He looks at me, then back at Vivienne. "You two eloped in Vegas, and you don't have to ask him." He rolls his lips and puts his hands to his mouth. "Please tell me that I'm right."

I look at Matthew, who looks like he's going to explode. "We did not elope," I confirm, looking at Vivienne, who comes to sit down beside me.

"Yet," she puts in. "We don't know what tomorrow holds."

"Vivienne Allison Grant," Matthew grits between clenched teeth. "Don't even joke about it."

I look over at Vivienne, who just shrugs. "Can we change the subject, please?" Matthew pleads.

"Gladly," I say. "I wanted to let you know that I've met with a couple of GMs over the course of the week." He nods at me. "And yesterday, I was approached by Nico."

Matthew laughs and shakes his head. "The guy is a thorn in my fucking side."

I can't help but laugh. "He did say that it would piss you off," I confirm.

"So you're getting back into the game?" Max asks me, and I look over at him.

"I never wanted to leave the game," I admit for the first time out loud. Matthew and Max just look at each other. "I have no idea what you read in the press or on Google."

"We don't go on Google," Matthew states. "Nor do

we believe anything that is in the press." He looks at Max. "Remember when you told them to fuck off and refused to give them even a quote."

"Assholes," Max mumbles, leaning back on the couch, putting one arm on the armrest and the other across the back of the couch.

"Good. I'd like to be the one who tells you my side of the story," I say, my hands starting to shake as the knots in my stomach get tight. She slips her hand into mine, and I look over at her and smile.

"You got this," she assures me as she blinks away tears.

I give her a sad smile before I turn and look back at Matthew and Max. "Two years ago, I was at the lowest I've ever been." I swallow down the lump in my throat. "My game was a mess; the press was always there to catch whatever fuckup I did. It was just barreling down. Every single day I went into the rink and tried to get someone to talk to. I tried my coach. I tried the assistant coach. I went to my captain. I went to the GM, and I was given the same answer." I close my eyes, thinking about how many times I tried to get help, how many times I reached out and just got kicked down again and again. "I was told to suck it up. I was told stop fucking up, and they will leave you alone."

Max shakes his head. "I felt very much alone. I felt like no one had my back. One night I skated out for the warm-up. I lasted two minutes before I had a full-blown panic attack. I'd had them at night in the privacy of my house, but now it was out there, and before the media caught it on camera, I went back to the locker room and faked sick. That night I went home and tried to end it all." I look down at my feet before looking up and facing them, hoping they don't think less of me. "My agent found me, and then I walked away. Didn't give a shit about anything."

"Xavier," Matthew says my name, and I brace myself for what is to come next. I have no idea what he is going to say. Fuck, he might not even be okay with me being with Vivienne. Her fingers tighten around my fingers, and when I look at her, she has tears running down her face. She hugs my arm and kisses my shoulder; only then do I turn back and look at Matthew. "They fucking failed you. There was no fucking way you should have gone through that. There are things in place to avoid that. There are people who you should have been talking to." He shakes his head. "I'm sorry that you went through that. Excuse my French, but that motherfucker." He looks at Max. "If that would have been my team and this happened, everyone who didn't report it would have been fired. Tossed out on their asses, without thinking twice." He shakes his head, and I don't know why, but I breathe a sigh of relief that he's not looking at me, telling me it is all my fault.

"Every single fucking person," Max agrees, sitting forward now, "from the coaching staff to the front office failed you."

"I second that," Cooper says, coming in. "I didn't mean to overhear; I was just wondering what my father was up to." He stares at me. "I'd love to have you here in Dallas."

"Where does that leave Vivienne?" Matthew asks me.

"I'm not making a decision without her. Even if I don't play again." I smile at her. "I want to get help to the players who need it. I have no idea where to even begin, but there needs to be more help available for us who struggle."

"I can work anywhere," Vivienne says from beside me.

"But your work is in New York," Matthew says to her.

She smiles at me. "I guess there is no time like the present."

"What does that mean?" Matthew asks. "Vivienne?"

"It means," she says, "I can go wherever I want to work because I work for myself." Matthew and Max share a look. "I'm a writer," she says, and my heart fills with pride.

"She's like not just a writer," I say, puffing out my chest. "But she's like a big deal."

"What in the fuck?" Cooper swears, putting his hands on his hips. "Mom," he yells behind him, "Franny, Chase!"

"Well, I guess we can say the spotlight is off you." She scrunches up her nose. "I love you."

"I love you more," I remind her and just like that the chaos erupts even more.

THIRTY-THREE

VIVIENNE

"SHE'S LIKE NOT just a writer," Xavier says from beside me. His voice is all animated, and his hands are in the air. "But she's like a big deal."

"What in the fuck?" Cooper swears, putting his hands on his hips. "Mom," he yells behind him, "Franny, Chase!" He turns to look at me, and all I can do is shake my head. I never thought I would tell my family. I mean, maybe eventually, I thought maybe, but listening to him come clean and bare his soul, I figured it was the perfect day.

"Well, I guess we can say the spotlight is off you." I scrunch up my nose. "I love you."

"I love you more," he reminds me and leans in to kiss me.

"What is all this yelling?" my mother asks, coming

into the room.

"If I'm going to do this." I stand up. "I need to do it in front of everyone so I don't repeat myself. Plus, I need to do it in front of Grandma and Grandpa."

I hold out my hand for Xavier, who stands up. "We aren't finished talking," my father informs Xavier, who just nods at him. "Thank you." He comes over and slaps his shoulder. "For trusting me with your secret."

"Figured if I'm going to elope with your daughter, might as well know what kind of man I am," he jokes with a straight face and then bursts out laughing.

"Too soon," my father says to him, "too soon."

"What happened?" Franny asks, coming into the foyer. "I heard you were in trouble."

"You will never guess," Cooper says, "what she does for a living."

"She edits things," Franny replies, and Cooper just shakes his head.

"Nope."

"Can I please be the one to tell everyone?" I hit his arm.

"Mom, she hit me." Cooper points at me, and she tells him to shush.

"Okay, well, we are all here and waiting," Chase urges. "They just brought out dessert, so can we move this along, please?"

I roll my eyes. "Well, as most of you know, I work in publishing." I look around the room, making sure my grandparents can see me. "And well, as much as it's what I do, it's not the full truth." I take a big, deep breath, and he squeezes my hand just like I did to him when he told my father his side of the story. "I really write murder mysteries." I look around the room. "And my name is Cooper Parker," I admit with tears in my eyes. My eyes go to my grandparents, who look at each other and smile. My grandfather leans down and kisses my grandmother's lips.

"Holy shit!" Franny exclaims, putting her hand to her mouth.

"You," my father says, "you write."

"I write books," I say finally.

"Amazing books," Xavier says proudly from beside me. "Trust me, I paid a lot of money for a signed copy."

"Holy shit balls," Cooper says, his phone in his hand. "She's written like a lot of books, and people have like fan clubs."

"I know," Xavier says, throwing his hands up. "I'm part of like three of them."

I shake my head while everyone starts coming at me with questions. "So you write the books?"

"She's in like thirty languages," Cooper reports, his eyes never leaving his phone.

"I think that means she's the most successful out of all four of us," Chase says, "and I'm a doctor."

"Speak for yourself," Franny says. "I had a sex tape." I roll my lips to stop myself from laughing.

"And you looked amazing," Alex says, holding up her hand to high-five her.

"You, too, Wilson." She turns to hold her hand up for him, and Dylan puts it down.

"Don't even think about it." He glares at her, and she sticks her tongue out at him.

"I don't even know why I like you," Alex pouts to him, and he wraps his arm around her shoulder, pulling her to him. Kissing her lips, she just smiles up at him.

"That's disgusting," Michael says. "That's my sister."

"Now you know how I feel," my father tells Michael, making everyone laugh. "It's so gross."

It takes about forty-five minutes before everyone slowly moves away from me. "You think you know someone," Franny says, shaking her head, "and then poof, she's a best-selling author." I roll my lips. "Oh my God." She gasps. "I need to read these and make sure you didn't steal any of my good quotes."

"Since when do you have good quotes?" Cooper asks. "Wait a minute." He turns to me. "Am I in the book?"

"Yes," I tell him. "I think it was in book three." His eyes go even bigger. "I made you a pirate. Gave you an eye patch and I think a hook." I look at Xavier, who closes his eyes. "And a peg leg. But don't worry, you died a happy, happy death." I try to keep the laughter out of my voice. "I think even with a smile on your face."

Xavier buries his face in my hair to laugh. "Mom!" Cooper turns, yelling for our mom and walking away from us.

I'm about to say something when I turn and hear a little girl come in, shrieking when she sees Abigail. Her blue eyes are crystal blue and her hair is in a ponytail on the top of her head. It takes me a minute to realize who it is. I smile when I see them hug, knowing how much

Abigail did for her when she was hurt a couple of years ago. It was a huge deal since her grandparents tried to sue Julia, who was her caseworker.

"Abigail," the little girl says, running to her and hugging her around her stomach.

"Penelope," Abigail replies, bending to kiss the little girl's head. Abigail hugs her around her shoulder.

"I missed you so much," Abigail says, looking up at her as if she hangs the stars. I look over to see Tristan walking into the room. His eyes light up just as much as Penelope's do when he sees Abigail. Tristan had no idea he fathered Penelope until a letter came out with his name. The minute he got the DNA results, he's been all in.

"You're here," he says to Abigail, who smiles at him.

"It was a last-minute trip," she tells him, trying not to look at him too long before looking down at Penelope. I feel like I'm interrupting a private moment.

"You got so big," she coos to Penelope. "Are you hungry?" The little girl nods her head. "See you guys later." She moves away from us, her hand in Penelope's. Tristan smiles at me, nodding before following the two of them to the kitchen.

I hear more commotion when Julia sees Penelope. Smiling, I turn back to look at Xavier. "Are you ready to go?" I ask Xavier, who just nods his head at me.

"After today, I need—" I put my hand in front of his mouth, not sure what he is going to say out loud. "Not that." He pushes my hand away from his mouth. "I mean, I could use that." He bends to kiss my lips. "But after I

FaceTime Beatrice."

"She's not talking to us," I remind him. We've been FaceTiming her every day since we left. She looks at the phone and then turns away, lying with her ass to us. "I'm going to have to get a lot of cookies to win her over again." Slipping my hand in his, we walk over to my parents to say goodbye.

"What time is your meeting tomorrow?" my father asks Xavier.

"Noon," he replies and my father nods his head.

"If you don't mind," my father starts, and for the first time, he looks unsure. "I'd love to come with you." Xavier looks at him, shocked. "Figured it would be good to have support at your back." If I could love my dad more, I would right now. I look over at Xavier, who blinks away the tears that are threatening to escape.

"I don't know what to say." He clears his throat, and I slip my hand in his, then I take my other hand, holding his arm and my lips to his bicep. "That would be great."

"What's going on here?" Max pipes up, coming to us and folding his arms over his chest.

"Nothing," my father says, "just making plans to go visit Nico with Xavier."

"Oh, count me in," he says. Xavier looks at them and then at me.

"You could say no," I mumble now to him, and Max pffts out.

"I'm his favorite," Max gloats. "You can tell them."

"Don't answer that," Michael advises, coming into the room. "Never answer any questions that either of them asks you." He looks at Max. "Mom is looking for you." Michael laughs. "It's been three point five seconds, she hasn't seen your face, and she's worried you got yourself into trouble."

"He's a walking, talking trouble sign," my father adds. "I'll come and get you at eleven."

"Oh, I want to come," Michael says, looking at them. "Are you going golfing?" He turns and yells for Dylan.

"No," Xavier says. "I have a meeting with Nico."

"Oh, you joining the team?" Michael says, not even knowing the backstory. "Vivienne going to finally call Dallas home?"

All eyes turn to me as my heart speeds up. No one has asked me the big question about what he would decide. Not to say I didn't think about it because I did. Every single time he walked out of the room to go to a meeting, it's all I thought about. Would he choose this city? Then I would google what is the best thing to do in the city. I would tell myself that I'm reading too much into it. Then I would try and write and have zero words because all I would be able to think about was what he was doing and how he was feeling. The eyes on me make my heart speed up even more. "Umm."

"We should get going," Xavier urges to help me escape the looks and the question.

Walking out of the house, I hold his hand as he drives back to the condo. He doesn't say a word, and neither do I. Instead, I sit the whole time, trying to think of the words to tell him. When I open the door and toss the keys on the table in the hall, he looks over at me. "I'm going to shower," I tell him, needing more time to catch my bearings.

Starting the shower, I undress, my head going a million miles a minute. "What if he doesn't want you to move with him?" I mumble to myself, looking to make sure I'm still alone. I get into the shower and take the longest shower I've ever taken in my life that wasn't filled with sex. When I get out and wrap myself in a towel, I step into the room, shocked that he's sitting there on the bench in the dark. "Jesus." I put my hand to my chest. "You scared the crap out of me." I stop walking when I see him looking down. "Are you okay?" He looks up at me, and the moonlight from outside only gives me a small glimpse of his eyes.

"Yeah." His voice cracks, and he laughs nervously. "Actually," he says with a sad smile, "no, it's not okay."

The minute he says the words, my heart sinks to my feet. "What's wrong?"

"I was sitting here thinking I should give you space." He starts talking, and I take a step toward him. "But then the other side of me was telling me to just tell you how I feel." He chuckles. "To be honest, I usually do this with Beatrice, but she's not talking to me right now."

I stop in front of him. "You can tell me anything," I assure him, but what I really want to say is, you can tell me anything as long as it's not that you don't want me anymore. I get down on my knees in front of him, wondering if he knows that he holds my heart in his hand.

"Today, your family asked you if you would move to Dallas." I swallow when he starts to talk, and from his tone, I have no idea if it's a good conversation or a bad one.

He looks into my eyes. "About that," I start to say, "this is so hard." I shake my head and clear my throat. "Which is silly since it's my job to think of words. Yet all the words are all jumbled on the paper."

"You don't need to move with me," he says to me. "I would never make you choose."

"What if I want to choose?" I put my heart out there one more time, not knowing if it's going to bite me in the ass or not. "What if I want to be where you are?" His eyes light up. "What if I told you I checked out every single city we went to?"

"I would say it makes me really fucking happy," he says, his hands coming to hold my face. I can't help the tears that fall. "But your home is in New York."

"My home is wherever we make it." I emphasize the we. "My home can be anywhere." He bends his head, his forehead touching mine. "My home is where you are." The words are even harder to say than I love you.

"I want you to be there with me," he admits to me. "I just didn't want to be a selfish bastard and ask you."

"I didn't want to be a pushy person and assume," I confess to him, and he laughs.

"If you didn't look like your sister, I would think they took the wrong baby from the hospital." I can't help but throw my head back and laugh.

"Don't kid yourself." I kiss his lips. "I'm one hundred percent Grant."

THIRTY-FOUR

Xavier

"HOW ARE YOU doing?" Matthew asks me when he steps out of the driver's seat. I close the back door of the SUV.

"Like I'm being strangled." I stretch the collar to my white shirt, unbuttoning it.

"You'll be fine," Max assures me when he joins us at the back of the car. "The minute you think it's too much." He looks at Matthew. "Scratch your nose or something."

"Or if it's too much, you get up and say, 'I need a minute.'" Matthew looks at Max, putting his hands on his hips. "Whatever it is," he reminds me, "you run this show." He points at me, and Max laughs at him.

"Yeah, you run this show until Matthew decides that you don't." He slaps my shoulder and squeezes, and I can't help but chuckle a little bit, but then the nerves come back and start eating away at my stomach. All I can do is nod at him as we turn and start walking to the door, Max and Matthew on either side of me. I honestly didn't think they would actually come to pick me up. I thought it was just said at the moment, but when Vivienne walked into the bathroom while I was getting dressed to tell me her father was there, I was speechless.

My heart beats faster and faster as we get closer and closer to the door. My feet even feel like they are getting heavier and heavier. Max reaches the door first and opens it, Matthew letting me go in after him, with Max following behind us.

The green carpet is all down the quiet hallway. The walls are filled with plays over the years. Dylan is in one of them, holding up the Cup. Michael in another one, and then in one of them, Cooper, Dylan, Michael, and Wilson, all off their feet in the air celebrating the win. The looks on their face is pure bliss. It's a look that every single kid who starts to play hockey chases. It's every little boy's dream to win the Cup, but then when you do it, it must be the ultimate feeling. "Well, well, well." Nico comes out of his office wearing blue dress pants with a white button-down shirt rolled up at the sleeves. "I want to say I'm surprised to see you two"—he puts his hands in his pockets and laughs—"but I'd be lying."

Matthew laughs at him, walking to him and holding out his hand. "Glad that you know me so well."

"I'm here to make sure that one"—Max points at Matthew—"stays in his lane." He holds out his hand to Nico, who smiles. "So you're all welcome."

"Matthew stay in his lane?" Nico jokes. "That's something I would be willing to pay to see." He turns to me. "Xavier." He holds out his hand. "Thank you for taking the time to meet with me."

I hold out my hand to shake his. "Thank you for wanting to sit with me."

"I'm assuming you want to do this in the conference room?" Nico asks. "There is more space." I nod and then hear the door close from behind me and look over to see Manning coming down the hallway, dressed in shorts and a polo shirt, very casual considering his title. Manning was the captain for Dallas for as long as I can remember. He won the Cup with them and then retired. Only after he retired did the news come out that he was the new GM of Dallas. He and Nico built a team that just got better and better through the years, winning two Cups back-to-back.

"There he is," Manning says, coming to me with a smile, the two of us have had our battles on the ice, but the respect for each other is very evident. "Look at you." He puts out his hand to shake mine, but he surprises me by pulling me in for a hug.

"How are you doing?" I say, trying to calm my blood pressure down.

"Good." He looks at Matthew and Max, nodding while they exchange handshakes. "What did I miss?" he asks, looking at Nico.

"We are heading to the conference room," Nico states. "Shall we do a tour?"

"That would be great." I try to not make a big deal of

this. Trying to tell myself that it's going to be fine either way.

We walk into the conference room, and I'm not surprised when Matthew and Max sit on each side of me. The support is so evident it's giving me that added security. "So," Nico starts, "you thinking of coming back to the league?" He puts his hands on the table. "From the word on the street, you were done."

It doesn't surprise me that he heard this, nor does it shock me. It also, for the first time, doesn't make me ashamed of the way I left. "I am," I answer him honestly. "I'm not going to lie, I'm probably rusty," I try to make a joke out of it, "but it's probably like riding a bike."

Manning leans back in his chair, laughing. "I'm not worried about that," he says, rocking. "I will tell you what I'm worried about."

I hold up my hand to stop him. "Let me just get straight to the elephant in the room." My neck is getting hot, and my hands are shaking a bit. "I'm not going to lie. It was not my ideal way to leave. But"—I look over at Matthew, who just nods at me—"I'm going to be one thousand percent transparent with you guys." The lump gets bigger in my throat, but I push through. "I'm not going to sit down and shit on the other team. But what I will say is my side." I thought telling them my story would be hard, but surprisingly, every single time I've said it, it gets easier and easier. Almost as if a weight was lifted from my body. "I was not in the best headspace. Press, well, you know, how press can be. Not the most supportive at times." They both laugh at that comment.

"I reached out for help, got none. Not one person wanted to step in and help me. I thought hockey was a band of brothers. I thought that it was one for all, all for one. I thought hockey was more than it was. That was my error in everything. I learned the hard way." I look down at my hands, surprised they stopped shaking. "Swallowed the pain every single night, felt more alone than I've felt in my whole life. Skated off during warm-up and almost lost my life that night." I don't think I need to spell it out because Nico hisses, but it's Manning who speaks first.

"For one," he declares, "you should have never gone through that. I've been lucky enough to be captain to a group of sensational guys. Not all were Boy Scouts. But push comes to shove, I would have thrown down for each and every single one of them."

"I know that this should surprise me," Nico speaks, "but knowing who runs the show there, I'm not. It's an old-school mentality." He hits the nail on the head. "When my father 'gifted,' me the team"—he uses quotations for gifted—"he had a GM who was stuck in the seventies. He also had a contract I had to stand behind. But he didn't do anything. I was my own GM. It took a whole thirty minutes of meeting with him to see that I was done with the old way of thinking. He was GM in name only until his contract was up. With that said, if one of my players went through what you just described and no one did anything, everyone would be fired. Period. There is no place for that in my organization, before and even more so now. Social media is a blessing and a curse. It brings the buzz for sure, but if you fuck up"—he shakes his head—"it's not just on the news for five seconds. It's replayed over and over again." I shake my head because he got exactly what I went through. "I'm sorry you went through that."

I nod at him and lay the rest of my cards on the table. "I've met with Vegas, Seattle, and also Arizona." Manning and Nico just look at me. "But if truth be told, I'd love to come to Dallas not just for myself, but for Vivienne. She has family here and a support system. So if you want me, I'm yours."

"Are you sure about this?" Matthew says from beside me.

"Never been surer of anything in my life than I am of Vivienne." I smile, thinking of her smile. I smile, thinking about her laugh. I smile, knowing she would do whatever I wanted to stand by my side. "I get one chance to love her, and I'm not going to fuck it up by bringing her to a city she doesn't know. So…" I turn back and look at Nico and Manning. "Ball is in your court." I start to get up and then stop. "Another thing." I hold up a finger. "I won't hide my struggles. If I'm having a bad day, I'm going to talk about it. If my anxiety gets the best of me, I'm not hiding it. It's covered up too much these days, and it's time that people see it's okay to not be okay." I take a second holding up my finger. "Also, I'm not shaving nor will I have my hair cut a certain way."

I look over at Max, who smiles at me and gets up, not saying anything. Everyone shakes hands, and only when we walk out of there and are in the garage does Max speak up. "You did good in there." He slaps my shoulder. "There is absolutely nothing I would have done differently."

"I'm assuming that what I told them is confidential?" I ask and then stop. "Actually, I don't even give a shit. It's my truth."

"Maybe now would be a good time to get your story out there," Matthew suggests from beside me when we stop at the SUV. "You should talk to Franny." I tilt my head to the side. "If there is anyone who can help you tell your truth in a respectful manner, it's her."

"I'll think about it," I tell him. I expect him to open the driver's door, but instead, he continues looking at me. "What you said about Vivienne." I wait for him to talk before continuing. "You mean it, right? I would hate to have to kick your ass." I throw my head back and laugh. "Does she know you were going to put your eggs all in one basket?" I shake my head.

"No," I tell him, "but I'll tell her now." I fold my hands over my chest. "And if she tells me she can't do it." I shrug. "I'll just call it a day and end it there."

"You would walk away from the game for her?" Max asks me.

"I've walked away from the game once for me." I swallow. "I would do it in a heartbeat for her. Wouldn't think twice about it. There is nothing more important to me than her and her happiness."

"Good to know," Matthew says, turning to get in the SUV. He drops me off three minutes later. "Come for dinner," he urges, and I just nod at him. "See you in a bit."

I walk into the lobby, going to the elevator, and press the PH button for the penthouse. I used the key she gave me before I left, walking into the penthouse. "Vivienne," I call her name, and I'm shocked when I look over and see our bags packed and waiting at the door. I don't have time to even think about it before I hear nails on the floor, and I look around the corner, seeing Beatrice coming for me. "Oh my!" I exclaim, getting down on one knee to greet her. She comes to me, her tail going nuts. "How's my girl?" I greet her, hugging her neck as she turns around and around in a circle in my arms. Her tongue coming out and licking my face over and over again. I look up seeing Vivienne leaning against the wall, wearing shorts and a T-shirt. Her hair is piled on her head, one foot on top of her other foot, the smile filling her face making my whole heart feel complete. "What did you do?"

"Well." She folds her arms over her chest. "Last night, you said that you usually talk to Beatrice about things. And I know that you are going to have to make big decisions." I stand up for a second, and Beatrice barks at me, so I get back down on one knee. "So I asked my dad to help me get her here." I look down at Beatrice, who is panting now. "Then I decided that with her here, we needed to have a backyard, so I rented a house next to my parents' house."

I stand up, walking over to her. "You've been a busy, busy bee." I bend to kiss her, and Beatrice barks at me.

I'm about to say something to her when Vivienne says to her, "Hey, sharing is caring. I brought you to him." I can't help but laugh, and I'm about to say something to her when the phone rings in my pocket.

I take it out and see that it's Nico calling. I look at Vivienne, whose eyes open big. "Hello," I answer, putting the call on speaker.

"Xavier." Nico's voice fills the room. "Did I catch you at a bad time?"

"Not really," I say, "but you are on speakerphone. Vivienne is here."

"I won't take much of your time. I just wanted to call and thank you for meeting with me." I swallow, thinking this is probably a phone call telling me I come with too much baggage. "Manning and I sat down after you left to go over a couple things." I look up at Vivienne, who steps closer to me and wraps her arms around my waist. "We took everything you said into consideration and weighed your demands." At this moment right here, I'm so nervous I think I'm going to get sick all over the place. My heart is racing, my stomach is lurching, my hands are shaking, and the back of my neck feels like it's on fire. "With that said, I'm sorry to say…" My ears ring as I brace for the bad news. "…you are going to be stuck with us." Vivienne's face goes into shock. "I'll call Miles now with an offer."

I can't help but smile as Vivienne puts her hands in front of her mouth and bends at her waist. My nerves from before are gone, and in their place is a happiness I don't think I've felt when it came to hockey for a long, long time. "You won't be sorry," I assure him, and he laughs.

"Enjoy the rest of the week," he says. "I expect you

on the ice next week. Call Wilson, do some ice time with the guys."

"On it," I reply, and I hang up on him, looking at Vivienne, who has tears streaming down her face.

"What just happened?" she asks me, trying not to sob.

"Well, I went in there and told him my story," I tell her. "Then I told him that the only place I would play would be here." She laughs and sobs all at the same time. "If you are going to follow me anywhere, you might as well do it with your own support system."

"You did this for me?" She wipes the tears away from her eyes, but more follow them right away.

"No." I shake my head and walk to her, grabbing her face in my hands. "I did it for us." I kiss her lips, tasting her tears. Beatrice barks beside us and walks between our legs. I look down at her. "And for you, too."

Epilogue One

Vivienne

Four months later

"HOW NERVOUS ARE you?" my mother says from beside me as I stand in the luxury box and wait for the team to come out. It's been four months since he took the offer from Dallas. Four months since he was all in, four months since we went back to New York to live the summer on the boat. It was just a little different this time. Instead of spending all day on the boat with me, he would leave to go and train. He trained from eight to four, six days a week. There is a light that has come back into his eyes I don't think he knows was gone. The nights would be just the two of us and, of course, Beatrice. He would get back and take me out for sunset cruises all the time. Until it was time for training camp, and then we had to say goodbye to the boats. It was also time to move all our things to Dallas. House hunting was a breeze because both of us only cared about having a bedroom and a yard for Beatrice. We left it in the hands of my aunt Zoe, and she did not disappoint. The house was five bedrooms with a media room and gym and a huge backyard with a pool for Beatrice.

"On a scale of one to ten"—I look over at her—"a million." I look ahead at the empty ice, wondering how he is doing. It's opening night. He was a bit nervous today when he got up.

"Hey," my father says, coming to stand by us. "He's got this." He puts his arm around me. "After that special last night." I look up and wipe away the tear that has fallen over my lashes. "There is no way in fuck one person will be sitting in their seat when they announce him." I can't help but smile with pride. After he signed with Dallas, he called Franny. There on FaceTime, he told her his story and asked if she would like an exclusive. She not only jumped on it but she also made sure he was the most comfortable he could be. So, where did we shoot it? On the deck of his boat, his home. It was also the first time she stepped in front of the camera. There was no way she was going to let anyone fuck with him. It was a first for both of them. She asked the questions she needed to and, a week later, sent us the show. I cried through the whole thing, feeling his pain and hurt, but then happy that the light was back. A smile was on his face all the time. Every single man in my family took the time to call and congratulate him. My grandfather thanked him for being so brave, and then he finally cried.

"I just want him to be okay," I say softly as I look and see the fans coming into the arena.

"Vivienne," my father says my name. "He has this, and if he doesn't, he has people around him making sure he's okay."

I don't say anything to him because the door opens, and my grandparents come in, and I'm shocked. "What are you doing here?" I ask them, knowing they were here last weekend. Even though they tried to make it to all the home openers, I didn't think they would come back.

"We had to come and support our boys," my grandmother declares, smiling at my father when he goes to give her a hug.

My grandfather hugs him and then comes over to me. "How are you doing?"

"I'm fine," I reply out of frustration, and he just laughs at me. "I'm not fine, fine, but I'm going to pretend I am."

"Well, if it helps," he says, "you aren't doing a good job at it." I can't help but laugh, and slowly, the room starts to fill with more and more people. When it's time for the skate, I walk down with the kids standing next to the glass.

He skates out after Cooper, coming over to the side and seeing me, his jersey pushed up his arms. He gives me a chin lift when he sees me and then asks me to turn around, and I can't help but laugh. I'm wearing jeans and a Dallas jersey, so I do the turn, and when I see his eyes again, he just laughs. "You better be wearing my name."

The kids call his name, and he makes sure to send

pucks over for all of them. When it's time for him to skate back out, I blow him a kiss, and he just nods at me. I walk back up with the kids, trying to tell myself that he's fine.

When the lights go off and the music starts, you can hear the whole place roar. The announcer starts talking, but all I can do is stare at the ice. Stare at the door I know he's going to be skating out of. The home opener is different than the other games. They go through the whole team, introducing you to every single member who makes the Oilers the team they are.

They introduce the coaching staff and then the equipment staff before starting on the players. They introduce the players who aren't playing tonight or who are injured. I don't even think I breathe for this. Each player comes out by number, from lowest to highest. I bounce on my toes when the numbers get closer and closer to his until I know it's his turn.

"Number twenty-two." The announcer says his number, and the crowd roars even louder than they have been. My feet tremble with their roars. I put my hands together, looking at the Jumbotron screen, seeing his face in the middle. I clap as loud as I can and cheer for him. "Playing the position of right wing." The fans start chanting Mighty Monty, a nickname Nico gave him when he announced that he was signing with Dallas. "Xavier Montgomery." The tears run down my cheeks like a stream of water running down the mountains. I don't even try to hide my emotion as I watch him walk from the tunnel toward the ice. He skates to the center of the ice, holding his stick up to the crowd, who hasn't stopped cheering for him. He puts his hand to his chest, touching his heart, before raising it to the crowd, who goes even louder. I smile and laugh through the tears when it finally dawns on me that his new number is the day that we met. He mentioned to me this morning that he changed his number which was a surprise. I thought it was bad luck to change numbers but apparently it wasn't, but this this is so much better.

"I don't know about you," my grandfather says to me, and I have to strain to hear. "But that sounds like he found his new home."

I smile, looking at him skating over to the bench. "You bet your ass he did." I clap as they introduce the rest of the team. Wilson, Cooper, and Michael each get the same applause. On the other hand, Dylan's is off the charts, but that's what happens when you're the best in the game.

The lights come back on, and the music blares out of the speakers. Dylan, Michael, and Xavier skate to the middle of the ice with Wilson.

My eyes stay on Xavier as he takes his place with his stick. Someone from the other team comes over to him and smiles at him. He smiles back as they hit helmets. Dylan takes his place in the middle and waits for the ref to drop the puck.

The ref drops the puck, and everyone finally sits down. I don't. Having so much energy in me, I can't sit. I watch Dylan pass the puck to Michael before skating forward and around his guy. Michael passes it back to

Wilson, who moves it up the boards toward the blue line. He passes it back to Dylan, who skates into the zone with the puck on his stick, moving it from side to side. Looking and passing it back to Wilson, he winds up and shoots at the net.

The shot is blocked by the goalie's pad that bounces back toward Xavier, who slaps it up over his pad and into the back of the net. If I thought the crowd was loud before, it's nothing like it is now. Xavier holds his fists together and roars out with happiness. Turning to look at the team, it isn't long before Dylan jumps on him, followed by Michael. Wilson comes over and taps his helmet before they skate to the bench and high-five everyone.

The announcer's voice now fills the place. "First goal of the game at one minute of play by Xavier Montgomery."

My father comes over to me right away and hugs me, and I can't help but sob in his arms. "He did it," I cry, unable to control the sobs.

"He did it," my father confirms, kissing my head. "Just like you knew he would."

"This isn't me," I tell him. "This is all him." I look toward the bench. "He did this all himself."

Epilogue Two

Xavier

Eight months later

I FINISH MY shift and get on the bench, my heart beating fast in my chest. I reach out, grabbing a green Gatorade bottle and spraying water in my mouth before looking up at the Jumbotron. There are two minutes and seventeen seconds left of the triple overtime. Game seven of the Stanley Cup Finals, both teams have given it all we have. Both teams are fucking exhausted, but this is what you fight for all year. Someone is hoisting that Cup tonight; the question is, who will be the hero?

I lean forward, watching the play, holding my breath the whole time. This season has been the best of my life. I thought coming back would be hard, and it was. I had to prove myself all over again. I had to do it through baby steps. The only difference was that I was vocal about the struggles. When it got to be too much, all I had to do was say the word, and I was taken out of the lineup for interviews. Surprisingly, the press was respectful of this, and no one tried to overstep. Through it all, I had the best woman by my side. She completed me in ways I didn't know were possible. She even tried to come out of her shell and ask me things. But the only thing she really cared about was if I was okay. I was more in love with her every single day that went on.

"Stone!" the coach yells for Dylan, who looks back at him. "I want your line on there with Wilson and Grant." I look over at him, wondering how the fuck this is going to work since Cooper plays as forward. "Grant, you good to play back?"

"Yeah," Cooper says as we get up and make the line change. Not fast enough because the other team skates into the zone, and it takes a second for us to get into position, but not before they get a shot at the net. Our eyes fly to the little black puck, which bounces off Steven, our goalie. Wilson is on the puck first, and the five of us now hustle back toward the other end.

He skates it out, looking over at Michael and passing it to him. The three of us skate against the two defensemen in front of us. I skate at the same pace as Michael, Dylan staying back just a touch. In case the puck gets intercepted, he's there to help the defense line. Michael passes the puck to me, but Dylan skates up and intercepts it, just like the play we did in practice a couple of days ago. He skates into the zone, rushing for the goalie.

The three forward players are all around him, leaving me empty. He glides closer to the goalie, going right, making the goalie slide over to him before he passes me the puck. The goalie slides across the ice, but it's too late, the puck has touched the blade of my stick, and I've sent it into the net. The horn fills the arena, but it's drowned out by the crowd behind the net that is banging on the glass. I jump into the air as Michael comes over and jumps with me. Dylan skates to the net to grab the puck before joining us.

I wish I could describe the feeling that is going through me. But I can't. Cooper joins us with Wilson, who jumps on us. Now the whole team is around me, surrounding me. The roar of the crowd is deafening, but it's even louder since we are at home and there are about thirty thousand fans outside now celebrating. My heart beats in my chest as the horn still blares. The emotion is off the charts.

We stand together as a group, as we did all year long, before breaking and skating to the middle of the ice to shake hands. Gloves are scattered over the ice, helmets thrown off, sticks tossed to the side. I take a second to skate to the bench and put my things down, looking up and seeing Nico and Manning high-fiving each other. Manning looks over at me in a split second, points his finger up to the crowd, and only then do I hear that they are chanting my name. "Son of a bitch," I say when tears form in my eyes, making Manning laugh.

I skate to the middle of the ice, getting in line and shaking the other players' hands. I look over to the side, seeing them opening the Zamboni door, where they are rolling out the red carpet and setting up the tables for the MVP of the playoffs, as well as the Stanley Cup. Everything is a blur right now, everything. I don't even want to look over to where I know Vivienne is watching me because I know that if I look at her, I'll be a sobbing mess.

I finally get to the end of the line and skate over to the bench, grabbing a Stanley Cup hat. Shaking my head in disbelief. "We fucking did it."

Dylan comes up to me. "You fucking did it."

"It was a team effort," I remind him before Cooper comes over and pushes my shoulder.

"The hero of the game," he says, making me laugh. "I still don't like you kissing my sister." That makes me laugh even harder.

The president of the NHL, Paul Garmin, comes out with a microphone in his hand, the announcer's voice comes on. "Ladies and gentlemen, please direct your attention to the ice for the award presentation to the most valuable player in the Stanley Cup Finals."

"Congratulations to Dallas on yet another Stanley Cup win," Paul starts and the crowd goes wild. "The award for the most valuable player of the playoffs. This person has shown perseverance on and off the ice. He is one of the top leading scorers in the playoffs, and he sure scored the big one tonight. Your award winner, Xavier Montgomery." I hear my name, but I'm not sure, or maybe I'm in shock because Cooper comes over and pushes me over toward the trophy.

My feet skate as if on autopilot. I shake my head in disbelief. I turn to point at all the guys on my team, all of the guys who made this happen. Paul extends his hand and I grab it, shaking it. The clicks of cameras go off all around us. "Congratulations," he tells me, picking up one side of the trophy, and I pick up the other. We turn to the camera, posing for pictures.

I don't have a chance to do anything before someone comes out from the press box with a microphone in his hand. "Xavier," he says, and the arena goes silent. "Congratulations." I nod at him. "What a season you've had."

I laugh at the irony of it all. "Considering I haven't played in two years, this is the cherry on the sundae." I look down at the ice, not sure I can look up, knowing tears are almost ready to start streaming down my face.

"Like Paul said, you had perseverance on and off the ice. Obviously, the highlight of the series will be your game-winning goal, but what will you remember most?"

"I mean, I don't think I would be here without Nico and Manning." I look over at them as they wear their suits with Stanley Cup hats on their heads. "They took me on, even with the black cloud hanging over me." They both nod at me. "And, of course, I couldn't have done it without my team." I look at the guys. "We battled hard each and every single game. Got knocked down a couple of times, but we came back stronger."

"You walked away from the game and then came back. Did you ever imagine this scenario?"

"Not even for a minute," I answer him honestly, not

sure what else I can say.

"Now, what are you going to do to celebrate?" he asks, and then I do it. I lift my eyes to the box where I know she is.

She stands there wearing my jersey, with her hands to her mouth, the tears running down her cheeks as she takes in this moment, Beatrice's leash in her hand. "I couldn't do this without my family." The words come out, and I see her smiling as she claps her hands. Beatrice barks, making everyone in the box laugh. "My dog, obviously, who has been a mascot of the team this year." The whole place laughs. I brought her in one day on an off day, and everyone fell in love with her. The PR guy of the team took a picture of her wearing a Dallas scarf, and it started. She would come to games after, and fans would go up to her. She loved every single second of the limelight. "But most importantly." I put my hands on my hips, turning my head and making sure her eyes are on me when I say the next part, "I'm going to try to get my girl to marry me," I say, and the whole place gasps. "Vivienne." I say her name as Matthew stands beside her with his arm around her as she shakes. "What do you say?" My own tears are coming down my face. "I got a Cup. I think it comes with a ring." I try to make a joke out of it, but the truth be told, I got her a ring last month and was just waiting for the right time to give it to her.

I never thought we would make it to the Stanley Cup Finals, and I was hoping to do it on the boat before the annual family vacation. That plan was scrapped since we are leaving for vacation right after the parade.

"Should we wait for an answer?" he says jokingly, and all I can do is touch my heart and then point to Vivienne. "We look forward to the news," he tells me, and I skate back to the team.

"You know what he's doing tonight?" Wilson looks at Cooper. "He's going to be sleeping with your sister." He beams with a smile. "Just like me." Cooper just glares at him.

"If you say a word," Michael warns beside Dylan, "I will throat punch you on the ice." Which makes all of us laugh.

The Stanley Cup comes out, and Cooper skates over as the team's captain. He shakes Paul's hand as he announces that the Dallas Oilers are Stanley Cup Champions.

He grabs the Cup from Paul and hoists it in the air. It's something that every single boy dreams about doing. He passes it to Dylan, who skates around with it. I just stand in the back when I look over and see some family members coming on the ice.

I spot Vivienne, who is there with Beatrice, as she is hugged by Nico and then Manning. It's my time with the Cup, and when I grab it in my hands, it's a lot heavier than I thought it would be. I hold it over my head as the crowd chants my name. I do a circle, then hand it off to Tristan, who takes it from me.

I skate through the people going to the bench and see her standing on the ice hugging Cooper. She must feel me staring at her because she turns and faces me. The smile on her face is so big her eyes squint at the side.

"You did it!" she exclaims, launching herself in my arms.

"We did it," I tell her, kissing her lips, and everything else around us disappears. It's just her and me. She buries her face in my neck as I spin her around, Beatrice jumping and barking at me. I put her down on her feet and turn to bend to hug Beatrice. "You did it also," I praise her, and everything in me tells me this is the moment, so I fall on one knee. "Think it's time," I tell Beatrice, who turns and sits next to me. "Vivienne," I say her name, and her eyes go big. "You came into my life when I was least expecting it. Killing me with kindness." I laugh through the tears. "I still remember when you looked at me and said 'Good talk.'" She laughs. "You have stood by my side like a pillar of strength every day since. I want to have all the babies with you. I want you to grow old with me." The cameras are now around us, clicking away. "Vivienne Grant, will you be my wife?"

She just nods, the sobs coming out of her as she bends to hold my face in her hands. "Xavier Montgomery." She says my name through tears. "I was made for you."

Ten days Later

"Are you sure this is okay?" Tristan looks at me, and I just nod my head. Over the past eight months, I've gotten really close to him. "It's a family vacation. I don't want to intrude."

"Please," I pfft at him. "Cooper," I call over to him as he empties his locker. "How many people are coming on the family trip?"

"Fuck if I know. I think we were up to eighty," Cooper says, shaking his head.

"So would two more matter?" I motion over to Tristan, and he just laughs.

"Fifteen more wouldn't matter at this point," Dylan interjects as Michael laughs.

"I'm dreading this plane ride," Michael groans, looking over at Tristan. "Just make sure you bring earplugs."

Tristan nods. "This sounds like so much fun," he says, laughing. "What's the worst that can happen?"

SOMETHING SO, THIS IS ONLY ONE & MADE FOR FAMILY TREE!

Hockey Series

SOMETHING SO SERIES

Something So Right

Parker & Cooper Stone

Matthew Grant (Something So Perfect)

Allison Grant (Something So Irresistible)

Zara Stone (This Is Crazy)

Zoe Stone (This Is Wild)

Justin Stone (This Is Forever)

Something So Perfect

Matthew Grant & Karrie Cooley

Cooper Grant (Only One Regret)

Frances Grant (Only One Love)

Vivienne Grant

Chase Grant

Something So Irresistible

Allison Grant & Max Horton

Michael Horton (Only One Mistake)

Alexandria Horton

Something So Unscripted

Denise Horton & Zack Morrow

Jack Morrow

Joshua Morrow

Elizabeth Morrow

THIS IS SERIES

This Is Crazy

Zara Stone & Evan Richards

Zoey Richards

This Is Wild

Zoe Stone & Viktor Petrov
Matthew Petrov
Zara Petrov
This Is Love
Vivienne Paradis & Mark Dimitris
Karrie Dimitris
Stefano Dimitris
Angelica Dimitris
This Is Forever
Caroline Woods & Justin Stone
Dylan Stone (Formally Woods)
Christopher Stone
Gabriella Stone
Abigail Stone
ONLY ONE SERIES
Only One Kiss
Candace Richards & Ralph Weber
Ariella Weber
Brookes Weber
Only One Chance
Layla Paterson & Miller Adams
Clarke Adams
Only One Night
Evelyn & Manning Stevenson
Jaxon Stevenson
Victoria Stevenson
Only One Touch
Becca & Nico Harrison
Phoenix Harrison
Dallas Harrison
Only One Regret
Erika & Cooper Grant
Emma Grant
Mia Grant

Parker Grant

Matthew Grant

Only One Mistake

Jillian & Michael Horton

Jamieson Horton

Only One Love

Frances Grant & Brad Wilson

Stella Wilson

Only One Forever

Dylan Stone & Alex Horton

Maddox Stone

Maya Stone

Maverick Stone

Made For Me

Julia & Chase Grant

Made For You

Vivienne Grant & Xavier Montgomery

Made For Us

Arabella Stone & Tristan Weise

Penelope

Payton

Made For Romeo

Romeo Beckett & Gabriella Stone

Mine to Take

Matthew Petrov & Sofia Barnes

Mine To Promise

Stefano Markos & Sadie

MADE FOR US

Abigail

It was time to celebrate.
After all my hard work, I was graduating at the top of my class.
Our family vacation was the perfect chance to relax.
Until I saw him get on the plane and my plans went out the window.
Tristan's everything I've always wanted but can never have.
One night was all we had together.
Now, I'm staring at the two pink lines wondering if I should even tell him.

Tristan

Six years ago, I was living for myself until I found out I had a two-year-old daughter.
Now, I love my life exactly how it is: me, my daughter, Penelope, and hockey.
Except—I've been in love with Abigail from afar for years.
She was the only one I trusted Penelope with.
One night with her is more than I deserve.
Now that I've had her, I know she was made for us.

Printed in Great Britain
by Amazon